12/2022

THE LAST UGLY PERSON
AND OTHER STORIES

ROGER B. THOMAS

The Last
Ugly Person

And Other Stories

IGNATIUS PRESS   SAN FRANCISCO

Cover design by Roxanne Mei Lum
Cover art by Christopher J. Pelicano

© 1991 Ignatius Press, San Francisco
All rights reserved
ISBN 0-89870-395-6
Library of Congress catalogue number 91-76725
Printed in the United States of America

Contents

Foreword

Very practical and very theoretical people are often impatient with the fact that seemingly mature adults spend a good deal of their time following the activities of imaginary agents, reading stories about events that never really happened to characters who do not exist. We all have moments when we sympathize with this Scrooge-like reaction to fiction, but such moments pass, our good sense is restored, and we turn with eager anticipation to such stories as these by Roger B. Thomas. If the case of the consumer of fiction is questioned, what must be said of the writer who labors over his stories and clearly regards what he is doing with the utmost seriousness?

Early in the century a dispute raged over some recently discovered prehistoric caves in France. Had their inhabitants been human or not? Chesterton, in *The Everlasting Man*, settled the matter in a swift and satisfying way. Look at the walls, he advised. The walls bore pictures, drawings of animals. Whoever drew those pictures was as human as you or I. Chesterton thus took artifacts as an infallible sign of the presence of humanity.

Think of those prehistoric hunters, then, returned from the arduous pursuit of prey. They are weary, they have been, let us hope, successful. They are certainly very practical men. Yet some among them begin to draw on the walls representations of the animals they have hunted and will hunt again. The rest presumably marvel at the pictures. They let them be. They ponder and enjoy them.

The human need for art is present here. Man is a creature who not only lives, directs his choices rationally, pursues goals.

He is also the only earthly being who reproduces the reality in which he is engaged. Our daily problems are never enough. We always multiply them by imagining variations on them. What would we do if . . .

If our doings were merely fugitive events, their meaning wholly exhausted by their occurrence, there would be no stories. But we know that what we do is decisive for who we are. The choices and decisions human agents make, particularly under great pressure, reveal what they are, they enforce or erode character.

All this is a pretty heavy way of putting before the reader the remarkable fictions of Roger B. Thomas. Any writer develops a distinctive voice, an angle of vision, a way of showing us who and what we are. There are techniques of story telling which show up more or less alike in all stories. Nowadays a bewildering number of people who have mastered those techniques and can produce serviceable facsimiles of stories. Without a distinctive voice or vision, however, mere mastery of the technique is minimally satisfying. I think Roger B. Thomas has a new and distinctive voice.

But first a word on his mastery of fictional technique. The four stories that make up this collection are marvelous on the level of skill alone. The vivid presentation of persons and events in "The Last Ugly Person" is remarkable. This is a story of more or less standard length, whereas "I Have Slaved for You" is a short short story, an extremely demanding sub-genre in which a wealth of information must be provided in a thousand or so words by indirection and implication. "Numaris" by contrast is a short novel, and "The Purging" a novella. It is as if Thomas wished to display the range of his artistry by offering us these four very different stories.

His voice, while distinctive, will evoke echoes of other writers, and this is only as it should be. Cave drawing becomes a genre and new drawings partly imitate old ones as well as nature. I thought of Ray Bradbury and at times of Flannery O'Connor. Furthermore, Thomas' work exhibits the truth of O'Connor's remark that all literature is anagogical. She meant that any story that will stick and stay, in our minds and in the tradition of fiction, points beyond the events it very concretely narrates to some (usually unstated) meaning of what is done in the story.

Reading these stories will enable you to see yourself and the world differently but truly. You will be introduced into the very special imagination of Roger B. Thomas. But through his images and artful use of language, he tells us truths which could not be conveyed in any other way.

Tolle et lege. You will be richly rewarded.

RALPH McINERNY

The Last Ugly Person

IT WASN'T REALLY RUNNING, but it was the best she could do. It had been so long since she had run or even walked a long way. Her hip ached and her side ached and her breath came in ragged, painful gasps that made little clouds in the crisp night air, white in the glaring light of the street lamps. Every now and again she had to stop, overtaken by a fit of coughing—deep, racking coughs that felt like they came from the bottom of her lungs. She wanted to stop, to rest and truly catch her breath, but she knew she couldn't. She knew they were looking for her, and if she stayed in one place too long they would find her and take her back.

So she kept running, though she did not know where she would go. She would have gone to the Nooks under the Chestnut Street bridge, but those were all paved over now, replaced by that rough concrete and those trees in the giant flowerpots— huge concrete pots, waist high, each with a little tree in it, all along the new concrete path where the Nooks used to be. Beautiful people ran and strolled along the pathway, and workers came from time to time to sweep up the leaves and twigs that dropped from the trees so the path would stay clean. Trees in pots. How ridiculous. She and Keith had laughed and laughed when they first saw them. Pet trees, Keith had called them. How Beautiful. Pet trees. They had laughed at the pet trees, all the time knowing that if they did not laugh, they would cry. The Nooks were gone. No longer could they huddle close together in the worn dirt snugholes, sharing for comfort a worn scrap of a blanket that wasn't much and worn scraps of lives that were even less, with the sting of the campfire smoke in their nostrils and the bite of the gin in their throats as they passed the flask around. They hadn't been much, the Nooks hadn't, but they had been the closest thing to a home that many of them knew, especially toward the end. So she and Keith had laughed at the pet trees, laughed loud and long, mourning for their lost Nooks.

Keith was gone now, of course, as were all the others. The Ugly places were all gone, and so were all the Ugly people. She had seen, so she knew. The reporters and politicians and all the people had cheered when they started cleaning up the Ugly places. They had taken pictures of the bulldozers that tore down the old buildings and watched the bricklayers work all day bricking up the alleys, and everyone had talked about how Beautiful it was going to be when they were finished. But there had been nobody to take pictures when the vans had come in the middle of the night to take away the Ugly people. They were all taken, two or three at a time. Anita and Shaggy Joe and Brooklyn—all of them gone. They took Keith, too, though he hadn't been in a mood to go peacefully, and they had had to beat him to get him in the van. She knew because she had watched from where she had hidden. They closed off all the alleys or tore down the buildings that made them. They took all the benches from the park and replaced them with those narrow concrete slab things that you couldn't lie down on. They even tore down old Androgetti's, which was a cruel blow. That had been a special place for her and many others, behind Mr. Androgetti's, between the dumpster and the back of the dry cleaners where the vents stayed so warm. Mr. Androgetti didn't mind, and sometimes he would bring out dinners that his Beautiful customers had barely touched. "A shame to waste them", he would say. "A shame to waste them." Then they would eat until their stomachs ached, toasting each other with milk cartons and talking in funny voices about the "fine Italian cuisine" they were eating. "fine Italian cuisine", just like it said on Mr. Androgetti's sign, except that Brooklyn always pronounced it "koo-seen-ee", knowing that it would make her laugh until she snorted her milk all over, and then they would all laugh the harder. But then something happened to Mr. Androgetti, and soon afterward the restaurant had darkened, and big trucks

4

had arrived to take away the stainless steel ovens. Then they had torn the restaurant down, making one less place to hide.

That was how they had found her in the end. When everyone else had been taken she was still free, but there were no places left to go. She would hide during the day and spend all night hunting up food and another hiding place, always watching for the cruising vans. Every morning it got worse, and she would nearly panic as dawn approached. For many days she found a hiding place just in time, but then her luck ran out. That one morning she had been bustling down Seventh, trying to make it to a spot that she hoped was still there, when a cruising van had turned the corner and caught her full in its lights. Quickly she had ducked into a doorway and squatted down, trying to make herself small, praying that she hadn't been spotted. Tightly she had closed her eyes as she prayed, as if making herself blind would prevent them from seeing. But it hadn't worked, and the van had pulled up right next to her. They had caught her. She didn't even look at them, for she knew what they looked like. The same crisp blue uniforms, the same rubber gloves, the same white doctor's masks, the same nightsticks like they had used on Keith. She hadn't resisted but had just stepped into the van like the man said. Another one had grabbed her bags and threw them into a big box at the back of the van.

"Sweet Jesus, sweet Jesus", she muttered as she stumbled along. Pains were shooting down her leg now, and every breath was like a knife in her heart, but still she ran. Carefully she watched the road ahead, ducking toward the storefronts whenever a car turned onto the street, but none of them had the high lights and shiny grill of a cruising van. Not that there were many cars on the street, or many people, either. At first she had worried about the people, that someone would recognize her as Ugly or see the flowered hospital gown and call the cruising vans. But nobody did, for nobody noticed her. They had all gotten so good at not seeing that she was invisible to them. Person after person, and sometimes couples, passed her, but nobody so much as glanced at her. There were advantages to being Ugly.

With a shiver she clutched the hospital gown about her

throat. It was too thin to keep her warm against the evening chill, too thin for anything but padding from her room to the dining hall to the counseling rooms in those stupid flip-flops that she hated. She wondered if the gowns weren't made of some kind of paper—they felt too crinkly-crispy to be cloth. That would be convenient—then they wouldn't have to be washed; they could just be burned. Stupid. Clothing out of paper. Nobody could keep warm in paper. Of course, they had never intended for anyone to wear these outside. But neither had they intended for her to duck down that stairway and wander down that hall, and they hadn't intended that someone would block that door open with a crate. She laughed in a way that hurt her chest and set her to coughing again. Wouldn't Stacey be furious!

Stacey had been the first face she saw after being taken in the van. When they got to the hospital, they had stripped her and hosed her down and checked her for lice, but that was all done by people in hospital scrubs who wore doctor's masks and talked to each other but never, never to her. Then a woman took her to her room. She knew it was a woman, though the mask covered her face and the loose clothes revealed no figure, for she could feel the hatred in the grip on her elbow. When you were Ugly, the men treated you like a thing, like a bag of garbage that needed disposing, but the women hated you. The woman had shoved her into her room and locked the door. It looked like a hospital room, with the green sheets on the bed and the chair and desk with the fake flowers on it, but she recognized a prison cell when she saw one. The door was locked, and the heavy glass windows wouldn't open, and there was nothing in the room heavy enough to break them, not even the chair, which was made of flimsy plastic. At least the room had been warm, so she had crawled between the sheets, which felt crinkly-papery like the gown, and went to sleep. The next morning another masked person came and took her to meet Stacey.

Stacey was Beautiful, of course, with bobbed blonde hair that bounced when she nodded her head, which was often, for she nodded whenever she smiled, and Stacey smiled a lot, showing perfect white teeth framed by perfect red lips. That was what she remembered about Stacey: perfect white teeth and perfect red lips and bouncing, bouncing blonde hair. She knew what Stacey was, of course—in the old days they would have called her a caseworker, but now they were called readjustment assistants. That was how Stacey had introduced herself—as "your readjustment assistant".

"And your name?" Stacey asked cheerfully, smiling and bouncing.

"Sal", she muttered.

"Sal?" Stacey repeated, her tone requesting more name than that. Sal had just looked at the floor. She didn't want to talk to any caseworker. She'd had enough of caseworkers in her day. They were always perky and happy and dripping helpfulness, just like Stacey, but they treated you like a fool. Stacey had done her best, with her upbeat tone and cheerful chatter and the occasional light touch on Sal's arm. She had honestly thought that Sal hadn't known why she would every so often tap with her pen at the board on the desk, and that Sal hadn't noticed the nearly invisible plastic gloves she wore so she wouldn't have to actually touch Sal's skin. Sal knew the type.

Stacey had tried so hard to seem helpful. She had smiled and chattered cheerfully about a "wonderful new life" and how lucky Sal was. She kept asking questions about Sal's past and how she had lived on the street: the places she had stayed, the people who had helped her, that sort of thing. Mostly Sal sat silently, staring at the floor, only occasionally mumbling some answer or other to a question. Once Sal had dared to ask when she would be allowed to go free. Stacey's face had filled with surprise, as if Sal had asked when she could go pick out her gravestone.

"Oh, Sal", Stacey had said, barely touching her arm. "You don't want to go back there." Then she had gone off some more with the "wonderful new life" talk, bubbling on about how Sal would have circumstances working for her instead of against her. She had almost made it sound nice, but then Sal remembered Keith being beaten by the nightsticks, and she wondered. She also wondered, though she did not ask, where everyone else was. She appeared to be the only one around, though there were obviously many more rooms, and the dining hall could hold far more people than just her. She was sure that her friends had been taken here but had been moved on to the "wonderful new life". She wondered if they had wanted to go, and if they liked it where they were.

There were more sessions with Stacey, though none so long as the first, which had lasted nearly an entire afternoon. The others—there had been about four of them—lasted about an hour each. Sal had just tolerated them, mostly staring at the floor and nodding or wagging her head in answer to some question. She found the sessions tiresome, and she could tell that Stacey did, too, for Stacey became more deliberately up-beat and cheerful with each one. Once, while being brought to the counseling room for a session, Sal had caught a glimpse of Stacey coming down a hallway for the meeting. Her face had looked lined and worried, especially about the eyes, and her walk had been slouching but almost frantic in its pace, as if she were being hunted. Sal had hardly recognized her, for she looked ten years older. Then she had ducked into a doorway, leaving Sal to wonder what terrible thing had happened. But when she had breezed through the door for the session, she was the same perky Stacey, perhaps even more so than ever. Sal was amazed and had spent the entire session wondering if Stacey kept a different face in her tote bag. It amused her to think of Stacey ducking into the washroom just before a session to slip on her nearly invisible protective gloves and her cheerful face, then stopping on the way out to strip them off and drop them in the burn bin.

Sal had only seen Stacey's real face one other time, and then only briefly, at their last session. Sal was being particularly stubborn at that one, and Stacey was being exceptionally cheer-ful, because the uselessness of it all was getting on both their nerves. Sal had been staring at Stacey's tote bag, which she brought with her everywhere and put on the floor by her feet during the sessions. At one particular point, partly out of true curiosity and partly out of sheer cussedness, Sal had abruptly reached down to grab at the tote bag.

"Hey!" Stacey had cried, her voice suddenly shrill and harsh. "Keep your mitts outta there!" She had kicked at Sal's hands and knocked the tote bag over, scattering the contents all over the floor. Sal saw that it was nothing more than the usual stuff—a plastic rain bonnet, a notebook, some other things. Then she saw the case. It was a white plastic case with no particular markings of the type that could hold anything from hair ties to sanitary supplies. It had fallen open, scattering its contents, and Sal had smiled. She recognized those. She remembered when she had smoked two packs a day. She hadn't seen any for years, though. It wasn't that they were illegal, just that they were so frowned upon that reputable shops didn't carry them. To get them you had to go to Ugly places to deal with Ugly people and pay a high price for them when you did.

So Stacey smoked. Not very Beautiful, Stacey. Somewhere else in that tote bag had to be the spray bottle of masking scent for hair and clothes and the neutral mouth drops to take the telltale odor off the breath. It wouldn't *do* for your Beautiful friends to know that you had such an Ugly habit, now would it? But now Sal knew. Yes, Ugly old Sal knew, and she had smiled at her knowledge.

Stacey had quickly stooped to pick up her scattered belongings and had given a quiet little gasp when she saw the cigarettes lying about the floor. She had quickly reached to hide them, at the same time glancing up to see if Sal had spotted them. Sal's smile told her everything, and for a brief instant—barely half a second—there had flashed across Stacey's upturned face a look of such sheer revulsion, of such cold and bitter hatred, that Sal gasped to see it. Stacey had quickly turned her face to the carpet, busying herself with repacking her bag, but Sal knew that in that instant she had seen Stacey's true attitude. Underneath all the cheerfulness and compassion and meaningful touches Stacey hated and feared Sal and all she represented, as the Beautifuls had always hated and feared the Uglies.

By the time the tote bag was back in order, so was Stacey's face, though a little stiffer and less cheerful than before. The session had ended swiftly, and Sal had returned to her room. On her way back from dinner that evening was when she had wandered away, found the vacant hall and open door, and made her escape.

Now, plunging down the shadowed street with her hip grinding and the pain in her chest bringing tears to her eyes, Sal wondered how wise that had been. She had no place to go and no clothes to wear and no food to eat. Nobody would help her, for as an Ugly she didn't really exist. They would surely hunt her down before the night was out. Yes, they'd hunt her down and take her back and put her in a real cell this time to make sure she didn't escape, and then where would she be? In worse shape than she had been before. But that didn't matter, she thought as she hobbled along. At least she was free. If only for a couple of hours, and probably for the last time, she was free.

Sal came to the corner of Ridgeway and cautiously peered around it, up and down the boulevard, looking for cruising vans. The only lights were far away down the street, too far to tell what they were, so she figured she was safe for a little way. She started to hobble north on Ridgeway, wondering how far she'd have to go before she found a place to hide, if she ever would. She remembered that a block and a half up on Ridgeway, right next to Herb & Anne's Music, had been a nice alley, well sheltered from the wind, but it had been one of the first to be bricked up, so she'd have to look farther. Her hobble had slowed to a fast walk, and she paused for breath more frequently, but she kept on.

Sal was just able to make out the sign over Herb & Anne's in the dim light when she noticed something strange. Just beyond it, where there should have been the glare of shiny new brick and mortar, there was a darkness that looked like shadow. Rubbing her eyes, she moved closer. Yes, there was no mistaking it—where there had been a clean new wall now yawned the familiar old alley mouth. Amazed, she approached it cautiously and examined the ground and building walls. There were no signs of the brick wall at all—no brick chips or mortar powder or any markings to indicate where it had been. The wall was gone without a trace, as if it had never been there. She wondered what had happened to it.

Sal did not stand still to wonder, though. However it had

happened, the alley was open again, a safe haven for a little while. She turned into it, breathing a sigh of relief as the shadows enfolded her. She was, in a manner, home again. The alley looked just the same as it once had, with dumpsters here and there and piles of crates laying about. She went deeper into it, nestling into the shadows like a kitten into a basket of warm sheets. It was good to be back.

Sal was about halfway down the alley when she caught the scent. At first she thought she was dreaming, but then she smelled it again, stronger this time. It couldn't be! She began to walk more slowly, peering around piles and into doorways, with the aroma growing stronger at each step. Finally, near the end of the alley, prudently sheltered behind a big dumpster, she found it. She stared in joy and wonder.

There, close to the wall so it wouldn't illuminate much, stood a rusty old bucket in which flickered a small fire. Hunkered down over the fire was a shadowed figure in shaggy clothes extending its hand over the flames and rubbing them in the warmth. Sal's heart leapt. Another Ugly! But from where? She had sworn she was the last one in the city, and for the past couple of weeks she had seen nobody else, familiar or unfamiliar, to indicate otherwise. But that didn't matter—at least she wasn't alone!

Sal must have made some noise as she stood watching in the shadows, for the figure turned a little and looked up at her. It was a man, and he was an Ugly, all right. He had a wrinkled, leathery face and a bushy gray mustache growing down over his mouth. His chin was covered with stubble, and his hair hung down in greasy, untrimmed locks from under the dirty old fedora on his head. The battered suit jacket he wore was too small for him, so the sleeves came a couple of inches short on his wrists, making his large, wrinkled hands all the more noticeable. His rheumy eyes looked very tired but nonetheless showed a sparkle of interest as he looked at Sal. They regarded each other before he nodded and spoke, rising to his feet as he did.

"Evenin', ma'am", he said in a gravelly voice, tipping his hat just a little.

"Evenin' ", she replied.

"Am I in your spot?" he asked, suddenly looking a little flustered.

"No, no." She waved her hands to ease his concern. "Not my spot. Not anybody's."

"You look a mite chilly", he said. "Come warm yourself."

"Don't mind if I do", she replied, stepping toward the bucket. He grabbed a nearby crate and set it on the ground. She sat on it and extended her chilled hands over the licking flames, sighing with pleasure as the warmth caressed them. The man hunkered down again and fed a couple more scraps of wood into the bucket.

"Name's Josh", he said.

"Sal", she responded. "You're new about, aren't you?"

"Yup", he nodded. "Just got here today."

"This isn't the best place to be right now", she said.

"Ain't no place very good to be right now", he replied. "Figure this as good a place as any." She nodded. They sat in silence for some minutes, watching the flickering flames. Finally he spoke again.

"Hungry?"

"Maybe a bit", Sal replied. Josh turned and rummaged in a plastic grocery bag by his elbow. He brought out a paper parcel that, when unwrapped, revealed itself to be a few pieces of deli chicken, the kind cooked with barbecue sauce. These had probably been scavenged from a dumpster somewhere, but they didn't look too old. Sal's mouth watered.

"Lemme heat 'em up a little", Josh said, rummaging in his bag some more. "Brings out the flavor." He brought forth a broken hanger, which he quickly twisted into a spit. Soon the chicken was warming over the fire, adding its spicy aroma to the musky scent of the woodsmoke. As the chicken heated, they talked about the various memorable meals they'd had and what food kept longest and cooked best over open fires. Then the chicken was done, and they ate it, juggling the pieces from hand to hand as they bit into them. It was just the way Sal liked it: spicy and juicy and just the tiniest bit charred in spots. She felt she had never tasted anything so delicious. When they finished the chicken, Josh brought out a couple more treasures from his bag—a few old dinner rolls and a small bottle of wine. The rolls were stale and crumbly but sweet, and they weren't too difficult to chew with a swig of wine to soften them. It made an interesting flavor, the light sweetness of the rolls and the tangy bite of the wine. So they concluded their meager supper, munching the rolls and passing the bottle back and forth.

When they were finished, the talk turned to the world around them. Sal described how things had been in the city: the cruising vans and how all the Uglies had been taken away. She described her own experience: the hospital that was a prison, the sessions with Stacey, her escape earlier that day. Josh nodded through it all, saying that it was much the same everywhere. He had just barely gotten out of the last city and had come here knowing that he would probably be caught, but there wasn't much that could be done about it. Sal found herself liking Josh more and more. His speech was quiet and gentle, without the anger that had always marked Keith's speech or the cynicism that lay behind every word that Brooklyn had ever spoken. Josh spoke honestly about the wrongs that others had committed, hiding nothing, but neither indulging in fierce bitterness like Anita always had. It was as if nothing that had been done to him could change who he was.

The night wore on. Sometimes they spoke together in quiet voices; sometimes they just sat together in silence. Sal, now comfortably warmed by the fire, grew pleasantly drowsy, but she didn't want to sleep. It was too pleasant just sitting, chatting with Josh, and warming herself over the bucket. It was just like old times in the Nooks, and she indulged in the fantasy that it would never end, though a small portion of her deep inside reminded her that it couldn't be that way.

Which it wasn't. After an unknown number of hours, as the stars wheeled above and only the least whisper of outside noises penetrated to the depths of the alley, their quiet conversation was abruptly interrupted by a very distinct noise, which had to be right at the alley mouth. Sal recognized it immediately: the sound of brakes squealing, quickly followed by the grinding sound of a vehicle being thrown into reverse. Then the grinding stopped, and the back wall of the alley, not twenty feet from where they sat, was illuminated by a bright white light—the kind cast by the searchlights that the cruising vans always carried.

Sal's heart pounded. Not daring to move, she glanced quickly at the fire and then at Josh, who simply shrugged. There was no use putting out the fire—they would be here in another minute. Seeing her panic, Josh reached over to her. She grabbed his hand in both of hers, drawing strength in her terror from his unshakable calmness.

Sal could hear them coming. Unlike the last crew, who had arrested her in efficient silence, these ones came noisily, talking loudly and banging on things. From the shadows cast by the searchlight on the back alley wall she could tell there were four of them. She was frightened, for though she couldn't hear their words at first, their voices sounded angry and cruel. They were breaking things as they came, smashing crates and kicking over barrels. Sal trembled, and Josh squeezed her hand in reassurance. They stopped about twenty yards away, close enough for Sal to discern their words, and one spoke.

"There", he said. "Smell that? I told you she'd be down here."

"She damn well better be, the bitch", said another voice. "We've wasted all night looking for her, thanks to those fools at the Center who can't do their jobs."

"Or those jerks in Reconstruction", said yet another. The voices were moving again, coming closer. "They were supposed to have sealed this alley months ago."

The voices were almost upon them. Sal clenched Josh's hand more tightly as the shadows on the wall grew smaller and more defined. Then around the corner of the dumpster stepped the four policemen, gloved and masked as the others had been. The foremost one pointed in triumph with his nightstick.

"See! I told you she was here!"

"Yeah, but what's this? Another one?" asked another.

"Damn!" swore one of the ones in the back. "Just what we need! S.I.D. told Central weeks ago that the streets had been sanitized."

"Sure, on the basis of your reports", retorted the second figure. "Good going—this means we'll be pulling troll patrols for three more weeks until they're satisfied."

"Quit the jawing. Let's get 'em in the van", snarled the first.

Throughout the exchange between the policemen Sal and Josh had just sat still, gazing up at their captors with resignation and fear. Now the foremost policeman stepped forward and kicked the bucket aside, scattering the little fire across the alley in a shower of sparks. He roughly grabbed Sal's arm and yanked her to her feet, tearing her hand from Josh's. The others came around and seized Josh, who offered no resistance. Nobody was being gentle this time. Sal was spun around and had her arms yanked behind her back, painfully twisting her shoulders. Her hands were tied tightly together with a cord or wire of some type that cut cruelly into her wrists. She glanced over her shoulders at Josh, only managing a momentary glance at him before the policeman cuffed her head a stinging blow to keep her looking forward. But from that moment Sal drew strength, for though Josh was being yanked about and tied up even as she was, and with more cuffs and blows, he still kept his serene gaze fixed on her, as if urging her to have courage. There was something deep and imperturbable behind those eyes, something that reassured her despite the circumstances.

Having tied them securely, the policemen then began dragging them down the alley toward the waiting van. Sal saw one of them reach down to sweep up Josh's plastic bag and fling it into the dumpster as they passed. The brightness of the searchlight hurt her eyes, so she had to bow her head as they got closer to the van. Two of the men climbed in first, then yanked them in behind, seating them at other ends of the van facing away from each other. The remaining two policemen got into the front, and the van began moving.

The ride was short, thought it seemed longer, because in the windowless van Sal could not watch their progress through the streets. She longed to talk to Josh, to ask how he was doing, or to hear even one word of encouragement, but the two policemen would not allow them to speak. When they got to their destination, the van door opened, but the policeman nearest Sal put his nightstick on her shoulder to indicate that she should stay where she was until Josh had been removed. From his grunts and gasps as they removed him she knew that they were not being gentle, probably punching him with the ends of their nightsticks. She felt sorry for him and for the fact that it was the pursuit of her that had led to his capture, but she was ashamed to realize that she was even more sorry for herself. She felt lonely and frightened without him. She knew that was silly, for there was nothing either one of them could do against the power that had captured them both, but she felt that way nonetheless.

After some minutes of sitting still in the darkness and silence with the nightstick resting heavily on her shoulder, Sal was pulled to her feet and shoved out of the van. She got only brief glimpses of her surroundings as she was hustled along: the van parked under a brick canopy, automatic glass doors that opened silently to let them through, the light green hallway walls illuminated by diffused fluorescent light, the sharp clack of the policemen's boots on the shining tile floor, the cool antiseptic smell of the air. It gave all the impression of a hospital except that there were very few people, and these wore not the blue-green dress of medical workers but the blue uniforms of the police. Everyone wore the doctor's masks, though, and the elbow-length rubber gloves.

After marching for some minutes, making a couple of turns along the way but never seeing anything but the sterile green halls, they arrived at a door with a small square window high up in its center. One of the policemen unlocked it while the other grasped her arms and cut the wrist cord; then she was shoved through and the door slammed and locked behind her.

There was no pretense this time: this was a prison cell. The bed was the sole piece of furniture; a sink and commode stood in the corner. There were no windows. The fluorescent light in the ceiling shed its rays on glossy enamel walls and shiny floor. Unlike most jails she had ever occupied, this one was unusually cold. Rubbing her sore wrists and noticing that she was bleeding a bit, she went over to the sink to rinse her hands. It had only cold water, and there was no towel, so she had to use toilet paper to dry her hands off. Then she went over and sat on the bed. There was nothing at all to do for anything. She tried to wonder what would happen next but found she couldn't. She couldn't even worry about Josh, or about herself, for that matter. Her mind was numb.

After sitting for a while, she realized that she was shivering. The thin blanket on the bed didn't look like much comfort, but she decided it would be better than nothing. She crawled under it, again noticing the crinkly sound of the paper-cloth sheets. The blanket was too thin and too short as well, but if she curled up and lay still, it would almost keep her warm. Then she discovered, to her surprise, that she wasn't sleepy. Normally she could sleep almost anywhere, but now, when she would have welcomed the release of sleep, she could not. So she lay still, feeling nothing, thinking nothing, wondering nothing.

After an indeterminate period of time that felt like hours but she knew could have been as little as forty-five minutes, the door clanked open again. Two masked policemen, who might have been the same ones who brought her here—there was no way of telling—stepped inside. One of them motioned to her with his nightstick, indicating that she should precede them out the door. Knowing there was no use in resisting, she rose and came along.

After another brief walk down the monotonously uniform hallways they came to another room. Sal was led into this with one policeman preceding her and one following. Inside was the first genuine room she had seen in the place, with real lightbulbs in real lamps, wallpaper, acoustic tile overhead, and a brown carpet underfoot. Toward the back of the room was a large polished wood desk, like one that would be found in any executive's office. This was completely bare except for a flat computer screen and keyboard off to one side. Behind the desk was a high-backed leather chair with nobody in it. About ten feet in front of this desk, roughly in the middle of the room, stood a more functional looking table facing the wooden desk, with two chairs and another computer screen and keyboard. Sal could see some of the characters blinking on the computer screen. On the right side of the room, facing the open space between the desk and the table, stood another table of similar design with two chairs, a screen, and a keyboard as well. At this table was seated a young man in uniform staring at the screen and diligently working the keyboard. To her surprise, he was not wearing a doctor's mask. At the back of the room to the left were a few plastic stacking chairs lined up against the wall. It was to these that Sal was led. She was seated in one of them, and the two on either side of her were picked up and moved aside so the police escorts could stand there, flanking her. She sat silently, hands in her lap, listening to the quiet click of the computer keyboard in the far corner and searching her mind to recall just what this room and furniture layout reminded her of.

The door through which she had just come opened again and through it came—Stacey! A very different Stacey, though—no tote bag with her, wearing a lab coat and a very different face. A professional face, Sal decided, straightforward and no nonsense and (Sal noticed) just the slightest bit fearful. Stacey did not look at anything in the room but walked directly to the table in the middle of the room, sat down at the keyboard, and began working with the computer. In a flash Sal remembered when she had last seen a room that looked like this: in a court! With the young man acting like the court recorder, Stacey looking like a lawyer, and the empty desk looking like a judge's bench, it had all the appearance of a courtroom. All that was lacking was the judge.

They did not wait long. The judge soon arrived through a door behind the young stenographer. He was a harsh-looking man with white hair, angry eyes, and a severe frown. He scowled once around the room when he entered, then stalked over to the desk and sat down, glancing with scorn at the computer screen. Though his suit was well pressed and his tie was in order, he wore the air of an unpleasant man who was unexpectedly called to an unwanted task. His words and tone confirmed this.

"Let's get this over with", he growled. The young man began reciting some numbers and references in a stiff, official-sounding voice, apparently reading from the computer screen.

The white-haired man then turned toward Stacey, who began speaking in a formal voice that Sal had never heard her use. Apparently she had a different voice to go with each face.

Sal could understand nothing of the conversation that followed. It was all in a jargon so cryptic that it might as well have been a foreign language. Terms such as *case* and *retrogression* and *sociologic inadaptability* were used often, as well as numerous references to this and that precedent. Through it all the white-haired man said little, spending most of the time glaring from one speaker to the other and exuding an air of angry impatience with the proceedings. Nobody wanted those fierce eyes resting on him for long, so he squirmed and spoke quickly when under the man's gaze. In the end it was Stacey who spoke the words that seemed to finish the proceedings.

"Therefore, it is the recommendation of the Institute that this case be resolved in accordance with Directive 427, Subsection G", she concluded with a note of relief.

The white-haired man stared at her for a moment, then responded, "Very well."

At this nearly everyone in the room visibly relaxed, but Sal felt a chill in her heart, as if whatever this decision meant, it didn't bode well for her. The white-haired man rose from the desk and turned to leave, saying as he did, "And may that be the end of it."

"Er, excuse me, sir". The policeman to Sal's left stepped forward, speaking in a quavery voice and fingering his nightstick nervously. The white-haired man fixed him with an icy stare.

"Yes, Sergeant?" he asked in an stony voice.

"We—er, we were wondering what to do about the other one", the policeman said hesitantly, as if reluctant to bring up the issue.

"Other one, Sergeant?" asked the white-haired man acidly. "Which other one?"

"During the resolution of this case, another item was discovered, sir. The item was preprocessed without incident, but . . ."

"This office was given to understand that this was a closed issue, Sergeant", the white-haired man barked back viciously. "Do you mean to tell me, with all your talk of unanticipated items, that the Center has misinformed this office? Is that what you mean to say, Sergeant?"

"No, no, sir", the terrified sergeant replied. "It's just that . . ."

"Then understand that this office is not interested in processing any more cases of this nature. Is that clear, Sergeant?" The white-haired man's voice was as cold as iced steel.

"Yes, sir, but . . ."

"I asked, is that clear?" The white-haired man lowered his voice to a quiet but very precise near-whisper that was somehow more terrifying than anything he had yet said.

"Yes, sir", the subdued sergeant said. Without another word the white-haired man swept from the room. Everyone who remained drew a deep breath. The sergeant turned to look at his companion and shrugged his shoulders, getting a shrug in return. Stacey stood up and turned around, looking pale and shaken (Probably needs a smoke, thought Sal). Both Stacey and the sergeant made for the door, the sergeant arriving first and holding the door, then passing out behind her. Never once during her entire time in the room had Stacey even glanced at Sal.

Uncertain of what to do, Sal looked up at the remaining policeman. He did not return her glance or show any sign of moving, so neither did she. The young man tapped away at his keyboard for a while, then finished and left by the same door that the white-haired man had used. Sal sat still in the silent room for some time with her silent guard at her shoulder. She didn't know what was coming next, but she knew it wasn't good.

After some time the sergeant returned, poking his head through the door and motioning to the other policeman to come along. He poked Sal with his nightstick, and she rose. When they stepped out into the hallway, they turned a different way than they had come from Sal's cell.

Cold terror rose within her. This was bad. This was very bad. She knew that the conversation before the white-haired man had been about her, and she guessed that something terrible had been decided. She found she was nearly panting in her fear, and her fingers were cold. She wanted out; she wanted to be free, to smell the blossoms on the plums in the park, or to see just one more sunset on the river—just one more, please, please! She felt like she was half dead, with part of her inside screaming and scrabbling with terror, desperately clutching after even one more breath of fresh air or ray of true sunlight, while the other part kept plodding along after her jailers. It seemed that her inward frenzy and outward inertia grew with every passing step.

They were now passing through corridors Sal had never seen before, occasionally blocked by frosted-glass walls with doors that were unlocked by a little white card being stuck in a slot. At last they came to a door that looked slightly different and opened itself when the card was used. Inside it was darker, and Sal drew back.

"What's—what's that?" she croaked, her throat constricted in terror. Neither man answered, instead seizing her by both arms and throwing her through the doorway. She tripped over a sill of some kind at the bottom of the door and sprawled headlong on the floor. The policemen did not follow her through. The door closed by itself, the mechanism hissing in the dark.

Sal saw quickly that the room was not completely dark but was very faintly illuminated by a red-amber light from some source that ran around the top of the walls where they met the ceiling. By this light she could faintly discern another figure in the room, a figure that was groping toward her.

"Are you all right?" the figure asked. Sal almost cried in her relief.

"Josh."

"Sal? Sal, are you hurt?" He was beside her now, helping her up. "That was quite a tumble you took." He assisted her over to a low dark thing that served as a bench.

"I'm okay, honest", she wheezed, settling herself on the bench. Josh had one arm around her shoulder and held her hands with the other. Panic engulfed her, and she wrung his hand in hers. "Josh, Josh, where is this place? What are they doing, Josh? It's something terrible, isn't it? Oh, Josh, I'm so scared, so scared." She was quivering with terror. All the time he kept stroking her shoulder and holding her hand firmly.

"There, it'll be all right, Sal. It'll be all right. I'm right with you", he murmured.

"Josh", she said. "Josh, I'm so sorry. If you hadn't been with me, they wouldn't have gotten you. You could still be free. I'm sorry, Josh—I'm sorry for everything, everything. Oh, Josh, what's going to happen to us?" She buried her face in his shoulder and sobbed.

"I'm right with you, Sal", he whispered. "Right with you. I won't go away; no, I'll stay right with you. I won't leave you; no, I won't . . ." His whispering increased in volume a little in an attempt to hide the quiet hissing. Sal knew what it was but found she could not be any more terrified than she already was. She even knew what the heavy drowsiness presaged, but with Josh comforting her she found her fear being displaced by a deep inner quiet. Then she noticed that the light was getting better, or her eyes were adapting to it, for through her tears she could just see Josh's hand holding hers in her lap. But no, it couldn't be Josh's hand—it was too clean, and young, and strong—and what was that mark on his wrist? Swiftly now the light was waxing, bright white, and pierced by fear of a quite different kind, she looked up, and saw.

And then she knew.

"Another five minutes, don't you think, Darryl?" he said. No answer came. "Darryl?" Scott swiveled in his chair, glancing around the control room. Darryl had ducked out, the bastard. How like him to leave just now. He swore quietly but fiercely at his missing coworker as he adjusted the gauges slightly to maintain the pressure. He'd better be back by the time they had to take a look, or there'd be hell to pay. That was always the worst part, especially if you looked too soon. Not that that would be a problem this time—there was no backlog, so they could take as much time as they wanted. Not that anyone wanted to spend a lot of time in this place. Scott tweaked another dial and stared at the observation window, inky black until they turned up the lights in the chamber beyond.

Darryl, meanwhile, was touching up his hair in the men's room down the hall. Almost end of shift—he could get out of these scrubs and into some decent rags, then head down to the university for breakfast at the Union. Maybe he could spot some young fillies and try out his new smile. With satisfaction he grinned into the mirror again, admiring the seamless job the dentist had done. Beautiful.

Suddenly he realized how long he had been gone. Cripes! He'd better get back, or Scott would have a bitching fit. He swept out the door and back down to the control room. He was sure glad this duty was ending—he couldn't take another shift with that jerk. He quietly eased the door open and stepped inside, peering left and right to locate Scott. Yup, there he was, seated at the controls, working away like a good boy. But what . . . ? Darryl could just barely see in the dim light of the controls reflecting against the observation window, but the reflection didn't need much light. In his trepidation the handle slipped from his hand, and the door swung to.

Scott heard the door slam and thought that Darryl was sure clumsy for someone trying to be sneaky.

"Actually made it back, handsome?" he sneered, not looking up from the controls. "When the going gets tough, the tough get going, eh? Just for that, you can be the first in there with the hose—how do you like that?" He looked up at Darryl's shadowy reflection in the angled glass of the observation window. Darryl gave no response for four heartbeats, then gave a strangled cry, yanked the door open, and dashed out. Scott wheeled in his chair just in time to see the door swing shut.

"What the hell is wrong with him?"

Darryl ran, gasping for breath, shutting his eyes, shutting his mind. It couldn't be. It couldn't be. That gargoyle thing that spoke with Scott's voice just couldn't be. He hadn't clearly seen until it looked up—he shook his head violently to erase the memory of the bared fangs and the leprous skin, the glaring red eyes, and the crabbed claws manipulating the knobs. It was a nightmare and worse than a nightmare, amplified by the lurid orange glow of the gas chamber controls. He didn't know what had happened, but he wanted to be far, far away from it.

Dashing around a corner and nearly stumbling in his haste, Darryl suddenly noticed that his feet were hurting as if they were being squeezed. What was the matter with his shoes? The pain was intensifying so quickly that despite his terror he had to stop, ducking into a doorway alcove. Not daring to sit, he pulled one foot up to his other knee and reached for the laces.

But that thing that grasped the laces was no hand but a scaly three-fingered appendage with sharp claws.

Gasping, Darryl made the mistake of looking to his left, where the fluorescent hall lighting against the glass beside the door made a near-perfect mirror.

Staring back at him was a long-snouted visage with fierce long teeth, coarse green scales, and nictitating membranes flickering down over cold reptilian eyes.

Darryl screamed and screamed and screamed and screamed.

Back in the control room, Scott started to rise to follow Darryl but was distracted by a sound that grew louder by the moment. It was coming from outside, and it didn't sound like the normal early-morning hubbub that could be expected at this time. Scott stepped over to the narrow window that was this room's only view of the outside world and pressed his face close against the glass to see better. Something was going on—in the dim light he could see people dashing everywhere out by the street. But were they people? They had to be, but there was something strange about them. Their forms didn't look quite right, and they were all running oddly. Lots of shouting, though, and more every minute. A riot? No, they weren't mobbing—in fact, they seemed to be running away from each other, dashing all about in their panic. Some were coming this way, screaming.

Suddenly Scott's heart jumped, for the outside screaming was joined by another shrill scream nearby, followed by another and another. Screams of pure horror were being torn from someone's throat—right down the hall, from the sound of it! Scott leaped to the control panel to turn up the lights and in doing so caught sight of his own reflection in the glow of the dials.

Slowly he raised knobby claws to feel the flabby, patchy skin of his face, while the mounting screams from the hallway echoed the realization in his own heart.

Meanwhile in the streets below the shrieking figures poured from the buildings to face the red dawn of a brand-new day.

Numaris

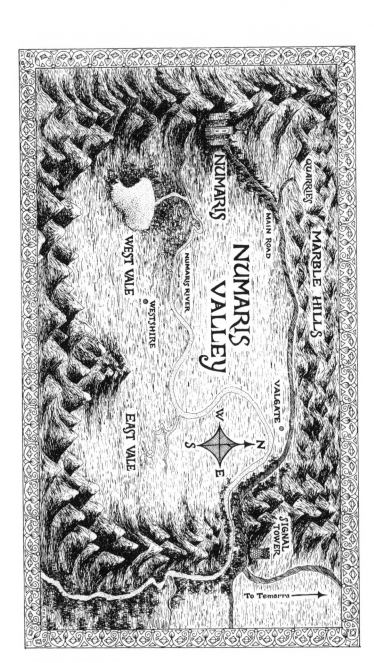

NUMARIS VALLEY

NUMARIS

WEST VALE

NUMARIS RIVER

WESTSHIRE

EAST VALE

MAIN ROAD

QUARRIES

MARBLE HILLS

VALGATE

SIGNAL TOWER

To Temarra →

N
W E
S

THE DAY BEGAN INAUSPICIOUSLY ENOUGH. As a mere field lieutenant in the Imperial Army, Sir William de Rowan was not asked to staff meetings to discuss missions or supply issues. He was also seldom chosen for the coveted message runs to the district or, more rarely, capital command posts, even though these provided the opportunity to rub shoulders with the staff officers and bring back the latest rumors, on which the field officer corps seemed to thrive. He could have had more such missions had he asked—he was assured it would help his career, which needed it—but he never asked, for deep inside him lay the conviction that an army officer should be fighting. So he stayed in camp, waiting for opportunities to take men into the field.

Which was why, in the dewy predawn of that fateful day, he mounted his gray destrier mare to lead a routine patrol out into the chill morning mist. Hardly anyone enjoyed patrol duty, least of all the squad doing it, but William took the billet often. He didn't mind it as much as some, especially since riding was a passion of his, and it was the countless hours of riding on his father's estate that had developed on his small frame the muscular carriage he now wore. At least riding was better than sitting around camp waiting for the meal bell.

His squad thought differently that morning, at least initially. The dozen or so junior officers and senior sergeants riding behind him did so in sullen silence, wrapping their riding cloaks tightly around themselves to ward off the cold. They were upset that he had made them wear mail, which was chilly in the early morning and hot in the long afternoon. The two dozen infantrymen trudging behind were none too pleased either, as he had made them bear their halberds for the patrol. He knew that most other officers allowed their patrols to travel lighter— some even led their men out unarmed and unarmored! The patrols were seen by most of his fellows as a vestigial ritual, but William never forgot that the Imperial Army was technically at war, and according to regulations the squad he led out was a light one, minimally armed for its duties.

As they walked on and the sun rose, the day warmed, and so did the squad's spirits. Cloaks were thrown back, and gay chatter accompanied the march. The infantry strolled along with their weapons across their shoulders, jawing about the camp games and the latest shipment of chow, not even pretending to march in company. William reminded himself that this was a patrol, not a parade, and did not reprimand their laxness. Spirits lifted more when, after traveling some miles along the valley road, they turned up the road toward the mountains. The men knew that though the initial climb was more difficult, the shaded mountain roads were the best place to be when the afternoon sun burned down.

So they marched on—down one hill and up another and finally into the woods. The climbing at first left the men no breath for talking, and once they entered the forest, as befitting such a solemn place, the conversations became more subdued than they had been on the open road. Immense oaks and maples towered over the men, spreading their branches across the road in a giant archway that let only a small amount of light through. The thub-thub of the horses' hooves on the hard-pounded dirt of the path seemed to reach barely into the forest before dying out in the deep shadows. They traveled more slowly, the horses' heads drooping and the men trudging quietly along behind. The morning's march had been tiring, and soon it would be time to stop for a bite and a rest.

The attack came when William was trying to recall the location of a good place to stop along the road. He was jolted from his thoughts by a brief sound, which he barely registered before it ceased. It came from the woods to his left, and as he was turning toward it, searching his mind for where he knew that sound from, he heard it again—and a long, black-feathered arrow buried itself in his horse's shoulder, inches from his thigh.

"Ambush!" someone yelled behind William, but he had no time to respond. Screaming in agony, his horse reared and turned, wrenching the reins from his hand as she tried to bite at the torment in her side. This proved well for William but ill for the horse, for in so doing she wheeled right into the path of an arrow that had been aimed for William himself. The shaft buried itself in the hapless animal's throat, and she collapsed to the ground, gasping her last in a bloody froth.

William had no time to think. His rider's instincts had taken over when his mount reared, twisting him to keep him in the saddle, and as the beast fell they forced his legs to kick themselves free of the stirrups and push himself away. He fell with the horse, and though his frantic scrambling wasn't the gallant leap he would have preferred to execute, at least he was free. He clumsily drew his sword and crouched behind the horse's twitching carcass to survey the situation.

It was grim. The squadron was milling around in panic and confusion, terrified cries filling the air as William's men fell beneath the murderous black arrows. His standard-bearer had taken one in the throat, laying him and the Imperial banneret in the dust. One other horse was down, and two more officers had been unhorsed. The remaining cavalry were wheeling about, swinging their swords and yelling, nearly slaughtering the foot soldiers in the process. The infantry was in no better shape. Some were trying to assist their comrades who had fallen, but most were attempting just to dodge both the lethal arrows of the enemy and the inept blundering of their superiors. Above all the trampling confusion sang the deadly melody of the bowstrings as his men were marked down by the invisible archers.

All this William noted in the space of three heartbeats. Cold dread twisted his insides, and the urge to slink away into the trees welled up strong within him. But no—the knowledge of his duty stayed with him. These were his men; they had trusted him, and he had led them into an ambush. Already the blood that was soaking into the dust was his responsibility—if his men were to live, it would be because he responded now.

The attack was coming from their left, the uphill side of the path, where the woods thinned out and the terrain was punctuated with boulders and rocky outcroppings. Somewhere among them lay the archers who were cutting down William's squadron. The proper tactical response would be to quick march his men back down the path to a place of safety and from there plan a counterattack. However, William knew that in the midst of the ambush there was little chance of his even getting the men's attention, much less forming them up and marching them anywhere. There, in that grim place where the very air bore death and each passing second brought more arrows to find throat and gullet, their only concern was to get somewhere—anywhere—that the arrows could not find them. Most of those who knew where they were going at all seemed to be trying to make it to the far side of the path, which had been on their right and was now behind William. There the ground sloped down, and the trees thickened again. Bushes and brambles filled in between the trees, providing ideal cover from the arrows. William looked at the thickets, and deep within him something triggered an alarm. His men were scrambling for the bushes, knowing them to be perfect for hiding and escaping. Yes, perfect for . . .

"Back!" William yelled, rising from behind his horse and brandishing his sword. Fear tightened the muscles in his throat, making his command sound more like a squeak, but he kept yelling. "Back! Away from the woods—toward the archers! Back!" He wasn't squeaking toward the end, and he could see that his deep-chested bellow was penetrating the din as men turned to look at him. They were hearing—but they weren't obeying. They still ran about in confusion, making for the underbrush behind. One man stumbled right past William, heedless of his shouting. Another attempted to, but William grabbed his arm and spun him around.

"Obey me, you fool!" he snarled, shaking his sword in the man's face. "Back! Can't you see? They're driving us!" The man's expression clearly showed that he saw little more than a saber waving inches from his nose, but he got the message. Wide eyed and gasping, he turned and stumbled back toward the middle of the path. Others noted this and began to turn as well, some even picking up the halberds they had dropped.

"Back! Form up!" William bellowed. "Dismount there! Stay away from the bushes!" Some men were still milling and trampling, but he could see that an officer's green still commanded some respect, for they were beginning to look for their stations in formation. He also knew it would command the enemy's attention and was keenly aware that a black arrow could end this rally at any moment. But he kept yelling, wondering in the back of his mind why fewer arrows seemed to be flying now. But before he had time to think on it he heard behind him the reason, which also confirmed his tactical intuition. He gripped his sword tighter and turned to face it.

Up from the shrubs and underbrush—the growth he had warned his men away from—charged a grim, snarling squad of black-clad soldiers. William had been right—the ambush had been well laid, and his men had nearly fallen for it. Had they scattered among the bushes, they would have been cut to pieces by these skulking butchers. William found grim satisfaction in knowing that he had discerned the enemy's strategy correctly, at the same time tasting the bitter irony that probably nobody would ever know of it. Outnumbered and caught by surprise, facing a vicious enemy with soft troops of his own and hostile archers at his back, William de Rowan felt in his bones that he would die there on that dusty path.

The enemy soldiers charged, snarling and screaming, closing quickly on the Imperial patrol. At least they must have been closing quickly, William reasoned absently, for to him they seemed to be taking forever to cross the twenty-odd feet of the path. It seemed that his senses were sharpened as well as slowed, for he could hear the slightest noise, even amidst the furious shouting of the enemy charge. His vision seemed keener, and he noticed disjointed details such as the shabbiness of the enemy's uniforms and how bad their teeth were. The Black Army, ancient enemy of the Empire, obviously treated their troops no differently than they did their slaves or other subjects: with beatings, starvation, and other maltreatment. This band had probably been sent with no supplies and few arms into Imperial territory to kill and destroy—and survive—as best they could. They were certainly looking forward to the plunder they would take from William's patrol. The weapons they were brandishing were old and broken, some merely heavy branches. Only one enemy soldier he could see had a decent sword. But there were more of them, and their ferocity more than compensated for their poor armament. William had little confidence that his camp-fat troops could withstand them. At least, he thought grimly as he gripped his saber tighter, he would ensure that there were fewer to leave this encounter.

So the enemy came on, their battle cries a raucous backdrop to William's musings. One wild-eyed soldier had obviously selected William as a target and came on with a blood-curdling shriek, knobbed battle club held high for the killing blow. William's blood was indeed nearly curdled, but his drill-trained muscles weren't, and without thinking he neatly sidestepped the bone-crushing downstroke and cut up into the man's midsection. The soldier wore no armor, so William's stroke cut cleanly through him until it struck his backbone with jarring force. The man's eyes registered dumb shock just before they glazed over, and he collapsed in a heap, clutching at the gash in his abdomen. William stepped back quickly, ducking a blow from a flail, and parrying the thrust of a crude spear. All was jump and twist and thrust and parry for some time, as he sought to stay alive and inflict as much damage as he could. There was no glamour here in the midst of battle; indeed, William felt rather foolish with all his hopping and leaping, more like a jester at a festival dance than an Imperial officer. He seemed to be doing some damage to the enemy—at least he was remembering to try for the maiming rather than the killing blow, for these were easier to inflict and get away from.

Out of the corner of his eye William saw with satisfaction that the squad had formed up into a proper defensive posture, with a double row of gleaming halberd heads keeping the Black Army force effectively at bay. His men were scared stiff, and the best of them was wielding his weapon like a green recruit, but the tight formation was making up for their errors and inexperience. William also noticed that the men were off to his right, which meant that he was out alone, away from their protection. He began to work his way toward them as best he could. The enemy soldiers, reasonably enough, sought to keep him isolated, so the struggle was extremely difficult and only got worse as he approached his own line. The closest call came when he was nearly there but slipped on some gore underfoot, falling to the ground mere feet from the protection of the halberds. The enemy sprang forward in triumph, foremost among them a black-bearded soldier with a brutal-looking dagger. When this fierce killer leaped on him with death written on his face, William was certain he was looking on the last thing his eyes would ever see. But a sudden flash said otherwise, as two well-thrust halberds caught the man in midleap, doing brutal things to his side and shoulder and shoving him backward to fall dead in the dust. Strong hands grasped William and pulled him back to the protection of the line. He scrambled to his feet, muttering his thanks to his rescuers, and looked about to assess the situation.

It was better than William had hoped for. All the men and horses who yet lived were behind or among the line of halberdiers. Those who had not made it lay bloodied on the path beside those who had been marked down by the arrows. A good number of enemy troops lay there as well, including a surprising number around where he had been fighting. Many of the enemy soldiers still remained, however, clustered together just beyond reach of the halberd line, howling and waving their weapons but not daring to attack the row of glistening blades. William realized that the ambush had been fought to a standoff.

He looked at his enemies with new eyes. Whereas before he had seen them as dread predators, willing and able to destroy him and his men at leisure, now he saw merely enemies—enemies who could kill but who could also be killed, and fought back against, and yes, even beaten. He saw fear in their eyes, as they clearly grasped the same fact. He saw something else in their eyes as well: cowardice. These boastful assassins were willing enough to hide in bushes or surround lone soldiers, but when it came to facing another armed force under battle conditions, they plainly didn't have the courage. William's blood burned in anger at the thought of these bullies burning farms and killing children because they hadn't the guts to face men in combat. His confidence rose.

"All squadron!" William bellowed. "Make second form! Backups match outers! Prepare to advance!" If he was facing nothing more than bullies, he could certainly show them some things. His assurance was contagious, and his men executed his orders sharply. If the Black Army was so fearsome, with all its hiding in underbrush, it was time to see how they handled a proper infantry charge.

At least that was what William's romantic mind told him. His practical mind had not forgotten those archers in the woods behind them, archers who were holding fire now only for fear of hitting their own men. Let the foot soldiers scatter or even withdraw a distance, and the arrows would begin to fly again. He had to ignore that, though—a fundamental tactical rule was to deal with the most immediate threat first, which in this case was the foot soldiers. He prepared to give the order to advance. Perhaps if he stayed close enough to the Black Army squadron, their archers would be hesitant to open fire until it was too late.

The enemy soldiers were obviously remembering the hidden archers as well, for they began backing off from the halberd line, opening the gap again. Sure enough, the archers began again—William's insides knotted at the horrid twang-zipp sound, though he took bitter satisfaction in noting that they had begun shooting too soon, as an arrow embedded itself in the throat of a Black Army soldier. What poor archery! he thought as two more of the enemy fell. But then it struck him that something was very odd here—the arrows were coming from the wrong direction! And they looked different! What was happening? In bewilderment William looked to his left, the direction from which the arrows seemed to be coming. There across the path, in perfect line formation, stood a company of archers firing with discipline and deadly accuracy—directly into the ranks of the enemy. He also noticed, though it did not register until later, that their hoods and boot tops were deep blue.

The situation dissolved into confusion. Before him the Black squadron was falling and scattering quickly. Behind him, in the woods, he could hear the sound of arrows flying amidst panicked cries and running. Making his best guess, he shouted his orders.

"First rank, charge! Run 'em down! Second rank and horse soldiers, about face! Fan out and prepare for action!"

The first rank obeyed promptly, letting out a mighty yell as they ran forward into the enemy's midst, slashing and hacking. The archers ceased fire, having slain half the foe and scattered the others to a point where arrows were little use anymore. It was sword and spear work now. The second rank were at first a bit confused by their orders but caught on soon enough. Now William had a rank of armed men facing the forest, ready to fight whatever came out of it.

They did not have long to wait. With cries and crashing men came stumbling out of the trees—men clad in black and carrying bows. Once again William had discerned correctly—whoever had set that company of archers across the path had also sent warriors around behind them to flush out the enemy bowmen. So the ambushers became the ambushed, and the Black Army archers had no stomach for that fight. Their panic redoubled when they saw the fierce blades of William's troops waiting for them, but they had no options left. William slashed the throat of one as he saw another go down with a blue-fletched arrow in his back. His men were dealing death blows left and right, while the woods rang with the cries of enemy archers cut down by the unexpected foe.

At last it grew quiet, and just within the edge of the wood William could see shadowy figures who did not appear to be coming out. His men looked inquiringly at him, obviously willing to go in after them if he gave the order, but he signaled them to stand down.

"Peace, men", he said. "Let's not be slaying our saviors." Behind him he could see no enemy soldiers, and the men from the first rank were attempting to form up on a path littered with bodies.

"Form up together down there." He indicated a spot down the path. "Modified parade. Stand by for orders."

At the sight of his men withdrawing, the figures in the forest shadows began emerging with understandable caution. Off to his right the bow company were coming slowly forward, bows still strung but with all their arrows in the quivers. William searched his mind frantically for the proper things to do and words to say. Black Army squadrons he knew how to handle. Blue Army forces, however, presented a different set of problems.

Hundreds of years before there had been only one army in the Empire, defending the borders and ruling until the King returned. But disputes arose among some of the officers regarding the manner in which some of the senior officers were ruling and whether their example was one that properly reflected the King's wishes. As it turned out, terrible abuses were going on, and later there were councils and courts-martial and many changes at Imperial Army headquarters, but not before some of the protesting officers split off and formed their own army, renouncing the rule of the Imperial officers and claiming the right to set up their own rule, one that would be run in closer conformance to the written wishes of the King.

The resulting rift nearly destroyed the Empire. Hundreds of officers and thousands of men joined the movement, calling themselves "the Faithful", after their determination to be faithful to the King's written commands. The Imperial forces called them simply "Rebels", since they had rebelled against the authority that the King himself had ordained. In time they took this name to themselves and wore it as proudly as the blue uniforms that they chose (Imperial forces wore primarily green). For years bitter battles between Rebel and Imperial armies tore at the fabric of the Empire. Records clearly showed that the most brutal battles in the history of the Empire were not those against the Black Army but those of the Blue and Green armies against one another.

In time the bloodletting slowed, and the Empire settled into an uneasy truce that saw the Rebel forces controlling certain tracts of territory and the Imperial forces controlling others, though loyalists of both colors remained scattered throughout the other's territories. After many councils and documents and confusing rulings, the Imperial government officially stated that the Rebels were indeed citizens of the Empire, for they sought to serve the King and to recognize the authority of his written rulings. It was difficult to ascertain what the Rebel forces stated, for there was little cohesion among them. Once the precedent of departure in the name of faithfulness was set, it was difficult to rescind, and it was used more and more commonly among the Rebel forces themselves, until literally thousands of independent commands existed within the Rebel territories.

By the time William joined the Imperial Army, little antipathy toward the Rebel forces remained among most of the Imperial troops. There was even some discussion among some of the younger officers about the strengths of the Blue Armies and how some of those traits could be woven into Imperial Army training. Among these voices was William's good friend and Academy barracks mate for three years, John Clay. John came from Farrish Province, which lay close to Rebel territory, and he had made the Rebels a particular study of his while in the Academy. This made some of the other cadets suspicious of his loyalties, but John was as Imperial as they came—it was just that growing up in such close proximity to the Rebels had made him more aware of their culture and outlook. He had even done his graduate project on the topic, vanishing for a couple of months to (it was rumored) enlist in a Rebel army incognito and ride with them in some campaigns. William had found it fascinating to talk to John, since he knew nothing about Rebels and was glad hear more about them. He was disappointed in one respect, though—he had hoped to gain some new strategic insights from the Rebel perspective only to find that the Rebels had not much to offer in the way of strategy.

"By and large they're very unsophisticated, William", John had explained. "Very charge-and-hack in their approach. Not much planning goes into most battles—in fact, some of them are quite suspicious of too much planning. But what they lose in strategy they almost make up for in spirit. Most of them are highly motivated in a way I wish our enlisteds were—or our officers, for that matter."

John, however, had been a rare exception in his views. Only

a small minority of Imperial troops thought that anything of value could be learned from the Rebels. An equally small minority, who were heard from more often because they were so vociferous, held that the Blue Armies were worse than the Black, or in league with them, and called for their complete extermination. The vast majority, like William, simply did not think of the Rebels one way or another. John had assured William that circumstances were much the same among the Rebel forces.

Which was why, on that hot afternoon with the sweat of battle still dripping off him and the stench of fresh blood in his nostrils, William knew that he had to act cautiously. The soldiers who had come to their aid were Rebels, and though there was no question that they had vanquished the Black forces, there was no way for him to know what would come next. The commander of this company was probably a reasonable man, or he would have let the Black Army slaughter William's men before moving in himself, but there was a chance that he would take advantage of his tactical superiority to capture or even destroy the Imperial squadron.

Making the matter more difficult for William was his inability to concentrate. The fierce rush of terror that had sustained him through the battle was wearing off, and he felt weak, sick, and anything but equal to the task at hand. Guilt and grief welled up within him at the thought of the men he had lost. Images of the fallen flashed through his mind—men lying still, their faces mashed against the ground, while their lifeless fingers clutched at the dust that so readily drank their blood. He had no idea how many he had lost, but from the weight on his heart it felt like it was more than half the squadron. How often in strategy reviews had he primly dissected the postencounter actions of the officers in command, glibly highlighting every mistake and transgression of policy! Yet here, now, having it happen to him, he repented every word. How could he have known of the weariness, the confusion, the grief for the lost, and the howling accuser within that screamed that if he had been a little faster, or a little smarter, or a little more competent, that even one more life could have been saved? He saw that the amazing thing was not that officers made blunders after battles but that they were able to do anything at all. He desperately wished that there were someone near with greater responsibility upon whose shoulders he could thrust the asphyxiating burden of decision, but there was no one. His was the command, the responsibility, the burden, and he did not know what to do. Through the confusion, however, one voice that overrode pride, and honor, and shame spoke clearly: there must be no more death. If he could do anything to avoid it, no more of his men would die.

The line of men was emerging from the woods, and their leader was easy to spot. He was a tall man with curly brown hair, clad all in blue and wearing some small insignia of rank on his shoulder. The man fixed William with serene blue eyes that betrayed nothing of his intentions. Deciding that the first move was his to make, William pulled himself together and executed the best salute he could muster.

"William de Rowan, Lieutenant, Imperial Army, First Division, Fifth Battalion, Fifth Regiment." He gave his rank and command in accordance with protocol. Then he shifted his grip on his sword, grasping it just below the hilts, and offering it to the commander in the universal symbol of surrender. "You have the advantage of me, sir. I ask only that you be kind to my men and allow us to tend to our wounded."

How the man received this was impossible to tell from his expression, which did not change. Saying nothing and gazing steadily at William, he extended a steady hand and took the saber. After examining it in deliberate silence for a long minute, he finally spoke.

"Klaus von Huber, Commander, Second Parliamentary Battalion", he replied evenly. Then he dispassionately offered the sword back to William. "And though I cannot speak for my fellow officers, I at least will not deprive a fighting man of his weapon while the blood of our common enemy is still wet upon it."

Without a word William took back his weapon and inwardly breathed a sigh of relief. It appeared that this Rebel force would not treat them as enemies.

"You mentioned your wounded", continued Commander von Huber. "Shall we attend to them?"

This was a necessary task that William felt competent to command, so he turned and gave the appropriate orders while the Rebel commander spoke briefly to one of his soldiers. Men of both uniforms scattered to tend to the forms lying about the path. In this silence following the din of battle every little sound could be heard: every rustle, every whimper. William's men and the Rebels were going from body to body, anxiously seeking for even the slightest movement or sign of life, tenderly responding when one was found and bowing in somber silence where there was none.

Standing beside Commander von Huber, William felt uneasy. The crushing weariness had not left him, but he felt he should be doing something. He turned and said, "If you'll excuse me, sir, perhaps I should join my men."

"You may do as you wish, sir", von Huber responded. "But I might suggest that you get that arm taken care of first." He nodded toward William's left shoulder. William looked down and saw, to his amazement, that his arm just below the shoulder was a hideous mass of torn green fabric and oozing blood. He had sustained a wound sometime during the fray and hadn't seen or even felt it.

"May not be too serious—could be just lost skin", von Huber continued. William knew that a wound's severity couldn't be reliably judged from its appearance, but he hoped the commander was right. He gazed dumbly at the injury as pain and nausea washed over him. Small wonder he had felt so sick. The wound hurt quite badly, but all William could seem to do was stare at it. He realized he was shaking, and his vision began blurring at the edges. Suddenly the Rebel officer grabbed his unwounded arm, and William realized he had been swaying where he stood.

"Let's get you bandaged up." Von Huber began leading William up the path toward where some of his men were clustered. "Don't worry about the shaking and dizziness—that's normal after a battle, especially if you took a wound." William said nothing, for the dizziness had indeed been worrying him, and he felt as if he were going to be sick, but it was nevertheless embarrassing that the Rebel had noticed his condition. They walked in silence for a moment; then William spoke.

"Thank you for saving our lives, Commander. That Black Army squadron had us a couple of ways, but you came along just in time. I wonder why that ambush was laid right there—they couldn't have known we were coming. And how did you get your men in place so fast?" William realized that he was on the verge of babbling, so he held his tongue.

"Well," von Huber responded slowly, "it was more bad fortune than good, at least for you. Our advance scouts had discovered that ambush, and we were moving our archers into position when your patrol walked right in. We moved as quickly as we could once the battle was joined, which was why it took so little time. As for why the ambush was right there—well, I suspect they were waiting for us rather than you."

"Waiting for you?" asked William. "Why would they be waiting for you?"

"About seventy good reasons", von Huber replied with just the hint of a smile playing about his mouth. "I'm rather surprised you haven't already asked what a Rebel force is doing so far from its home territory."

William thought quietly for a moment. The commander was right—this was deep within Imperial territory. It was very unusual to find any Rebels at all in this area, much less a force of fighting strength. This unusual situation was getting odder by the minute. Seeing that von Huber was enjoying his role as riddlemaster, William kept silent and waited for the answer to unfold.

"Our land borders that of the Kingsmen, who are locked in arduous battle with the Black Army, even as we are. In order to assist them in their struggle, we have assembled a supply train to take to their battle sites. It was judged that the difficult passes of the Stony Mountains would be too difficult for the train, and the roads through the Kanesian Valley would have taken us too near the fighting and exposed the cargo to risk. Thus we chose the longer but safer route through Imperial territory. This had the additional advantage of allowing us to travel by Imperial roadways, which have a high reputation for being well maintained and kept safe from marauders by vigilant Imperial patrols." The commander's final sentence was delivered so dryly that William almost laughed despite his pain. That at least explained the screen of advance scouts: though the Empire and Parliamentarians were not actively at war, it would be uncomfortable if not hazardous for a supply train with an armed escort to be found marching through Imperial territory. William suddenly realized that this Rebel commander was in a situation at least as difficult as his own.

"It must be a precious cargo indeed to warrant such a circuitous route", William said. If he remembered his maps correctly, the route von Huber had described was at least triple the length of either of the two rejected alternatives.

"Indeed", the Rebel replied, pointing up the path in the direction they were headed. William looked and saw coming around a bend a small herd of donkeys followed by bullock carts. All were laden down with . . .

"Women!" William quietly exclaimed. He was amazed. Living in camp as he did, he hardly ever saw women. To see them here, on the edge of a skirmish, seemed even more incongruous.

"Field-skilled battle surgeons", corrected von Huber. "And medical supplies as well."

Medical corps! This explained much. Veteran Imperial commanders valued one medical corpswoman over five Academy lieutenants, and William knew the Rebels had even fewer than the Empire. Small wonder they took the route they did and sent a full battle wing as escort.

William watched with amazement as two senior corpswomen sized up the casualties of the skirmish and swung into action. Dismounting their white mules, they took complete control of the situation, their white and blue robes flying about them as they gave their orders. They were clearly in their element, taking command of junior corpswomen, foot soldiers, and even Rebel officers. White-clad figures swarmed past William and von Huber, and William could see massive donkey packs being opened to access medical supplies. Von Huber made a discreet signal that William was certain hadn't been seen, but in short order a young corpswoman clutching a handful of white bandage cloth and a canteen came scurrying over, blustering as she came.

"Horrid, horrid", she exclaimed. "How utterly horrid that those devils should attack in broad daylight. In the middle of the day!"

"Yes, horrid", von Huber replied. "Now, Sister, if you could examine the lieutenant's shoulder, which was wounded in the battle . . ." The presence of a real wound on a genuine battle victim sobered her considerably, and she took refuge in her profession. Motioning them over to a nearby tree, she continued in a calmer voice.

"Ye'll be seated here, sir", she said. "Can we get this hauberk off? I'll be havin' to clean some metal from this, so if ye'll stay for a moment, Commander . . ."

Von Huber helped William sit down against the maple. The change of position made William's head swim so badly that he nearly toppled over where he sat. He felt his mail hauberk and jerkin being eased off his good arm and around behind his shoulders, then ever so gently down his wounded arm. William gasped as the fabric came loose from his wound, and spears of fire lanced down his arm. All he could remember of the minutes that followed were fleeting images swimming in a sea of crimson agony: von Huber's strong arms pinning him as he struggled against them, the glistening steel of a surgical knife digging into his arm, the cold of water washing first his arm and then his face, the bright red of his blood staining the corpswoman's robes. Finally it was over, and the fiery pain subsided to a dull throb, as the white gauze was wound around his shoulder. He felt nauseated and exhausted.

"Sorry to have to do that t' ye, sir", the corpswoman said. "But ye had some mail rings in yer arm, an' t' leave 'em there would've meant infection an' possibly th' loss o' the arm." William knew that and also knew that her skilled assistance had probably saved his career if not his life. He wanted to say some words of thanks to her but could only stare at the white bandage girdling his arm and the tender hands now tying it tight. He was grateful when von Huber dismissed the woman with appropriate thanks and offered him another sip of water. He took it, leaned his head back against the tree, and closed his eyes—only to snap them open again as a surge of nausea swept over him. He struggled to maintain control of his stomach but failed, and he found himself retching onto the moss at his side while von Huber supported him by his good shoulder.

At last the retching ceased, leaving William more exhausted than ever. He gratefully accepted another sip of water. He was embarrassed at getting sick all over and wondered what the Rebel Commander must think of him.

"As you can see," he gasped, "Academy training produces soldiers of steel nerve and iron constitution. Want to sign up?" He looked over to see von Huber grinning at his jest.

"This must be your first battle wound", he replied. "That always happens. In fact, I was expecting you to lose your lunch all over the corpswoman, as was she. I'm glad you waited."

William simply nodded in response and leaned back against the tree again, being careful to keep his eyes open this time. He rested for a moment, then suddenly shot up straight.

"My men! I'm . . ." he started, but the Rebel pushed him back.

"Your men are in the best of hands, Lieutenant", von Huber said. "You just rest for now. We'll get you started soon enough. Your men won't be helped by an officer who's too sick to march them back to camp. I'll go see to a couple of details and be right back with you." So the Rebel moved on, leaving a grateful William to rest in the shade of the tree, taking an occasional drink from the canteen that had been left beside him. He watched with interest as the soldiers of both colors assisted the corpswomen in tending to the wounded. The concept of women near a battle site was strange to him, but these were seemingly unaffected by even the most gruesome wounds. He watched as one removed an arrow from a man's groin while four other soldiers held the man down. He knew of battle-seasoned veterans who would blanch at dealing with such a wound, yet this woman no bigger than a camp page was gently but firmly easing the arrow out, ignoring the man's cries and struggles. Finally it came, spurting blood all over, which the corpswoman stanched with calm professionalism.

Such scenes were being repeated all over the battle site. William counted and was encouraged—of his squadron of thirty-seven, only four appeared to be dead, and about ten more had seriously disabling wounds. Everyone seemed to have shed some blood in the fray, but most of the wounds seemed minor. At least they should be able to march their own wounded back to camp.

This brought William back to the problem of how to get out of this situation. The technically illegal Rebel supply train didn't make his life any easier. As an Imperial officer, he was required to report such incursions, and von Huber—William looked around until he spotted the Rebel commander, engaged in subdued but intense conversations with his noncoms—had to know that. Yet William was understandably reluctant to sink fangs into the back of one who had carried him. He'd love just to part ways and forget about it all, but he couldn't guarantee that his men would keep quiet about the camp. Besides that, the decision wasn't his to make. Von Huber had the tactical superiority here, which meant he could dictate what would happen to the Imperial squadron. William reasoned that the Rebel's options boiled down to four: release them, disable them and leave them here, take them along as prisoners, or kill them all in cold blood. He didn't think von Huber would take the last course, if for no other reason than that it wouldn't solve his problems. Any one of the last three choices meant the patrol wouldn't return to camp on time, which would have the countryside swarming with search parties by the next dawn, and that would ensure that the supply train would not reach its destination. As far as William could see, the only reasonable choice they had was to let him return to the Imperial camp with his patrol. Hopefully the Rebels would prove to be reasonable people.

Commander von Huber returned, stirring William from his musings. Beside him stood one of the senior corpswomen, looking rather nervous.

"Lieutenant, this is Medical Sister Bethanna." Von Huber introduced the woman, who made an unsteady little bow.

"I fear, Lieutenant," Sister Bethanna said gravely, "that we could not save five of your men. Four others have extremely serious wounds and will probably not live though the night. Of the rest, six are maimed badly enough to require special transport. The rest, including yourself, should be able to march back to your camp, providing it is not too far."

"Thank you, Sister", William responded. "But I believe you will find our death count to be six. One of my men bolted into those far bushes during the ambush, where he was certainly slain. Please realize, however, that it would have been far worse for us had your corps not stepped in when you did. For myself and my men I thank you deeply."

Sister Bethanna flushed red, bowed again, and retired muttering about insufficient facilities. Von Huber squatted down beside Williams, anxiety tugging at the corners of his eyes. He was obviously feeling some tremendous pressure.

"Well, Commander," William said, "have you taken enough argument from those of your noncoms who think it would have been better to let the Black forces finish us off before you stepped in?" He looked directly at the Rebel as he said this and watched the look of feigned shock melt away to grim acknowledgment.

"I'm glad you understand what I'm dealing with", von Huber replied. "I'm in a narrow pass here, and no mistake."

"Beyond question", William said. "You won't kill us, and you can't take us captive or tie us up unless you want to be dodging search parties for the rest of your journey—which would be short. That means you've got to let us go and trust us to keep quiet—something that's tough to do when you don't even know me."

"Indeed", von Huber replied. "Have you any thoughts?"

"I think you have no other option. You must trust us. I can assure you that I will do everything short of insubordination to keep your presence in Imperial territory a secret, but I cannot speak for my men. I can request them to keep silent, but I cannot ask them to lie if directly questioned, and you know how men talk about camp. We would try to keep quiet out of simple gratitude for what you have done for us, but I simply cannot guarantee it. That is the best I can offer."

The Rebel commander pondered this silently for some time, then nodded and gazed steadily at William with ice-blue eyes.

"As you have stated, Lieutenant, we must trust you", he said. "Furthermore, in my heart I want to trust you. Let it be as you have said. You shall return to your camp with your patrol and our fate in your hands." William nodded assent, saying nothing. The Rebel stood and offered his hand to William, who winced and stood stiffly, reeling slightly with weakness and nausea. He gritted his teeth and forced his muscles to obey. His left arm throbbed when he kept it still and twinged shooting fire when he tried to move it.

"We'll rig a sling for that", von Huber said, noticing William favoring the arm. "One other concern—your dead. Do I remember correctly that the Imperial custom is to bury the fallen at the battle site with only simple markings?"

"That is correct", said William. "To be buried 'plain grave' is a great honor."

"I had set my men to digging graves for your five, but we'll need another if what you told Sister Bethanna bears out. Up in this clearing ahead." William was being led up the path a bit and then off to the eastern side, uphill into the sparser trees and rocks. All around him soldiers were busy—primarily Rebel blues, but some in Imperial green, most of these with bandages. They were collecting equipment, finding comrades, and trying to regain their bearings. William noticed some of his men clustered around a noncom. He motioned to them to come along behind. His dead would at least have an Imperial honor guard.

There, in a clearing illuminated by brilliant sunlight, five dark holes gashed the dry earth, and a group of men were already working on a sixth. Beside the new graves lay the ones who would soon occupy them. They had been somewhat cleaned of the gore of battle, and their weapons were arranged about them in ceremonial order. William and von Huber walked up to the leftmost body, the only officer among the fallen. It was McTannan, who had taken the arrow in the throat. The wound was partly covered by the collar of his cape, and someone had closed his eyes and eased from his face the grimace of death. His hands were folded over the hilt of his saber, which was lain on his chest in the customary manner. Soberly William looked down on the first man to die under his command. It was not a comfortable feeling. He had not been particularly close to McTannan, considering him a bit of a grouser, but the feisty sublieutenant had known how to celebrate, and the officer's mess would be a duller place without his stories and jokes.

"Is it still Imperial custom", von Huber interrupted William's reverie, "to bury the dead with their weapons?" William was puzzled by this question until he noticed how intently the Rebel was examining the saber. Being standard Imperial issue, it was neither as ornate nor as sturdy as the custom-made swords that some officers wore, but even so it was still several grades above the sword that von Huber wielded. His was a sturdy, serviceable fighting tool, but the finish of the metal indicated that it had been forged by the village blacksmith and the handle crafted by the local cooper. The balance looked atrocious, and he probably spent most evenings just keeping the thing sharp. But such was the nature of supply and weaponry among the Rebel forces, and as a result von Huber was about to bury a finer weapon than he would probably ever take into battle. William could understand his struggle.

"It is, usually", William answered. "There is another custom, however, that if a warrior falls in combat and there is another who can continue the fight, the fallen one's weapon is given to the other. This is known as burial with empty hands. It is usually practiced within a family, from one brother to another, but it can be any comrade in arms. All that is required is that the one receiving the weapon pledge to continue the battle for the King and Empire", he looked piercingly at the Rebel commander. "It is considered a great honor to be buried with empty hands, and I know that each of these would be anxious to have their weapons continue the good fight, even if they cannot." Von Huber merely nodded in response.

A disturbance off to their right drew their attentions, and they saw two men coming into the clearing carrying a blood-stained and dripping cloak between them, stretcher style. The gruesome burden was carried to the sixth grave while one of William's sergeants approached him.

"We—we found him, sir", the sergeant stammered, swallowing frequently. "It was Kerrol. We had to look about some—the savages . . ."

William waved his hand to cut short the narrative. It was obvious what the savages had done. He rose and walked down the row of bodies, gazing at each one in turn and trying to remember something about the man himself. There was Jones, who always seemed to be able to locate extra rations, even on long forced marches. Barr, the quiet one, whose ability to start campfires under the worst of conditions was legendary. Winshore lay next to him—who would tell this man's wife and little daughter that Daddy wouldn't be coming home any more? And there was Belt—strong as an ox, but with an easy manner and gentle smile that would never be seen again, thanks to a black-feathered arrow. And last lay the luckless Kerrol, a bloodied bundle whose open, honest face would forever be just a memory to his comrades. William felt the weight of his office keenly. It may have been just a simple day patrol, but these men had trusted him with their lives, and he had failed them.

Turning, he saw that his men were assembled in the clearing, as were most of the Rebels. He indicated to von Huber that they might as well begin the burial ceremony. The appropriate commands were given, and the troops paraded into position. William had to struggle to recall the entire ceremony, but he managed. One discomforting thing was that while the Imperial troops knew the proper responses at the proper times, the Rebel troops were quite at a loss and stood stock still, looking very uncomfortable, while the ceremony proceeded around them. At the point where the honor guard would lower the fallen into their graves, William stopped, turned to von Huber, and saluted.

"At this point, Commander, we would inter our comrades", he said. "But we have wounded to tend, and time grows short. With your kind permission we will halt here and return to our camp. If your men could attend to returning the fallen to their graves, we would thank you."

"That we will gladly do, sir", von Huber replied, saluting in return. "We salute you and your fallen."

"And we salute you, and thank you for your assistance", said William. "Your squad saved our lives, Commander. For that we cannot thank you enough. Go in the King's peace." With that he wheeled and gave the commands to his noncoms to retire the men. He could tell that both his troops and the Rebels were somewhat startled by his abruptness, but he wanted to get his men out of the clearing and on the road as quickly as possible. The men turned and marched as well as they were able with their wounds, but even if they had been completely fit, it would have taken some time to get the patrol squadron on the road home. As it was, with easing the worst of the wounded onto the remaining horses and fixing dressings for the march (including a sling for William's arm), it was nearly half an hour before they were trudging back down the trail up which they had so confidently marched some hours earlier.

William remembered the return march as little more than a bad dream. All became a dark, throbbing agony as they walked slowly back to their camp. Wounds ached and tore, and those on the horses whimpered and groaned with every jolt. They rested frequently, hanging their heads as they sat by the side of the road, oblivious to the flies that swarmed around them. At one of these stops William tried to impress on the men the importance of keeping the presence of the Rebels a secret. The men simply stared at him as he spoke, and he didn't feel very convincing, but in the end they seemed to understand. Then they marched again, and rested, and marched again. The hot afternoon sun burned down, baking the fields and the roads and the wounded men. William became convinced that it would never end, that he would forever be walking, the horses' hooves would forever be kicking up little puffs of dust as they fell, and his arm would forever be aching. The land seemed devoid of inhabitants; the many peasants and field workers they had passed on the way out had left the fields to escape the afternoon heat. What few were left fled in terror when they saw the battered men, obviously unwilling to come near a party whom fate had treated so brutally. This discouraged William tremendously, for he remembered the six who would never march again and that they had paid that price so that these could live in peace.

One incident restored some hope, however. They came upon a woman harvesting some fruit from a tree. At first she responded as all the others had: dropping her apron load, she put her hands to her mouth in wide-eyed horror at the sight of the wounds and blood, then picked up her skirts and ran into the house. But after a couple of minutes she emerged again, burdened with a shoulder-yoke that carried two brimming buckets of water and shrieking at two boys who followed behind her, struggling with more buckets. These were brought to the roadside near the patrol, and the men stopped to drink and wash their dusty heads. Their thirst was by now tremendous, and what water remained in their canteens was warm and stale. The most badly wounded got to drink first, then those walking. When William's turn came, he felt sure that he had never tasted any wine so good as that cool well water. The woman said little but stood aside wringing her hands and staring with wide eyes, clearly terrified of the soldiers. When a bucket was emptied, she would send her sons off to refill it, and so the entire patrol drank and was refreshed. When at last they were finished and had refilled their canteens, William thanked the woman many times for her kindness. He would have given her some gift or token, but it was obvious that all she wanted was to be away from the soldiers, so they moved on.

Throughout the gruesome journey William carried an additional burden. The crushing grief and yammering guilt, temporarily displaced by his wound and the concerns of the burial, returned with a vengeance. Over and over again he reviewed the attack, reliving every horrifying moment, gnawing and worrying at the questions of responsibility and competence that haunted him. Was there anything he could have done? Was there any sign of the ambush that he should have noticed? Had he delayed too long giving orders, or should he have pursued different tactics that would have saved more lives? He dreaded reporting the loss of the men and the accusatory questions that would surely follow in the review session. In addition, he had the matter of the Rebel convoy, whose presence he

53

was going to attempt to hide. That would make things doubly difficult.

To distract himself from the throbbing of his wound, and also to get off the fruitless activity of rerunning the battle in his mind, he pondered the question of Commander von Huber and the Rebels. The more he thought about it, the odder their behavior seemed. It would have been far more to their advantage to allow the Black Army to slaughter William's squadron before stepping in, as well as far more in character, if some of the fire-breathing anti-Rebel Imperialists were to be believed. Even John Clay, favorably disposed as he was to some of the Rebel ideas, harbored no illusions about the fact that many Blue Army units considered themselves to be still in a state of war with the Empire and believed that all of them should be treated with caution in a battlefield environment. Yet by all appearances the Rebels had deliberately and knowingly, intervened to save William's men from destruction. Why had they done that? William knew that they could not have feared his squadron's tactical strength—what had been their motive? Then there was the question of the squadron being allowed to return to their base despite the obvious danger to the Rebels. His pragmatic side argued that the Rebels had taken the only available option under the circumstances, but he could not shake the impression that Commander von Huber had honestly wished to allow them to return to their base unhindered.

This was new and disturbing thinking to William. Being raised in a solidly Imperial household and trained at the Academy, William's lifelong attitude toward the Rebels was one of benign ignorance: he simply did not think about them. He understood that they existed and that the Empire had decreed that, though different from the Imperial troops, they were not exactly enemies as the Black Army was, but he never concerned himself with their existence because he didn't have to. Even in the Academy, when John and others had ventured the revolutionary concept that something of value could be learned from the Blue Armies, William's interest had been academic and somewhat distant. He never dreamed that he would be so closely impacted by Rebels. Now he wondered many things:

What were their principles of strategy? What motivated them? Why and how were they different from, and how were they similar to, the Empire? What sort of troops served in the Rebel armies, and why did they serve there? It began to dawn on him that this ignorance represented an immense gap in his own experience that made him uncomfortable. What else might he not know that could endanger himself or his men? He pondered these questions as they plodded down the hot, dusty road.

So they marched, on through the heat and dust and ache. Slowly the sun dropped from the sky, and the evening breeze from the mountains began blowing at their backs. The shadows lengthened beside them, and still they plodded on. At long last, as the sun was setting in a blaze of gold and crimson, they saw ahead of them the banners and campfires of the base encampment. This cheered them, and they pressed on a little faster, though they had felt they were on the last of their strength before. They had to stop shortly, however, for one of the worst of the wounded began cramping and vomiting blood, and they had to ease him gently off the horse to tend him. William was afraid that they would lose him within sight of the camp gates, but he stabilized and even seemed improved, so they loaded him back on the horse and continued.

At last they topped the final ridge and looked down on the camp gates, where William saw that there were a good many torches and much activity around the front guardhouses. He wondered at this until he heard a great shout go up and a squadron of cavalry break loose from the crowd and begin galloping up the road toward them, followed by foot soldiers and medical corpsmen, who came at a dead run. Then he realized that his patrol was the cause of the commotion. They were long overdue, and it was obvious that search parties were being assembled. Now, within sight of home and with assistance descending on him rapidly, part of him wondered if it might not be best to stop here in the road and wait for help. But when he turned to his men, he saw that those who could were already beginning to form up and march more smartly. They obviously were going to return with some honor if it took the last of their strength to do it. William's heart swelled with pride at the sight, and he drew his sword. Wheeling to take position to the right of the columns as protocol dictated, he wryly noted that even after fighting a battle, burying six of their own in a clearing, and marching back hungry, thirsty, and wounded, his squadron was returning to camp more smartly than they had left it. It amazed him, but he felt that he understood something of it as well. The pride and fierce joy that welled in his heart showed him more clearly why it was that men endured so much and sacrificed so terribly just for the opportunity to lead men into battle.

The sudden change in the demeanor of the men startled those who were racing toward them. Those who had thought they were coming to the rescue of a patrol on its last legs instead found themselves hindering the path of a stern military unit. There was much milling and trampling for a moment, but when it became obvious that the patrol was going to continue regardless of who was in the way, the cavalry and others pressed aside to make a path. Abruptly, and to the surprise of all, including William, the wounded men broke into a robust marching chant. Not knowing how to respond, the rescue-squad-turned-honor-guard stared blankly for a minute, then began to raise a cheer—haltingly at first, then swelling as it caught on. As bright flame will flicker through dense smoke, turning a pile of smoldering logs into a blazing bonfire, so the cheering spread to the gate and through the camp, changing a mood of anxiety and annoyance into one of triumph and exultation. The story was not yet known, but whatever had happened, William's patrol had suffered hardship and trial yet triumphed over it well enough to return. The cheering soldiers parted before the patrol to make an open path to the gate and beyond, down which William marched with his men, their eyes shining with wonder.

So it was that William returned from his routine patrol.

Once inside the gate things quickly dissolved into total confusion. The medical staff finally closed in on the seriously wounded, and curious troops crowded about, yammering questions and breaking up the formation. William was surrounded by a sea of grasping hands and glistening faces, dark eyes luminous in the torchlight. Wheeling about in alarm, he was relieved to see that his men were being taken care of by the soldiers surrounding them. Nobody was taking care of him, however—questions were being shouted; faces were popping in and out of his field of vision; hands were clutching at him. One even grabbed his upper arm where it was bandaged, causing him nearly to faint with pain. Just as he was becoming convinced he would never escape the crowd, a massive figure loomed before him, calling his name.

"Lieutenant de Rowan! Lieutenant de Rowan!" William recognized the man as one of Commandant Lloyd's aides, a sturdy sergeant.

"Here!" William shouted above the din. The man turned and saluted.

"Commandant Lloyd requests your presence in his quarters immediately, sir!"

"Very well", William responded. Seeing that the man, having delivered his message, was turning to depart, William cried out and grabbed his arm. "Here—take me to him!" The man turned briefly, surveyed the mass confusion, and proceeded to use his size to bull a path through the crowd. William followed behind, still holding the man's arm.

Proceeding in this manner, they arrived at the command complex in short order. William's escort left him outside the front flap of the commandant's personal quarters, which had a strategy room inside where the commandant frequently held meetings. Catching his breath for a moment, William started to straighten out his uniform jacket, then abruptly stopped himself. He was returning from a battle, and the commandant would be furious if he learned that the report were delayed even one minute because of some lieutenant's preening. Squaring his shoulders, he walked in.

The strategy room had, as did most of the tents, a wooden floor. It was lit by many cut-glass shielded candles, which, despite their number, managed to cast a multitude of flickering shadows that teased and tricked William's already exhausted eyes. The back of the tent, opposite where he had entered, was most shadowed, and he could see it filling up with camp officers entering by the rear flaps. It was a standing camp tradition that patrol debriefings were open to any officer who might be interested in attending. This was a seldom-used privilege, but it was obvious that this time, with a patrol staying out late and coming back wounded and battle-weary, not many were going to pass up the opportunity to hear the story firsthand. William's heart sank at the sight of the curious faces—this was going to be difficult enough without all the questions this audience was certain to ask.

In front of the gathering crowd of officers, dead in the center of the room, stood one chair, slightly more ornate than a common camp chair, in which sat a grizzled man who quietly gazed at William with piercing dark eyes. His close-cropped hair was flecked with gray, and he wore the insignia of a commandant on his worn but neat uniform. He sat silently, resting his chin on steepled fingers while the murmuring of the officers behind him grew louder. He didn't seem to be doing anything about it, which made William uncomfortable. After half a minute of expectantly waiting for someone to give him a cue, William decided simply to proceed as best he could. Adjusting his arm in the sling, he came to attention, saluted, and said, "Field Lieutenant de Rowan returning from scheduled patrol duty, sir."

"Report", replied the seated man.

Commandant Lloyd had always been an enigma to William, as he was to most of the officer corps. A full field commandant of his length of service and battle experience was rarely found outside a headquarters unit, much less living in the field with his battalion. Others commanded from a distance, visiting the bivouacs on occasion but mostly keeping to their residences or command posts. Commandant Lloyd lived right in the camp and, as far as anyone knew, had no permanent residence. Granted, his tent was comfortable, his wine had its own cellar beneath his private mess, and his banquet tent was the site of many glittering receptions, but still he remained the only commandant to live—and insist that his officers live—with the troops. The more cynical officers whispered that this was due to some secret scandal that barred him from headquarters duty. Others wondered if it were some unusual career move designed to bypass the usual time-in-grade promotion pattern.

But a few—William among them—wondered if the real reason might not be that he actually enjoyed field life, that he was a true warrior who wanted to be near the battle and to other warriors.

Whatever the reason, there was one thing it assuredly wasn't: incompetence. Commandant Lloyd was a disciplined and effective commander with a penetrating eye for strategy and tactics. When William was first assigned to the battalion, this had excited him, for strategy was his passion, but he quickly learned that to speak out at one of the strategy review sessions was to invite unpleasant attention. The commandant would brutally dissect any commentary, often subjecting the commentator to a grueling cross-examination during which every thought and assumption was held up for painstaking inspection. William got caught in a couple of such sessions and thought he did rather well under the circumstances—until he noticed that any show of competence, rather than satisfying the commandant, seemed to provoke him instead. Soon William's presence at strategy review sessions was essentially mandatory (officially it was optional), for more often than not he would be singled out to expound on some point of the day's lesson and at times was even told to conduct the session under the commandant's relentless scrutiny. The knowledge that this could happen at any time kept William's nose in the books and journals almost constantly. Not that he minded that part of it—such was his love of strategy that he could so lose himself in studying and planning that he would forget meals—but at times he grumbled to himself about the unfairness of it—he was just trying to be a good officer, and the battalion commander had him singled out for attention that bordered on abuse. Meanwhile the slackers—the pretty-boy officers who were just buying time here, preening themselves for the headquarters jobs they coveted so badly—these were treated cordially and sent along, never to be grilled or embarrassed or put on the spot by that gruff gray voice. William wondered what he had done that so incurred the commandant's disfavor.

Whatever it was, William realized, it had to be trivial compared to the trouble he'd gotten himself into now. As he stood alone in front of the room, the object of scrutiny by dozens of eyes, but especially the commandant's piercing gaze, he realized that the most rigorous strategy session he'd ever endured would seem like a singing lesson after the interrogation he was certain to receive now. To make it worse, he was going to try to lie in the midst of it to protect Commander von Huber and the Rebel caravan. He swallowed hard, wondering at himself for being such a fool as to think that his problems would be over once he got back to camp.

There was nothing to do but begin. Swallowing once more, William began his narrative from the outfitting of the patrol after the relief of the dawn watch. He gave all the pertinent facts in the proper order, just like the scenario description for a strategy session, except that this scenario had actually happened to him and had cost some of his men their lives. Through it all the commandant simply gazed at him, absorbing every word and never interrupting. This was customary, since questions were never allowed during a scenario description. William's confidence grew as he continued, and as he approached the conclusion he felt sure he could handle any questions that might arise. Nobody had any reason to suspect him of anything extraordinary, and he convinced himself that he had only imagined a brief flicker in the commandant's eyes when he had glossed over the intervention of the Rebel forces. Finally he finished his account, saluted again, and stood awaiting questions with only the slightest bit of anxiety, which he hoped would be attributed to postengagement nerves.

"You say you were southbound . . ." began one of the captains in the crowd, but to the utter astonishment of all present—especially William—Commandant Lloyd thrust up an arresting hand and barked abruptly, "No questions! Can't you see the man's wounded? You there," this to a foppish major standing near, "bring that stool for the lieutenant. Someone else bring some food and wine!" All this was in a tone that brooked no delay, and the items were swiftly delivered. "Now you're all dismissed. Review of this action will continue at a later time, providing the lieutenant is fit to talk to us, and I choose to invite you." The room emptied quickly, as it always did when the commandant spoke like that, and William found himself alone with his commander.

"Have a bite", the commandant said in an almost paternal tone. He poured two goblets of wine while William, suddenly ravenous, took some bites from a roll. "Go easy on the wine until you get some food in you." William was dumbfounded—this was a side of the man he had never before seen. He sipped the wine as the commandant took the other glass and began strolling about the tent.

"Aye, fighting's hungry work, so it's important to remember to eat, since in the excitement one can sometimes forget", the commandant said to nobody in particular in a rambling tone. He wandered back to the chair and sat down again. "So refresh yourself. I'll let you go off to the medics shortly—right after you tell me what else happened on that forest path."

William froze in midbite, his eyes riveted on the commandant, his heart pounding. The senior officer smiled quietly and continued.

"You're your father's son, young William, and a warrior to the core, but not enough of one to fight your way out of an ambush like that. Also, that bandage on your arm is far too well tied for a field dressing."

William's face flushed hot with embarrassment, and he nearly panicked to think that his story could be seen through so easily. He licked his lips slowly, wondering who else had put that together and what reason he could give for lying to his commander. Commandant Lloyd chuckled again.

"You needn't worry—none of the others has enough experience to know what it takes to get out of a hammer-and-anvil ambush, much less to know that you don't have it. I've no doubt that you have a good reason to keep quiet about whatever happened, but", here his voice hardened almost imperceptibly, "it would be most unwise to keep it quiet from your commandant."

Taking a deep breath, William filled in the remainder of the tale, this time with far less confidence than before, all the while bitterly regretting the word he had given to von Huber, which he now had to break. Once again the commandant listened straight through, riveting William with his steady gaze, never interrupting. Even after William was finished, the senior officer continued gazing at him for some time before standing to again walk about the tent, deep in thought.

"Parliamentarian, eh? And the commander again?" he said at last.

"Von Huber, sir. Klaus von Huber", William replied.

"Yes, yes—von Huber. A medical convoy, eh?" the commandant mused, sinking back into thought. He muttered to himself, leaning over the map table and stroking his chin. At last he stood straight and turned to William.

"You did well not to speak of this publicly", he said. "I would like to meet this von Huber, though whether to thank him or be thanked by him I wouldn't know. He saved you some lives, but you did him a favor by springing that trap that was laid for him and his convoy. It does solve the major mystery of the incident, though, which was why your patrol was ambushed." He fell silent again and turned back to the map, studying it carefully. This lasted for some minutes, and William began to wonder if he had been forgotten, or was supposed to leave, or should stay a little longer, when the commandant again straightened and turned to him.

"Get some rest, Lieutenant. Have the medics look at that wound. They'll probably want you off duty until it is healed up a little. Listen to them but stand ready to attend the command tent at my call."

Thus dismissed, William saluted and turned, once again feeling the depth of his weariness. Outside of the command tent in the cool night air, he was glad to see that the clamor surrounding the patrol's return had died completely, returning the camp to its usual evening watch quiet. He was just another field lieutenant now, unnoticed by those passing by on their business. He absently strolled past the tents, knowing he should be going somewhere but unsure of exactly where. His arm throbbed, and his throat ached, and he felt chilled all over. A nearby campfire flickered invitingly, and he squatted down beside it to warm himself, while he tried to recall where he should be going and what he should do when he got there. It was something important, he knew, and in just a minute he'd remember—as soon as he could tear his eyes away from the dancing flames . . .

"Beg pardon, sir", the voice came from nowhere, but it was the hand on the shoulder that startled William so much that he jumped.

"My horse!" he shouted, turning so quickly that he wrenched his arm grasping at the man—who quickly grabbed his good shoulder to prevent him from rising too quickly. A wave of pain and dizziness washed over William, who clutched at the strong arm to keep from falling. When his vision cleared, he recognized the muscular sergeant who had escorted him from the gate to the commandant's tent.

"Beg pardon, sir," the man repeated, "but I seem to remember you marched into camp. Perhaps one of the wounded was on . . ."

"No, no", William replied, suddenly remembering the truth. "She was killed. Right under me, Sergeant—a black arrow through her throat. A black arrow", his vision began to blur again, and he felt himself swaying where he stood. The sergeant's strong arm wrapped around his good shoulder to steady him, and he felt himself being led away from the fire.

"Where are you taking me?" William asked, trying to focus on the rows of strange tents. "My quarters aren't this way. What's your name, anyway?"

"Beauchamp, sir. First Sergeant Beauchamp. An' I thought a visit to the medics might be in order, what with that wound and all."

William pondered this for a moment, though concentration was getting difficult for him. Wound. Medics. They mustn't learn that . . . that . . . oh, bother. He couldn't remember what it was they shouldn't learn.

"I just hope", he mumbled to himself as he stumbled along, "that they have warm beds."

"I'm sure they do, sir", responded the sergeant.

The medics did have warm beds, but he recalled little of them later. He dimly remembered a tent hung with white and full of bustling white-clad figures. He recalled a twinge or two of

63

pain when his dressing was changed and then the blessed relief of a soft mattress and plenty of blankets.

The next day William had a slight fever, which he didn't even notice but which the medics used as an excuse to keep him abed all day. They also informed him that he would be off duty for a couple of weeks at least, as the wound went well into the muscle fibers, which would take that amount of time to reknit. This annoyed William tremendously, not only because inactivity was worse torment for him than torture but also because the camp was astir with the assembling and provisioning of a major field expedition. He had no delusions about being able to ride with a company again so soon, but he desperately wished to be part of the planning and packing. He pestered his white-clad jailers (as he came to view them) with demands for news, and from the scraps they grudgingly relayed he gathered that the day had dawned with orders for a full-force turnout with the intention of discovering how the Black Army forces had managed to intrude so deeply into Imperial territory. At first William was alarmed to hear this, fearing that the commandant had decided to follow after the Rebel convoy. After all, he had not said anything about his intentions, and the Rebels were technically trespassing by their unauthorized passage through Imperial territory. But a few minutes' thought dispelled William's concerns—if the commandant had wanted to apprehend the convoy, he would have sent a squadron or two of light cavalry out before daybreak. This expedition was infantry and heavy cavalry and would not be departing until midafternoon, which meant that the commandant meant to cover for William and allow the Rebels to reach their destination.

Later in the day the expedition thundered off, leaving a nearly empty camp containing a hundred or so cooks, a few score staff officers and their aides, a few dozen medics, and one restless field lieutenant. He had been placed on indefinite sick roll, but he also remembered being told to expect a summons to the command tent at any time. Were that call to come, he wanted to ensure that he showed no mark of weakness or sloth. In the days that followed he attempted to prepare for this by exercising strenuously despite the medic's warnings and even sneaking out from time to time for an illicit run around camp. This was also his method of conveying scorn for the medics and their mother-hen tendencies. His defiance culminated in his performing rapier drills in his ward with a tent rod, thoroughly alarming the medics and bringing down the wrath of the chief medic, a gray-haired major of imposing stature and gruff attitude.

"See here, young man", he scolded, his bushy eyebrows jutting at William. "A fine fool you'll look if the commandant requests your services, and I have to report you incapable due to disregarding prescribed treatment! Men have stood court-martial for that!" He then laid out an exercise plan to strengthen the wounded arm and shoulder. Properly cowed, William submitted to this, for the old major was obviously accustomed to dealing with cocky young warriors and brooked no nonsense. He was also accustomed to designing treatments, as William quickly discovered when he undertook the prescribed regimen. It was obvious that his self-initiated exercise had been unconsciously favoring his damaged side, depriving it of the workout it needed while allowing him to feel self-righteous about how well he was progressing. The major's exercises quickly set him straight on that, for they were both painful and tiring, and it took all his discipline to keep at them. But they worked, and after a couple of days he could begin to feel the results.

A constant companion during his recuperation was Sergeant Beauchamp. He had dropped by the medical tent on the first day, and William, certain that he was being summoned before the commandant, struggled to get up. But it was not a summons, only a personal visit "to see how the lieutenant was gettin' by" (though William suspected that Beauchamp, being the commandant's aide, was getting some word back to the command tent). At first he came once a day, but as William's strength grew he began to come in the morning and evening to talk with William and encourage him in his recovery. William greatly appreciated this, for the sergeant understood (as the medics did not) that a soldier's anxiety increased with ignorance, so he brought daily news of the expedition's progress as well as other news from around the camp. As they talked,

William was increasingly impressed by the sergeant's grasp of affairs. Though his manner was simple and straightforward, and he wore the homespun look of so many field sergeants, he had an understanding of subtleties of strategy and politics that outstripped William's. He casually expounded on the political intrigues at staff headquarters as well as the personalities of the people involved. He discussed at length the circumstances along the Rebel borders, showing a keen grasp of the histories of the various conflicts as well as the military, cultural, and even economic factors involved. Seeing an opportunity to fill in some of the gap in his own understanding of the Rebels, William pumped the sergeant extensively for information.

"Oh, they're bad, all right", the sergeant replied once when William asked just how bad the Rebel-Imperial relations were. "T' be sure, we're not lynching an' burning each other's villages as we once were, but the borders are mighty tense. Most o' the peace comes from lack of contact—we and the Blues just don't see each other enough. But there still be parties on both sides pushin' for the enlistment, voluntary or no, or annihilation of t'other. No—the blood's not fresh on the ground any more, but it's still bad enough. Oh, someone like yourself could probably walk through a Rebel city in your uniform, an' where fifty years ago you would've been killed, now you'd probably make it through alive—though you'd leave on a stretcher." The sergeant's understanding of the Rebels was so keen that William suspected he had seen action in that arena, but when questioned, Beauchamp grew silent about his service record there.

After a week of semiconvalescence and five days of reconstructive therapy under the eye of the medics, William was finally released to return to his own quarters with a warning to continue the exercises for three more weeks. He was glad to return, though he missed his two tentmates, who were still out with the expedition and would not be back for another three days. He would have loved to join them, but despite its progress his arm was still sore, and he knew he wouldn't be back in action for weeks.

The next day when Beauchamp came to visit, William took

him along to see the stablemaster. As a cavalry officer he had brought his own mount into service with him, but since she had been killed in battle he was entitled to draw another from the Imperial stables. This did not excite him, for the stock kept by the stable staff was never cared for as well as the personal mounts, and rarely was there a beast truly suitable for battlefield work. They were mostly brood mares, light runners kept for message work, and the occasional stud that was too surly to train. To make matters worse, William would have to deal directly with the stablemaster, Major Tysen. Normally he would have worked with one of the sergeants or soldiers who manned the stable, but they were all afield with the expedition, leaving only some stableboys and Tysen himself. He was a bitter old supply officer who considered all officers nuisances scheming to wheedle him out of precious tack and leather. Nobody dealt with Major Tysen unless he had to, but William needed a horse so he had no option.

"A replacement steed? Have you the authorization papers?" the major sneered when presented with William's request.

"They should have been delivered some days ago, sir", William replied.

"Indeed? I seem to have no recollection . . ."

"I delivered them into your hand myself, sir", broke in Sergeant Beauchamp, who was standing at attention behind William. "Day before yesterday. They were the papers signed by Commandant Lloyd."

"Assuredly, Sergeant." The major eyed Beauchamp icily as he began rummaging around in the papers on his desk. Beauchamp had no fear of being on the major's bad side because he knew quite well that the old man didn't have a good one. After some minutes of searching, the papers were located.

"Killed in combat, eh?" Tysen asked after skimming the report. "What cause? Broken neck?"

"Arrow in the throat, sir", William replied evenly, pointedly ignoring the implication that he had been running.

"Hmm, yes", muttered Tysen. "Terrible thing to happen to a perfectly good horse." He continued examining the paperwork for some time before putting it down and fixing William with a steady gaze. "The problem, Lieutenant, is that I have no horse to give you—or at least none that you would find suitable."

William and Beauchamp exchanged glances as the major rose to his feet. They had anticipated this.

"Quite possibly, sir, but we'd like a look all the same", replied William. So they proceeded to the corrals, where the major's word was proven as good as they had expected. Older mares with swaybacks and sad eyes filled the yard, along with an occasional horse that was too light to be a war steed, obviously being kept until ready for the message stable.

"You are welcome to make your selection from my available stock", Major Tysen nearly gloated when he saw William's resigned discouragement. Together they walked all around the corrals, watching for any sign of a suitable animal but finding none. At last they were preparing to leave, when William spotted a swift-moving shadow flashing in a far corral.

"What's that? Down there in the end pen?" he asked.

"Oh, that one", Tysen replied sourly, as if the mention of the topic upset him more than usual. "He was sent with the last general distribution. A young stallion."

That told William nearly everything. A young stallion was almost no use in the camp. As a rule they were too unruly for messenger work and too distractible for war training. They tended to savage the geldings, and the mares got unmanageable when one was near. It was a rare stallion who could be trained for anything useful short of stud work, and even then the older ones were preferred. He nearly wrote off the possibility right then, but on a hunch he replied, "Let's have a look at him anyway."

They wandered down to where the coal-black horse dashed and wheeled about within his pen. He was certainly beautiful, but he didn't look like he'd ever be a good war steed. He had a good form and strong muscles, but his frame was a bit small, and he looked far too skittish. They watched him for a while, and even as William was resigning himself to having to purchase a mount from his own funds, a part of him began to wonder if this steed might not be worth a try.

"He's certainly nimble enough", William said. "And spirited."

"Aye, he's spirited, all right", Beauchamp replied. They watched for a while longer before William made his decision.

"I'll take this one." Beauchamp and the major stared at William in amazement. He stared back. "Unless there is some problem, Major?"

"No, no—I'll go draw up the papers", Major Tysen replied, still puzzled. He scurried away quickly, obviously delighted to be so easily rid of two problems at once.

"He'll be a handful, sir. You might not be able to train him", Beauchamp said in a cautioning tone.

"I know, Beauchamp. But even if I can't, I'll be able to trade him against a more useful mount. Besides, my father always said I had a hand for animals. I won't be doing anything for some weeks anyway." He tenderly touched his bandaged shoulder. "So I might as well train a horse."

In the end it took almost that long to break the spirited stallion. The first week was spent just winning his trust, with William spending hours in the corral so the horse could get accustomed to his presence. Finally, from a combination of familiarity and hunger, the horse came to nibble the carrots held in William's outstretched hand. From there William's innate charm with animals began to take over, and soon he was saddling and walking the beast around to familiarize him with carrying a load.

"D'ye have a name for him, sir?" asked Beauchamp one day as he watched William feed the horse a treat of turnips after a particularly successful session.

"No", replied William, patting the horse's neck affectionately. "I ought to call him 'Coney'. He certainly eats like one." It was true—the horse's appetite was voracious, and he preferred green vegetables above any other food. It was a totally unsuitable name for a battle steed, especially a stallion, but the remark was one of those that, coming at the right time, lodged where it was not intended. Soon "Coney" was the name by which the animal was known.

The field expedition had returned two weeks after it had set out, having found neither any Black Army soldiers nor any sign of how they had entered into Imperial territory. If anything was reported regarding the Rebel convoy, William heard nothing of it, and neither did Beauchamp, whom William had let in on the story. It was decided to patrol the area of the attack more diligently and possibly to establish a garrison along the road.

The camp returned to its routine. William could not yet rejoin his company due to his wound and lack of a battle-trained mount, but since the medics had certified him capable of light duty, he was assigned to the camp master-at-arms. He was not excited by this duty, thinking it more suitable for a staff officer or enlisted man, but orders were orders. The MA was glad to have him, since it was uncommon to have a temporary assignee with a mount, and proceeded to use him for all manner of assignments that needed a rider. This, though tedious, was not unbearable, for it gave him a chance to ride and also to allow him and Coney to get accustomed to each other—a necessary step before they undertook battle training together. It also gave William, whose interest in cartography was ongoing, an opportunity to verify further the staff maps of the regions through which he was sent. He took to taking a complete portfolio along whenever he went out, making notations and corrections as he traveled, and returning the results to the mapmakers.

Thus it was that William was sent one quiet morning to meet a supply convoy that was due in later that week. The convoy was coming from division headquarters with provisions, weapons, and armor. The Supply Corps had a long-standing policy of sending at least one officer to meet and escort incoming convoys, since the last few miles of the route passed through a couple of villages, and the muleteers who ran the convoys would at times "lose" supplies while traveling through populated areas, which would throw the supply officers' books out of balance and infuriate them no end. William wondered if it wouldn't be better to "lose" some of the supplies regardless of what it did to the books, for the camp was bulging with so many idle weapons and unused materials that it was a major chore simply to care for them in the storehouses.

But that was not William's concern. All he had to do was meet the convoy and escort it home. Since the rendezvous point was a good two days away, William packed plenty of provisions for some overnight camping. In order to give Coney some cross-country as well as road training, he avoided the roads, relying instead on maps and field navigation. The first day was delightful, riding through meadows, over hills, and through small woods. They stopped only briefly for lunch, then rode until late afternoon, when they made camp in a small thicket, and William made a cheery fire to keep them warm against the evening chill. After an open-cooked supper, he curled up in his bedroll as the stars winked into sight in the indigo sky overhead and wondered how he ever could have forgotten what fun it was just to camp and why it had been so long since he had done it.

It was still dark the next morning when William's body woke him to remind him why. Thick dew drenched his blanket and all his gear. His muscles, out of tone from spending so much time in camp, were dreadfully cramped. The wound in his arm ached in a manner that told him he'd have a cold-sensitive scar for the rest of his life. He spent ten minutes just getting out from under the blanket. He was enough of a campaigner to know that one of the best cures for cramped muscles was to get riding again, so he saddled up Coney and got moving. There wasn't even a hint of light in the eastern sky, but he remembered his star patterns well and used them to turn toward the road. With the chill mists curling around him and the dew on the long grass soaking him to his knees, he wanted to get out of the fields as quickly as he could.

The sun was just yellowing the eastern horizon when William came to the road just on the edge of a pine forest, into which it ran off into the murky depths. Turning up the road he cantered along, stretching and twisting to get the last of the kinks out of his muscles. The road rose steadily as it went on through the forest, and occasional breaks in the trees gave him glimpses of the spectacular sunrise off to his right, where the dawn over the mist-filled valley painted the sky in hues of rose and violet. It was a magnificent morning, still and quiet, and William felt like the only person in the world. He stopped at one clear spot simply to admire the spectacle of the sun breaking the horizon, and it was there that he spotted the smoke.

71

Up ahead, to the right of the road on the downhill side, from among a broad thicket of pine, rose several thin columns of campfire smoke into the still morning air. There were only the slightest traces of vapor rising, indicating properly constructed fires, kindled with only the driest wood and kept hot and pure—critical to keeping the smoke from being spotted by an enemy. In fact, it was only the particular combination of morning mist and angle of sunlight that had betrayed them at all. The trails left by the warm air rising through the morning mist were un-mistakable—there were scores of them coming from the pine woods.

At first William wondered if he was seeing the supply train's night camp, but he quickly dismissed the idea. There were far too many smoke trails, and muleteers would never take so much care with their fires. A supply train camp would be marked by a single column of dark, stinking smoke rising from a central fire in which all the camp's garbage would be burned. Fighting forces were the only people so meticulous with their fires. He racked his brain to recall if any training bivouacs were scheduled for this region, but he could remember none. Then with a chill that came from deep within him he recalled how far Black Army troops had penetrated into Imperial territory. He needed to investigate those campfires, and he needed to do it cautiously. For a moment he regretted that he had come out with no armor and only a belt knife for a weapon, but he quickly dismissed that as folly. Stealth was his only weapon now—even full armor and field weapons would not avail him against a force big enough to have that many campfires.

Dismounting quietly, William took a moment to tie up his stirrups so they wouldn't jingle, then carefully led Coney into the scrub growth beside the road. He moved cautiously and watched everywhere, knowing that a force trained well enough to build proper campfires would certainly have sentries out, and he might already be within their pickets. The roadside scrub soon gave way to the peculiar needle-carpeted openness of the pine woods, which always made William nervous. His train-ing and personal experience on maneuvers in pine woods all told him that they were an ideal environment for stealth, but his spine continued to tell him that the open spaces were too revealing, that enemies were always lurking behind him. He proceeded nonetheless, leading Coney by the bridle from tree to tree toward the campfires, moving as slowly as was reasonable for his movement not to be noticed. He was grateful for the dawn mist that yet shrouded the trunks of the trees while the morning sun painted their tops golden.

At length William came near to where he judged the outer campfires to be located. He still could see nothing, but he proceeded with even more caution now, advancing very slowly and straining his eyes into the mist ahead. Very faintly he thought he could discern dim shapes, some of them moving. He leaned forward for a better look.

William's ears registered the distinctive whizz a split second before his hand felt the strong thunk. A hundred instincts screamed at him to move, but his battle training clamped down on them all, and he didn't move a muscle except to turn his head slowly just enough to see the quivering arrow embedded in the tree trunk two inches above his hand.

The fletching was bright blue.

"That's right, mate—hold that station, or the next one finds your kidney", a voice growled behind him. William struggled to control his breathing and his grip on Coney's bridle—now was not the time for the stallion to pick up on his terror and start getting unmanageable. He could scarcely hear the footfalls of the sentries as they approached, but ripples of cold terror shot up his spine, as his deepest fears kept telling him that there was no reason that the next arrow shouldn't strike at any time. It took every ounce of his self-control not to jump at the hissing sound of a blade being drawn from its scabbard not four feet behind him. He steeled himself for a swift blow.

"All right, mate, let's have a look at you", the voice commanded, and William slowly turned, keeping the hand he had held on the tree in plain view while the other still held Coney's bridle. There behind him stood two uniformed figures, one holding a long knife and the other a bow with an arrow nocked but undrawn. The one with the knife was tall with a lantern jaw and close-cropped black hair, while the other was shorter

73

and wore a short brown beard that matched his brown hair. Their uniforms were simple and trimmed in blue with few insignia. They both glared at him with naked hostility that swiftly turned to wonder as they caught sight of his uniform through the gap in his riding cloak. The tall one's lips drew back in a menacing grin.

"Well, well—see what we've caught, Clarke", he said. "We go watching for Black Army spies and find an Imperial officer—not that there's much difference, eh? You just spread your arms out there, Green Man, and we'll see what weapons you're carrying today."

William obeyed, holding out his arms to spread his cloak and show the single dagger. The dark-haired soldier eyed him suspiciously but stepped close enough to snatch the blade from its sheath.

"Nothing more that this, my dandy? Not up to fighting? No, I imagine you prefer skulking and spying", the man snarled. "Fine knife, though. It'll come in handy. Now . . ." here he thrust his knife toward William's midriff. "What were you sneaking around here for? Who sent you?"

William, obliged by the accepted customs of conflict to give only his name, remained silent. He was not going to say anything to this belligerent Rebel about his true mission, benign though it was. He simply gazed at his captors.

"Not talkin', eh?" the tall soldier growled. "We'll . . ."

"Maybe the colonel will want to talk to him, Sarge", offered the brown-haired soldier. "He mentioned that he wanted to see anyone found about the camp."

The tall one studied his comrade for a moment, as if pondering something, then replied, "You're right, Clarke. We'll take him to the colonel. Here, you bind him, and I'll take the horse." The sergeant stepped forward to take the bridle, while Clarke pulled a leather thong from a pouch at his side.

Clarke turned William toward the tree trunk and began tying his hands behind him. William felt a distinct difference in the attitudes of the two soldiers, for Clarke seemed the more gentle of the two, which made William glad he had been chosen to do the binding.

"Be careful with him", William said to the sergeant. He was astounded at how squeaky his voice sounded. "He's a stallion, and not fully trained."

The Sergeant glared at him. "I've handled enough horseflesh in my day, pretty man", he snarled, grabbing Coney's reins so abruptly that the stallion shied, proving his statement false.

Clarke finished his tying, but much to William's dismay the Sergeant decided to inspect the knots. "See here, Clarke, you'll have to tie tighter than that. He'll twist right out of these", the sergeant said. This was not true, for though the thong was not uncomfortable, it was as secure as any that William had ever felt, and he would not have been able to escape it. Nonetheless, the sergeant handed Coney's reins to Clarke and began retying the thong, drawing it so tight that it cut into William's skin and started his hands throbbing in pain. In doing so the sergeant also jostled William's wounded arm, sending a shock of pain down his side that caused him to gasp.

"Too tight for you there?" the sergeant sneered, pulling a knot tighter as he spoke.

"My wound—left shoulder", William replied through gritted teeth.

"Wound? An Imperial officer?" the sergeant said sarcastically. "Couldn't have been in a battle, eh, Clarke? What'd you do—fall off a barstool?" With that he grasped William by both shoulders and shoved him toward the camp. William nearly fainted with the pain but managed to keep his feet. Out of the corner of his eye he saw Clarke coming along with a deliberately neutral expression, which William guessed meant tacit disapproval of his superior's behavior, giving him some hope that all the Rebels in this camp were not as sadistic as this sergeant.

That was the only hope William had on that grim walk. After the immediate terror for his life subsided, he settled into a deep gloom that was not aided by the throbbing agony in his arm and hands. He had no idea what army these soldiers belonged to, but the sergeant at least seemed to be one of those who never got word that the Wars of Rebellion had ended. Now William was being led as a captive into an entire camp full of these Rebels with no clue as to their intentions. His treatment so far gave every indication that he would be treated as a prisoner of war at least, and possibly as a spy—which could mean execution, his tightening stomach told him. He forced himself to ignore that possibility. He was in full uniform, and no state of war existed between the Empire and any Rebel force, so they couldn't accuse him of spying. But then again, not being at war also meant that large armed Rebel encampments should not be found deep within Imperial territory, as this one was. What if they were planning an attack on the Empire, and he was unfortunate enough to stumble across the invasion force? That would make his chances slim indeed. He recalled how reasonable Commander von Huber had been and how those Rebels had treated him like a fellow soldier despite the color of his uniform, but that merely stirred up his own doubts as to what had motivated the Parliamentarians.

William grimly reflected that he seemed to be having no luck at all when it came to Rebels. He had lived nearly his entire life without giving them a second thought, and now within the span of a few weeks he had had two encounters with them, neither under auspicious circumstances. His mind seethed with fear, frustration, anger, and a good portion of self-disgust. He tried to force himself to think strategically, which was what he was supposedly good at, but found that strategic thinking is much easier when one is detached from the situation. What a difference there was between the concept of fear and discouragement as a factor in a battle plan and actually being in the grip of those emotions! He forced himself to reason—he should be looking for weaknesses in his enemy's circumstances and strengths in his so he could come up with a strategy to capitalize on that. "Know your enemy, know yourself" was the central strategic principle, and tactical one as well, for as one of his Academy professors had put it, "Tactics is simply strategy on the hoof."

The difficulty was that he was almost totally ignorant about the Rebels, never having bothered to learn because he never thought he would need to know. Cursing his folly, he furiously searched his memory to recall what he could of his conversations with John Clay, hoping to recall any shred of knowledge that might help him in his present plight. Only one or two stuck out in his mind.

"The critical thing to keep in mind about the Faithful, Bill," John had explained one evening over a mug of ale, "is that they have almost no concept of serving the King within an army. Their whole thinking revolves around the personal oath of allegiance to the King. Now it's true that we take a personal oath of allegiance as well, but that oath also enlists us in the army. That isn't as much a part of their thinking. For them armies are thrown together as loose confederations of fighters, often held together by the personal charisma of a particular officer. Some of the older ones, such as the Parliamentarians or King's Faithfuls, have stabilized over the years to where they have a fairly established hierarchy, methods of selecting officers, training regimens, and all the rest, to a point where they look much like us. But underneath it is a very different understanding of what it means to serve the King."

"But how can they ignore history?" William had asked. "The instructions are clear—not only did the King demand personal loyalty, but also he created an army to rule in his absence."

"The Blues know that, but they look at it differently", John had answered. "For them an army is a secondary thing, existing only to facilitate their individual fight for the King. That's why there's so much instability in their ranks—if a soldier doesn't feel that his army is being run in a way that helps him fight, he finds another. Hence discipline can be quite loose, as commanders won't enforce it for fear of driving away their men. Strategy also suffers, since any good strategy requires some troops to attack, some to retreat, and some to stand and wait. Blue soldiers don't like to hear that—they all want to fight, so they often end up charging as a disorganized mass, each trying to do as much hacking as they can."

"That's no way to run a campaign!" William had exclaimed. "You can't tailor a strategy to allow for every soldier's desire to fight or not! It's a wonder they win anything at all!"

"You and I know that, but they have a different perspective",

John had continued. "As for how they win anything—mostly that hinges on their fierce personal devotion to the King. You'd be astonished at how much difference it can make, having soldiers as devoted as many of the Blues are. I've seen some of them do almost superhuman things out of sheer love of the King." John's admiration had shown so clearly at that point that William had felt envious and a bit defensive.

"We've had plenty of soldiers, officers and enlisted, whose personal devotion matched that of any Rebel", he had replied rather testily.

"True, true", John had replied. "But they're more the exception, eh? Our thinking mostly hinges on our enlistment in the army rather than on our oath of allegiance, doesn't it? I think that's something we can learn from the Blues."

That conversation had moved on to other topics, but William had never forgotten it, mostly because the perspective that John had tried to explain was so alien to his thinking that he could not grasp it at all. He didn't know what good it would do him right now, except to remind him that he was dealing with people who did not think like he did, but that was at least something.

They were now emerging from the mist into the camp proper, where William saw encamped before him more Rebel troops than he had ever seen. The camp was far bigger than the smoke trails had led him to believe. It obviously housed hundreds and hundreds of troops in its tents, and they were all arising and buckling down to the day's work. Soldiers were gathering about the campfires to warm themselves and eat some gruel from wooden bowls. They looked with curiosity at William as he was led past. From all William could observe the camp was especially well ordered, with the tents laid out neatly and staked well, the lances and other tall weapons stacked in neat piles in front of the tents, and plenty of clean straw laying about. There was no noticeable garbage, and the paths on which they walked were free of debris. William took special note of the buckets of water placed about and of how clean the men were. This always indicated good order within a bivouac. So did the absence of hubbub and confusion—the soldiers went about their business with a quiet but cheerful efficiency that spoke of good discipline.

But clean and orderly as the camp was, it was clearly very poorly supplied. The clothing the men wore was clean but could hardly be called uniform. There was no consistency among them—some wore full blue uniforms, though they were rarely alike, while others wore only blue shirts, and yet others wore blue scarves or strips of blue cloth sewn to their sleeves. The tents, too, obviously came from a variety of sources and had seen much use in their day. They were of various sizes and hues, and though all were clean, many were patched and sewn. The weapons particularly were in poor condition. The spear stacks had all manner of weapons in them, from decorative halberds to rude sticks to pruning hooks—which were dangerous in their way but hardly battlefield weapons. William even thought he saw a pitchfork in one stack. They passed a soldier who was diligently attempting to fletch his own arrow with yarn and the best he could find from a bag of feathers that looked like the result of last night's plucking. Clean and orderly though they might be, the Rebel force was clearly lacking good supply sources. In particular William noted the lack of provisions. Nowhere were the bubbling soup kettles and roasting fowl that could be found over campfires in even the most transient Imperial field encampments. All he could see being eaten was gruel from wooden bowls, which explained the clean campfires but caused William to wonder about how long this force could stay in the field.

After walking in silence for some distance through the camp, they came upon a single large tent that was clearly the command tent, since there was none other of its like within sight. William thought this odd, for even in temporary Imperial encampments the command tent was always surrounded by lesser conference and staff tents, which made up the command complex. Here, this single tent seemed to be all there was. William was also surprised that there was no guard in front of the flap. Coming up to the tent, the private tied Coney to a nearby tree while the sergeant busied himself unstrapping the saddlebags. Then he took William's wounded arm roughly and pulled him right through the flap.

The inside of the tent was murky, and it was some time before William could see properly, for the morning sun outside had grown quite bright while within the tent the only illumination was a single candle hung from a tent pole. As his eyes adapted, he saw a table set up on the far side of the tent beneath the candle. On the table were spread various parchments, and over it leaned two men, who seemed to have been examining the parchments but had both turned to see the cause of the intrusion. Off to one side stood a smaller table and some stools as well as the remains of a recently eaten breakfast, again of the same gruel he had seen throughout the camp.

He was fascinated by the two men. One was tall and slim with white hair and the lines of many years on his lean face. His eyes were keen, and his bearing was noble. He was taller than the sergeant, which made him much taller than William. He wore a full uniform, one of the few William had seen that could truly be called regular. On it were insignia and decorations that spoke of rank and experience, and though the insignia were alien to him, William guessed that this was the colonel. The other man was much shorter, as short as William, and stockier. His hair was black, as were his eyes, and they glittered with a keenness that was neither cruel nor suspicious but seemed only very active and inquisitive. He wore a true uniform as well, and from its simpler design William guessed that he was a senior enlisted man, possibly the equivalent of a senior or staff sergeant in the Imperial forces.

Both these men gazed in silence at William and the sergeant—who was now standing at stiff attention—for some moments before the taller one spoke.

"Yes, Sergeant?" His voice was clear and commanding but gentle, though to William it also seemed to contain a touch of the dramatic. If he was annoyed by the interruption, his voice did not betray it.

"Caught a spy, sir", the sergeant replied with smug satisfaction. His manner had changed. Before he had been imperious and sadistic; now he was imperious and ingratiating. It was clear that he relished the opportunity to report to his commanding officer. "He was sneaking around the edge of

camp before dawn, and I caught him. He was carrying these."
He hustled forward to hand over William's dagger and saddlebags. The colonel glanced at the items with minimal interest,
looked over at the staff sergeant beside him, then turned back
to William.

"Yes, er", he said, obviously at a loss as to how to handle this
unexpected circumstance. "Thank you, Sergeant. Very diligent
of you. Please seat him over there, and we will attend to the
matter presently."

"Yes, sir", replied the sergeant, obviously crestfallen that his
arrest caused no more disturbance than it did. He pulled William
across the room—again by the wounded arm—and seated him
on one of the stools. The sergeant then took station behind
him, and another uncomfortable silence reigned for some moments before the colonel spoke again.

"Is there anything else, Sergeant?" The tone of dismissal was
obvious in his voice.

"Won't you be needing me to guard the prisoner, sir?" Now
the sergeant seemed near desperation, as if being sent forth from
the tent into anonymity were a criminal sentence. Once again
the colonel glanced at the staff sergeant, then at the well-tied
William, who was clearly no danger to anyone, then back at
the sergeant.

"Very well, Sergeant, you may stay", he said with resignation.

"But make yourself useful and open these flaps to let some
light in", the staff sergeant barked. This was quickly done, and
the two turned back to the parchments on the table, ignoring
William and his captor for the time.

William's first moment of rest in hours only heightened his
discomfort. His arm ached, his hands throbbed, his shoulders
were being wrenched back, and with every movement the
leather thong cut more deeply into his wrist until he could feel
blood dripping down his fingers. He was also terribly thirsty.
All these physical pains crowded out the despondency that had
gripped him before. He tried to focus on a plan to get back
to his own camp, on what the two men leaning over the table
were saying, on anything but his torments, but his mind refused

to cooperate. Making matters worse were a pitcher of water and cups that stood on the table not two feet from him. After some minutes of this he finally decided that asking would harm nothing.

"May I have some water?" he asked. The dryness of his throat caused his request to come out more quietly than he expected, so the two men at the table did not respond, though he was certain that the sergeant standing stiffly behind him had heard.

"May I please have some water?" he asked again, louder this time, causing his request to come out more like a bark. The two men stopped their discussion and looked; the colonel at William, the staff sergeant at the sergeant. Silence reigned for a minute before the staff sergeant finally spoke.

"You heard the man, Sergeant", he said, his voice dripping with disgust. "Give him a drink." The sergeant, obviously flustered under the scrutiny of his superiors, muttered something under his breath but poured a cup full of water. William was just wondering how the sergeant was going to deal with his tied hands when the answer became obvious—he held the full cup up to William's lips in a clumsy attempt to give him a drink. At this the staff sergeant exploded.

"Oh, for pity's sake!" he exclaimed as he stormed over, shoving the cowed sergeant aside and spilling the water. William gasped as the staff sergeant fumbled with the thong, sending pain shooting up his arms. When it became obvious how tightly the thong was tied, the staff sergeant stopped and asked in a cold voice, "Who tied this thong?"

"I—I did", the sergeant stammered.

"Get outside", came the reply in a tone so controlled it was obvious that a thunderstorm of fury was being contained. "I'll deal with you in a minute." Then William heard the unsheathing of a knife and the careful probing of the tip, cutting away at the leather while staying clear of his flesh.

"This may tighten a bit as I cut", the staff sergeant was explaining. "But it won't be bad. What'll really hurt is when the blood returns to your hands. You'd better be on your knees when that happens." Then the last thong was cut and William realized how right the man was. He was bringing his hands forward to massage them when his breath was taken away by a searing sheet of pain. Blinded, he dropped to his knees and leaned against the stool upon which he had just been seated. His hands felt aflame and throbbed with a brutal persistence that blocked out all else. He was only dimly aware of his surroundings—that the staff sergeant was gone, that there was a great deal of angry shouting outside the tent, that the colonel was hovering about, broadcasting extreme distress at William's agony yet unsure of what to do about it. Slowly the pain abated enough for him to be more aware of other sensations—the first of which was cool water being poured over his hands and wrists.

"That's right, sir", he heard the staff sergeant say. "Just keep pouring the water over his hands. It'll help them hurt less, and it'll wash some of the blood away." It was true; William's hands did hurt less under the water. He even ventured to flex them a little, which was painful, but he persisted because it felt so good to be able to move them.

"The trick is to keep them up." The staff sergeant was now addressing William. "They throb less that way." He began chafing William's wrists and hands, which was painful but helped restore movement quickly. After a couple of minutes he was able to sit on the stool again and feebly grasp a cup to get the drink he had requested. The colonel and staff sergeant faced him nervously.

"Sir, I wish to deeply apologize for the inexcusable behavior of my sergeant", the colonel said gravely and somewhat dramatically, "I don't know who you are or why you are here, but no matter what, you did not deserve to be treated with that type of brutality. Please accept my deepest apologies."

"I've warned you about that man Harold", the staff sergeant said to the colonel before William could reply. "He's got a mean streak a foot long right through him." William was amazed at the egalitarian manner that the staff sergeant used toward his superior. No Imperial enlisted man would have dared to speak to an officer, especially a colonel, so casually, but the Rebel officer did not seem to think it unusual.

"That you have, Jacobs", he replied. Then to William he said, "Please accept our assurances that he will be disciplined to the fullest extent of our regulations. Brutality to prisoners is not accepted in this army."

So there it was. As far as these people were concerned he was a prisoner, even though he was an Imperial officer carrying out his duty in Imperial territory. The arrogance of such an attitude infuriated him, but he decided that tact would make more headway than confrontation.

"Thank you", he said. "I am Field Lieutenant William de Rowan of the Imperial Army, First Division, Fifth Battalion." He wondered if that would serve to remind them in whose territory they were trespassing. The colonel gave no indication that it reminded him of anything.

"Colonel Stephen Cole, Commanding, First Freeman's Army, at your service", he replied with a bow. "This is Staff Sergeant Joseph Jacobs, my aide and strategist."

"Call me Joe", said the staff sergeant with a wide grin. William nodded in response, again surprised by the man's easy familiarity. He seemed quite amiable, and William found himself warming to the man, if for no other reason than that he found it almost impossible to believe that this pleasant fellow could consign anyone, even an Imperial officer, to the gallows.

"To which command is this army attached? I've not heard of the Freeman's Army." William ventured a question, hoping that they wouldn't notice that it wasn't what a prisoner normally asked. He guessed correctly, for the colonel responded quickly with a bit of stiffness and a bit of pride.

"We own no command, sir. This army is an independent force."

Ah—that told William much of what he needed to know. From what John had told him, independent armies were self-contained commands that reported to no hierarchy at all, not even the loose ones that were found in some of the Rebel armies. Sometimes such armies would form confederations for the duration of a campaign or two, but they were far more likely to be found fighting alone. They were known for their valor in battle and their fierce loyalty to their commanders but had the usual dismal record for strategic knowledge and (as William had already seen) supply capability. They also had the worst record for tolerance of Imperial or other commands. If word ever came of an attack by Rebels on Imperial territory, there was almost certain to be an independent force behind it. They were almost completely guided by the nature and personality of the commander, sometimes disbanding entirely if he was killed or went elsewhere. That was important to remember, because it meant that this colonel had life-and-death control over him. William was somewhat encouraged by this, for this man too seemed decent enough—he had neither breathed fire nor spat nails upon hearing that he had an Imperial officer in his custody—but William knew he would have to be careful nonetheless.

"We would offer you some refreshment, Lieutenant, but we have broken our fast already, and our fire has been extinguished", Joe said, indicating the dishes on the table. "We have some field rations, however . . ."

"No matter. I have some provisions in my saddlebags there, if you don't mind my getting them", William replied.

"Not at all", said the colonel.

The staff sergeant handed William the bags, in which he dug around for a bit trying to find his rations. But the bag was too tightly packed, so he moved some of the items on the small table aside and dumped the bag onto it. His portfolio was the first thing to fall out, the black oiled map cases spilling all over the floor. The staff sergeant stooped to pick them up for him.

"What are these?" he asked casually, turning the case over in his hands.

"Just maps", William replied.

"Maps?" Joe said so quickly that William looked up in surprise. The staff sergeant was eying the case with a hungry expression, as if it contained a great treasure. Then he noticed William's scrutiny and quickly put the cases on the table and turned back to the colonel.

Mystified by this incident, William pondered it as he set up his "small" breakfast of cheese, jerky, biscuit, apples, and a small flagon of wine. Hungry as he was, his attention was more on the staff sergeant's unusual reaction to the discovery that William had maps. Why would a map elicit a reaction like that? After a minute or so it came to him: the supply issue! The Rebels were so ill supplied, especially an independent force such as this, that strategic supplies such as maps were certain to be quite rare and probably poor quality when available at all. The Rebels didn't have the advantage of a cartographic staff in every battalion headquarters, much less a standard portfolio from which to draw. It made William feel rather smug to realize that he, a mere lieutenant, was riding around with an entire portfolio of maps that a Rebel colonel and his entire army lacked. Then he realized that this, perhaps, could be a strategic advantage. He had something the Rebels apparently needed—perhaps he could bargain for his freedom with it. At first he almost dismissed the idea, for though the Rebels showed no sign of doing so, they could certainly take whatever maps they wished without any bargaining at all. Then he remembered that all the notations on the maps were written in Imperial Ceremonial, the archaic language of the Empire that was still used for official documents, ceremonies, and maps. Even if the Rebels took the maps, they would certainly still need him to translate for them. Now there was a possibility, provided that such bargaining didn't constitute treason. That was a stickier question, on which William deliberated for some time. Finally he came to the conclusion that it would not be a breach of trust if he were to work out some bargain with the Rebels as long as they were not planning an attack on the Empire. He did not think they were doing this, or they would have been far more anxious about his presence from the start, but he could not be sure. He decided to see what he could learn about their objectives from the conversation over the table.

They were talking strategy, of course, which William always found interesting, but what he found even more intriguing were the terms that they used. His lifelong impression of the strategic capability of Rebels, somewhat reinforced by conversations with John Clay, was that they were little more than simpleminded enthusiasts who dashed about from one feeble campaign to another with little concern for goals or government. Yet the colonel and staff sergeant were discussing an upcoming battle in terms that could have been lifted from any

Imperial strategy text. Phrases like "the goal of this campaign is the swift liberation of the enslaved population from the yoke of the Black Army" and "the stroke must be swift and complete—there can be no question of coexistence with the Black Army" were common, phrases similar to ones he had included in countless strategic recommendations. This did not fit William's expectations, especially coming from people with such an obviously simplistic approach to fighting as these Independents had. But what really surprised him was that these people used the phrases not as standard recitation of approved combat doctrine but as if they really meant them.

William slowly realized that he was hearing people who had done what he was always urging his fellow officers to do—make the shift from scholar to soldier. It was a running joke in the Imperial Army to refer to certain officers as "never having left the Academy", and in truth it was possible to do so, even in the field corps. For such officers the war remained a lifelong academic exercise, with theoretical battles played out in strategic journals by means of interminable series of articles—polished and perfect in doctrine but never actually executed. Indeed, there were officers of flag rank who retired having never drawn a sword in anger. It frustrated William to see that many of his colleagues emulated this and saw it as the duty of officers endlessly to refine and reformulate strategy. How often had he encouraged them to get out into the field and execute those strategies? For which they had branded him a fanatic, and he had to be brought captive into a Rebel camp to find soldiers who were willing actually to do something. His heart warmed to the colonel and his sergeant, for they were obviously soldiers before they were anything else.

One thing William quickly noticed was how frequently the conversation was punctuated by admissions of limitations: "Of course, the map is rather vague about that" and "We're not sure what lies in here" were the sort of comments being made. He even thought he noticed Joe casting furtive glances back at the map cases piled on the table next to William. This emboldened him—if they were desperate, bargaining would go much more smoothly. He fished about in his mind, trying to come up with an enticing opening offer to get the Rebels interested. He felt very inept at this, since he had never considered himself much of a schemer, and in the end he just cleared his throat and stammered out a question.

"Excuse me, but I couldn't help hearing—are you having trouble with your maps?" he asked. The two rebels looked at each other in mystification, then both spoke at once.

"Our maps are adequate for . . ." began the colonel in a stilted, almost offended tone.

"Our maps are sorely lacking", cut in Joe with customary directness. "Why do you ask?"

"You're welcome to take a look at these, if you wish", William replied. Both men's eyes lit up, the colonel's with an anxious hope and Joe's with an eager fire. Once again they both spoke at once.

"Thank you, Lieutenant, but . . ." said the colonel.

"Are these Academy maps?" asked Joe, opening one up. The colonel, meanwhile, was looking at the black oilskin cases with the green Imperial Army seals with a suspicious eye.

"Sergeant, I'm not sure about this", he said, touching one of the map cases as if it were a coiled snake. "This Green Army material—if the men were to find out . . ."

"Sir, these are Academy maps, drawn by the best Imperial cartographers!" exclaimed Joe, spreading one out on the table. "Look at this detail! See how precise it is! We simply don't have anything like them!"

It was true. There was no comparison between the amateurish Rebel chart and the precise Imperial version. The Rebel chart was drawn on poor paper with carbon and inferior ink, while the Imperial map was precisely lettered and noted on fine parchment. Joe was in ecstasy over the potential of such resources, and even the colonel, who was obviously fighting an internal struggle about accepting help from the Empire, had to admit that the product in question was clearly superior.

"Look at this", raved Joe. "Just look at this! You could coordinate troop movements to the hour with a map this detailed. What do these markings mean?" This last question was addressed to William.

"Those are terrain markings", he explained. "These indicate how passable the rocks are, and these here tell what this water is like. For instance, this set of markings indicates that a lightly loaded squad in fair condition could pass this trail in half a day and ford this river here, while a fully loaded squad would take a full day and have to ferry their supplies across. The notation is cryptic and takes a while to learn but is unbeatable once mastered." William was growing excited—the enthusiastic reception of the offer of the maps was going to make his job easier. He began to look for an opportunity to make an offer to bargain for his freedom.

"Can you believe it! Can you believe it!" the little sergeant bubbled in his excitement. Even the colonel was smiling now, but suddenly he frowned.

"And this writing here?" he asked, pointing to some writing near a spot on the map. There were some notations in Imperial Ceremonial, the very existence of which made some Rebels nervous.

"Those are strategic specifications about that city—the population, available resources, major roads running through it—that sort of data. For some reason our cartographers still use Ceremonial when making notations, though I'm not sure why." This was true—William had always wondered why common speech could not be used just as easily. The Ceremonial was just as well in this case, however, since the particular map they were examining was of the border areas with some Rebel territories, and the notations included some straightforward references to Rebel troop strength and strategic tendencies. Some of the comments were quite unflattering, and William was grateful that the Rebels could not read them. He decided to try to hook them with the most enticing bait of all, hoping he had the skill to get them to bargain with him.

"I doubt if this is the map you need", William said. "I've all sorts of them in here—what is your target? I'll get you the one that contains it."

The sudden silence and glances exchanged by the Rebels made William quickly aware of the sensitivity of the question he had just asked. Here he was, for all intents a captive enemy, asking the leading strategists of an army to reveal their intentions. He suddenly realized how much he had endangered his own position, and his mind raced, trying to think up an adequate way to retrieve the question. Then the Rebels came to an unspoken decision.

"Numaris", Joe said quietly.

William was stunned. He stared at the sergeant for some moments in dumb amazement. Numaris! It had been two generations since Numaris was lost to the Black Army and thirty-three years since the attempted reconquest had resulted in one of the most humiliating defeats ever suffered by the Empire. To this day it was nearly impossible to get veterans of the battle to talk about it. William knew his father had been there and suspected from the few hints he had ever dropped that Commandant Lloyd had also been part of the battle. William had always had an interest in Numaris, partly because it was so shrouded in secrecy. He had made it a particular study while in the Academy, unearthing every fact he could find in an attempt to discover how the city had fallen and why it apparently defied reconquest. His graduate project had been a critique of the strategy and tactics of the lost battle that went into such detail that he had had to get special clearances to examine classified dispatches and postmortems in order to complete it. What he had found was startling and explained why most of the documentation on Numaris remained secret. His project had been classified when it was completed, and though he heard hints from his graduate mentor that it had received high praise from the reviewing officers, it had never been published or publicly reviewed, even in abridged form, so he had never received any recognition for the work. It did, however, give him enough background to appreciate the value—and difficulty—of the prize the Rebels were attempting to recapture.

Numaris! He had never seen the city, but the poetic descriptions of it painted exquisite pictures in his mind. Surrounded by mountains, the city rose above the fertile valley in which dwelt the once happy and industrious population who were its subjects. Built almost completely from the rose-tinted marble that was quarried from the nearby hills, the city and its valley had been the pride of the Chalis Province. Not being on the shipping routes had prevented it from developing into a major trade center like Chalis City or Temarra, so instead it had become a center of learning and the seat of three major academies. The quarry and agriculture of the valley had kept the city prosperous, while the integrity of the academies had built its reputation as a center of knowledge. Eventually the decision had been made to move the government of Chalis Province to Numaris. Thus the city had reigned, a queen among cities, until its fall to the Black Army. Now the precious marble came no more from the valley, the light of the academies was darkened, and those citizens of Numaris who survived the conquest lived as slaves of their conquerors.

Numaris! Part of his mind raged against the idea—who did these Rebels think they were? How did they, with their pitchforks and porridge, think they could succeed where a superbly supplied, impeccably coordinated assault had failed? But another part of him could see that, despite their lack of sophistication, the tone and demeanor of the fighting men before him were of those who had carefully considered a difficult task and had chosen to proceed with it regardless of cost.

William shook himself. He had been staring at the sergeant for more than a minute while these thoughts ran through his head. They seemed to be anticipating a reaction, but all he could do was stammer.

"Numaris?"

"Yes, Lieutenant", replied the colonel firmly. "The good citizens of that valley have lived and died in bitter slavery for too long. It is past time for them to be liberated, which we propose to do—or die in the process." Now William stared at the colonel, for his manner had transformed from that of a disturbed, unsure official to that of a stern, certain leader with his eyes firmly fixed on a goal. In an instant William saw that he had misjudged the man; though he could be unsettled by the day-to-day details of running an installation, he clearly had great compassion for the downtrodden as well as a tremendous vision to free them and was able to communicate that vision to others. William's respect for the man soared. He had often commented to colleagues that the Imperial Army seemed to value administrative ability over true leadership. Here he had a chance to see a true leader, and he was not going to scorn him.

"That's a tall order", he replied quietly.

"We know", nodded Joe in response.

"Map twelve", William said, reaching for the pouch, while Joe folded up and laid the others aside. They spread the map of Numaris Valley out on the table.

Numaris lay at the extreme western end of a valley that was about twelve miles long by eight miles wide at the widest point. The valley was shaped something like a fat gourd laid from east to west, with the neck to the east, the thicker body to the west, and a short spur of hills jutting up from the south that separated the valley into two vales. The valley was almost entirely a fertile plain that was home to hundreds of small farms. These were kept watered by uncountable streams that trickled down from the surrounding mountains. A small lake lay in the southwest corner of the valley, about three miles from Numaris itself, out of which ran the river that flowed down the valley and out through its rocky mouth—the river that had proven the bane of the Imperial Army. Numaris itself was built right up against the western mountains, so the cliffs formed the western and much of the southern walls. The city's sole gate opened north-eastward, toward the famous quarries, which were located in the crumbled hills that formed the northern wall of the valley. Unlike the majestic and forbidding peaks that swept up from the green plain on the south and west, the Marble Hills were lower and more verdant, even housing some manors and orchards on their lower slopes. There were no major roads going all the way over the hills, however, which made them impassable for cavalry, and only a small band of the most determined infantry could pass over them through the ill-kept shepherd paths. The only substantial route for traffic in and out of the valley remained the main road, which passed down the valley from the gates of Numaris to the eastern gap, which was extremely narrow, only wide enough for the road and the river. This constricted entrance to the valley had long been the best defense that Numaris had. The city had built a garrison tower at the mouth of the valley outside the mountains and had placed across the gap a perfunctory barrier that was no true defense but rather a delimiter of the authority of the government of Numaris for the purposes of taxation and commerce. The question of a defensive gate across the mouth of the valley had been raised from time to time—indeed, the rumor still circulated that the Black Army was finally constructing one—but from his studies William knew that one would never be built because it was not necessary. Other factors rendered the valley nearly impregnable.

As the three soldiers examined the maps side by side, the contrast between them was even more obvious. Where the Rebel map was dirty, smudged, and approximated, the Imperial chart was precise, clean, and copiously notated. The terrain markings were excruciatingly accurate, since the entire valley had long been Imperial territory, and every yard had been carefully mapped, including obscure footpaths and even geological features. Joe was elated beyond words, bubbling almost total nonsense at this unanticipated bounty.

This should have been the point at which William made the offer to bargain his assistance for his freedom, but in fact he had quickly forgotten that whole plan. Here was a strategy session much to his liking, with determined soldiers planning a real battle in an arena with which he was extremely familiar. Any of his Academy classmates could have predicted the results and would have laughed as they did so. William de Rowan was the strategic demon of his class, at times driving impromptu sessions far into the night just to get a certain strategy honed to perfection. When wrapped up in planning he could forget to eat, sleep, or relieve himself until one thing or the other drove him to agony. In fact, there was only one thing that could distract the excruciatingly conscientious William from his duties, and the Rebels had inadvertently placed it right in front of him. Had they deliberately set out to distract him they could not have set up a better situation for that purpose. He was almost quivering with excitement at the prospect of planning a real battle.

"Tell me," William asked as nonchalantly as he could, "what is your plan of attack?"

Again Joe hesitated a moment, glancing at his superior. Receiving a confirming nod, he launched into his narrative. William was impressed with Joe's crisp professionalism and the confidence he exuded as he spoke and could see that, noncom or not, here was a soldier who was the match of many majors that he knew.

"To begin with, of course, we'll have to take out this garrison tower. We figured to do that quickly and quietly, to minimize the possibility of them alerting the city by signal fire", Joe explained, gesturing to the appropriate spot on the map. "That means a night attack, with a couple of grapnel men coming from their blind side. We would also attack at the gate, hoping to get inside before they had a chance to shut it. Next would come . . ." he proceeded to outline the planned assault in great detail, including precise strategic references to formations and advance sequences. William was impressed with Joe's intuition for strategy, all the more because he had always believed Rebels to be strategic rustics with no grasp of battlefield subtlety. William allowed the entire plan to unfold, asking no questions and nodding only at intervals. At last Joe finished his explanation and looked with expectation into William's face.

"Well?" he asked, obviously anxious for a reassuring opinion. "What do you think?"

William was silent. He reached down and tweaked the map a little so he could see it better. Both Rebels gazed at him as he examined the map silently. At length he spoke quietly, just barely above a whisper, never taking his eyes off the map.

"What do I think? What do I think?" His voice grew firmer. "I think your men will die. Their heads will be smashed against the rocks, their standards will be trampled beneath the hooves of their enemies, their blood will soak into the sand, and you will go down to cruel defeat."

The Rebels gaped at him. The colonel looked as if he had just been slapped across the face, while Joe looked crushed. Dead silence filled the room for half a minute.

"I didn't think it was that bad a plan", muttered the colonel indignantly. "In fact, I . . ."

"The plan?" William broke in sharply. "The plan? The plan is just fine, as far as it goes. Imperial strategists couldn't do better—in fact, they didn't. The plan is essentially identical to the one drawn up by the Imperial Army for the retaking of Numaris over thirty years ago—and it will fail for the same reasons. No, it isn't the plan that will defeat you; it's the geography. That will kill you just as it killed the Imperial Army back then."

"What happened?" asked Joe.

"The assault on the valley began, as you intend, with a silent attack on the garrison tower. We thought we knew all about it, since we had built it, but the Black Army had made some modifications. Where the top had been an open battlement, it had been turned into a massive bonfire platform. The trapdoor was firmly locked from below, and a hole had been cut through the center of the floor. The hole was about a foot in diameter, and over it was piled an immense load of dried branches, tarred rags, and other inflammables. From the underside of this pile a length of tarred rag dropped through the hole to the chamber below, where it could be ignited by anyone with a torch."

"Which means they can ignite their signal fire without exposing anyone to enemy steel", Joe interrupted. "Very clever."

"Precisely, and that's just what they did. The minute they heard our men on their roof, they lit the rag, firing the brush-pile and nearly cooking everyone up there. They had to climb back down their grapnel lines much more quickly than they had ascended them. The resulting fire was quite a sight, alerting the army in Numaris that something was up. We eventually took the tower, but only after a floor-by-floor fight that took the whole night."

"In other words, there is no taking that tower by enough surprise to prevent a signal getting off", Joe concluded.

"Best we can tell, no. If you can figure out a way, please let us know, but our best minds have worked at it ever since and have found it so practical a design for its purpose that over the past thirty years we've adapted all our signal towers to match it. But that was only the start of the troubles. Bad as it was to lose the chance to snuff that signal, our real problems came from not reading our own map notations closely enough.

"The critical feature was the river. Notice how it meanders across the valley floor until right here, where it cuts up to the northern hills and hugs close to them for this final portion of the valley. Now, everyone we talked to about the river assured us that it was broad, lazy, and easily fordable down its entire length."

"That seems odd," Joe said, "considering that it's the only drainage for all this high land."

"Good observation", replied William, impressed by the sergeant's deductive skills. "But it's the soil that makes the difference. The whole valley is deep in rich soil that soaks up most of the water, which is what makes it such good farmland. At any rate, we forgot that almost all of the population lives in the western two-thirds of the valley, and those few who live in the east live mostly to the south, away from the road and river. That meant that the reports we got applied only to the western portion of the river, and they were true as far as they went. What we didn't realize was that when the river makes this veer northward, it also changes its nature. It turns from a shallow, lazy stream to a deep, violent, and rocky torrent."

"That is completely unfordable", Joe said grimly.

"Exactly", replied William. "We should have taken a clue from the violence of the river where it exits the valley, but we didn't. I notice that your map doesn't have any notations to indicate the nature of the river. Ours did, but nobody considered them important enough. We were so wrapped up with our maneuvers and supply lines that we ignored the simple geography—and lost an army because of it.

"Our plan was essentially the same as yours—get through the gap, fan out to hug the high ground, then progress down the valley with the main forces along the north and south walls and a dividing force moving up the middle, forcing opposition to the right or left where they could be crushed by arrows and flanking charges.

"What actually happened was that the minute our forces

broke through the gap, we found ourselves pinned to the north wall by the river. Unable to fan out as we planned, our entire force was held to the road for about three miles, until the river veered south again and the valley opened up right here", William pointed to the spot on the map.

"Where the enemy was waiting for you", said Joe.

"In spades. They have only a small garrison at Valgate, mostly pikemen and longbowmen, but since they held the wide end of the bottleneck, they could get three pikes on every one of our horses, plus volley arrows at us over the heads of the pikemen. Our heavy cavalry, who had led the charge so as to punch through any opposition, found themselves pushed onto the pikes by the foot soldiers coming behind. They were slaughtered nearly to a man, soldiers and horses both." William fell silent for a moment, remembering with sorrow the eyewitness accounts he had read of that grim hour.

"And then?" asked Joe.

"By that time the cavalry had arrived from Numaris. The pikemen stood aside, and the cavalry charged our foot soldiers. It turned into a rout. You must understand that an entire army was strung out along the three mile stretch of road, an army that had been intended to spread out across the valley floor. It was so long that nobody knew what was going on at the other end, so while the front ranks were turning to flee, the rear kept marching forward, resulting in massive confusion. The Black cavalry cut through this like a knife through lard, slaughtering hundreds and scattering the rest to either side. The ones that went in the river all drowned, while those driven into the rocks were hunted down by the Black infantry that followed. The few who escaped the carnage were the ones who evaded the pursuit and got away through the hills.

"The defeat was total. Our men were so dismayed that they offered essentially no resistance, so the Black cavalry swept from one end of the column to the other, massacring as they went. By the time they got close to the end, the rearmost ranks caught on to what was happening and fled, but they were chased and cut down at the mouth of the valley. Then the cavalry turned back to assist the infantry in the 'cleanup'—butchering the wounded, despoiling the bodies, and chaining any captives to be dragged off into slavery."

Finishing his account, William fell mute. Silence reigned in the tent, punctuated only by the transient noises of the camp outside. Grief lay thick on the hearts of all three men.

"That's—that's horrible", said the colonel. "I had heard that the Empire had suffered a defeat at Numaris, but I had no idea . . ." He trailed off into silence. William looked at him. No idea of what, Colonel? No idea that they were flesh-and-blood men, King's troops just like you? No idea that it was more than just two armies, both of which you considered enemies, killing each other? No idea that it would someday affect you?

"Well," Joe interrupted William's thoughts, "that thoroughly destroys our plans. One question, though—if the critical combat juncture is this bottleneck where the river veers south, why only a small garrison there? Why not put the bulk of the defending force there, so they wouldn't have to make the run from Numaris?"

"Actually, it used to be that way when the Empire first occupied the valley. The main force was quartered in Valgate, hence its name, with only ceremonial companies within Numaris itself. But over the years the strategic importance of that site was forgotten, and the bulk of the Imperial troops moved to the city. After that fell, the Black forces kept that pattern, but probably for different reasons. Being a hostile occupation force, they must keep large numbers of troops near the populated areas to police them. But with the signaling from the tower, the setup they have works fine—the garrison can hold the bottleneck plenty long enough for reinforcements to arrive."

"Something I've always wondered, Lieutenant—exactly how did Numaris fall?" asked Colonel Cole. William pondered a moment before replying.

"Treachery." The chill in William's voice told of another story, one that was not going to be told at that time, and the uneasy quiet fell again.

"Your information", Joe once again broke the silence. "has been most helpful, sir, most helpful. Your knowledge about the battle and the area is most impressive."

"I did my graduate project on the defeat at Numaris", William explained.

"Good thing for us that you did", said the colonel. "I thank you as well, Lieutenant. It appears we will need to rethink our strategy."

"Unless", Joe cut in with a mischievous grin, "you've got some ideas." The colonel looked alarmed at this and appeared to be starting to speak when William quickly responded.

"In fact, the purpose of a graduate project is to develop a strategy for a campaign. Mine was a strategy to retake Numaris, avoiding the errors of the defeat."

"Really?" Joe responded enthusiastically. "Tell us about it!"

"Sergeant," interrupted the colonel sharply, "I wish to speak with you outside immediately!" The commander had reached a high level of agitation over something that William could not perceive. The Rebels stepped outside, leaving William to ponder the map and recall the strategy he had developed for retaking Numaris.

In a glade outside, beyond earshot of the tent, a heated discussion was taking place between the colonel and his sergeant.

"Sergeant," began the colonel, "your request of that Imperial lieutenant was out of line and completely inappropriate!"

"With all due respect, sir," replied Joe, "that's an Academy-trained strategist in there! We don't have anyone with anything close to that kind of training! Did you hear how thorough his description of that battle was? He's the sharpest strategic thinker that's ever been in this camp. And what's more, he's already got a plan for the very campaign we hope to pursue! What possible harm could there be in listening?"

"I'm not questioning his competence, Sergeant, or his dedication", the colonel replied. "It's just that—that I'm not comfortable with this Imperial strategy. Who knows what sources have been used to construct it?"

"What difference does it make, sir?" asked Joe. "We can always check it against our own manuals to ensure it doesn't violate any of our tenets of strategy." One of the most common accusations exchanged between the Imperial and Rebel armies was that of impure strategies—each accused the other of drawing from "tainted" sources, polluting the pure principles of strategy left by the King.

"What we have here is an unbeatable opportunity, sir", Joe continued. "The King himself couldn't have set this up any neater. Why don't we at least listen to his plan, then take what we can use?"

"What worries me", the colonel was obviously wavering, "is what if the men were to find out? What would they say if they knew that we were using Imperial strategies?" Rebel troops, especially those who enlisted in independent forces, were deeply suspicious of "overstrategizing"—a trait that had spelled the doom of many of their campaigns.

"What difference does it make?" Joe responded hotly. "And who has to know, anyway? If the strategy is sound and pure, should anyone care whom we consulted? Besides, you yourself have told them that Imperial subjects are Kingdom citizens just like they are . . ."

"Some of them *can* be", interjected the colonel.

"At any rate, if they can be citizens just like we can, can't we accept help from them?" Joe was speaking sharply now. "Besides, it isn't like we're asking him to ride with us—we just want to get some ideas."

"I'm just not certain", said the colonel. "If the men were to find out, they might start deserting, or mutiny."

"Then let 'em desert!" rejoined Joe hotly. "Or let 'em go charging down the road to Numaris to die just like those Imperial troops did! I tell you, sir, I'm totally dedicated to this army and our mission, but knowing what we do now, I cannot recommend proceeding with our current strategy. It would be suicide to try it. If you want me to draw up another one, it'll be six to eight weeks at least. Or you could find another strategist and take your chances with him. Or we could listen to this young Imperial officer, who seems willing to help us despite our disgraceful treatment of him, and make use of the gift that has been dropped into our lap."

"Six to eight weeks is quite a while", mused the colonel. "Are you sure it would take that long?"

"At least—and that's providing we borrow the lieutenant's

map, and even then I can't guarantee it'll be any better than our current plan", Joe replied.

"But we have no guarantee that what he has is practical, either", reasoned the colonel. "After all, it is only a school project."

"School project!" exclaimed Joe. "Colonel, those Academy graduate projects are year-long ordeals that involve interviews with veteran strategists, field internships, and exhaustive studies in the Academy archives. All the resources of the Imperial Army are at their disposal. They are considered the premier strategic works of the Empire. If this lieutenant did a project on the retaking of Numaris, then be assured that it is one of the finest works on the subject in existence—or he wouldn't have gotten his commission."

The colonel pondered in silence. After about a minute Joe again spoke.

"Six to eight weeks at least, sir—no telling what the men will think of lying idle that long."

"All right", snapped the colonel with the annoyance of a man forced to choose between undesirable alternatives. "We'll listen, but be careful."

Returning to the tent, they found William bent over the table, absorbed in thought and oblivious to the tension around him. Joe joined him, looking over his shoulder at the map, while the colonel stood off to one side, eying the proceedings as if from a distance.

"What sort of plan did you have for retaking the valley, Lieutenant?" Joe asked casually, effectively disguising the apprehension in his voice.

"The assault I envision", began William enthusiastically, "can be launched only by a daring commander with determined troops. It necessitates dividing the attack force into either three or four groups, depending on how thorough an attack is to be launched. The attack must be closely coordinated between all the groups to ensure success. In essence, it entails a decoy force to proceed down the main road, a cutoff force stationed in the rocks to the north side of the road here, another force on the south side of the valley entrance just over the river, and, if the troops are available, yet another assault force for a special attack."

"However can you expect to coordinate movements between forces spread all over the valley like that?" asked Joe.

"That would be a big problem, except that the enemy takes care of that by means of the signal from the tower", replied William. "In signaling to the city for assistance, they would also signal to the attacking troops to begin their movements.

"The geographic advantage of the defenders is the last couple miles of road here, where the Imperial Army met defeat. Because the defenders hold the wide end of the bottleneck where the river veers south, they can hold it against all attack, and because they are defending only the valley, they can plug the road here at the eastern end of the gap such that it cannot be penetrated. Because of the broken nature of the cliffs at the north of the gap, the only weak point in the whole scenario is their south flank. The river runs swift, narrow, and deep here, and the ground to the south of the river not only is rock almost to the water's edge but also is slightly higher than the road and river, meaning that any sort of charge would be downhill into a raging torrent that is too deep to ford."

"Sounds like a substantial weak point", said Joe, perceiving that William's careful description was not for nothing.

"That's what everyone's thought so far. But look at the geography carefully. The gap here, at its narrowest, is only about fifty to seventy yards wide from the south bank of the river to the north edge of the road. There is about a ten-yard width of smooth riverbank along the south edge of the river before it starts getting rocky. The south riverbank stands ten to twenty feet above the road. Now—you think about it."

Joe gazed thoughtfully at the map for some time before he slowly turned to William with a fire in his eyes and whispered, "Archers."

"Precisely", replied William. "That narrow stretch where the south bank parallels the road runs roughly three hundred yards along the gap. If a cavalry regiment were trapped in there with longbowmen along the south bank . . ."

"They'd be mowed down like cattle!" Joe nearly shouted in his excitement.

"That's the idea. But cavalry doesn't just stand there to be cut down, so you have to plug both ends of the gap. That's where the infantry comes in. To lure them out you have to send an impressive-looking force marching down the road just like a pack of fools, except that after a token fight at the bottleneck you'll want them to turn tail and run back to the gap. The Black cavalry and infantry will give chase, right to the eastern end of the gap, where your force will stop, pick up the weapons they left there, and turn to face their pursuers."

"Won't the enemy be suspicious of a force that flees so easily?" asked Joe.

"A really smart one might", replied William. "But I've found that under these circumstances people normally see what they're expecting to see. A Rebel regiment that takes on a defending garrison but turns and flees at the sight of heavy cavalry reinforcements is just what might be anticipated, so hopefully they won't see anything more than that. In fact, if I may say it, here is a place where you Rebels' reputation for poor strategy would work to your advantage. With luck and some good acting, the Black forces won't see any strategic significance in your retreat, and neither will they see the troops you have hidden in the hills to the north of the road. These will remain out of sight until the Black force thunders by; then they will descend with their pikes to close the western end of the gap. Then, with troops blocking both ends and archers firing into the middle, the Black Army will perish." There was no talk of surrender. The Black forces neither asked nor gave quarter unless they were gathering for their slave markets.

The two Rebels stood pondering the map and William's plan. Joe spoke first.

"Looks very tight. What are the problems?" William was once again impressed. This was classic review technique: the creator of a strategy should understand its weaknesses better than anyone else. In fact, the bulk of the strategy should be devoted to addressing them.

"Placement. Coordination. Duration." William replied. "The

whole strategy hinges on the assault forces being exactly where they should be. They have to work in concert without communication, for that would betray the hidden forces and destroy the strategy. The task of getting the forces to the proper places without being detected calls for long marches through difficult terrain, draining both stamina and supplies. It gets even worse if you add in the fourth assault."

"That being?"

"Numaris itself. Once the Black Army is defeated, the city still needs to be taken. Fortunately, our intelligence tells us that they are so confident that their only threat is from the east that when they get the signal from the tower, they virtually empty the city to repulse the attack. Only a company or so is left within the city proper. Unfortunately, a company is all that's needed to hold the gates for quite a while against almost any force, especially one without siege equipment." He didn't go on to explain that one Black Army technique for discouraging sieges was to slaughter city inhabitants and hurl their bodies over the wall onto the besiegers.

"So what's your solution?"

"A rear assault. The west and southwest walls of Numaris are simply the mountains against which it is built. This is a sure enough defense against a conventional attack, but a lightly armed force could scale the western mountain, which is lower, and drop down into one of the least-watched areas of the city. Against the regular force it would be impossible, but if they struck when the majority of the garrison was out of the city, they'd stand a chance against the company that remained. Now, this looks like a nice stroke, but it has all the disadvantages that have already been mentioned and two more as well. The first is that the soldiers have to be two-thirds mountaineers just to make the assault. The mountain would be a challenge to anyone simply climbing it, and these men would have to fight at the end of the climb. It would take a lot of skill, stamina, and determination to do it."

"And the second drawback?" Joe asked.

"No retreat", William replied, smiling grimly. "It's a succeed-or-suicide mission. Once the force is in the city, the only way out is through. It's essentially impossible to go back over the mountain." William was surprised to see the two Rebels brighten up at this prospect. Most Imperial officers grew grim at the suggestion of such an action; these two clearly relished the idea.

"There are, of course, many more details involved", William continued. "This is just a brief overview. The actual document gets far more specific, down to the detailing and deployment of the individual platoons. These would have to be adjusted to fit your actual personnel availability, but it could be done."

"Tell me, Lieutenant," asked Colonel Cole, "if this plan is such a masterpiece, why hasn't it been tried by the Imperial Army? Surely they wish to retake Numaris."

"You will recall, Colonel," replied William, who even through his enthusiasm wondered at the note of suspicion in the question, "that the first specification for this plan is a daring commander leading determined troops. Both are in short supply at Imperial headquarters right now. As with all plans that have a potential for great success, this one has a potential for dismal failure. A missed cue or a poor troop placement would bring the entire strategy crashing down in disaster. The commander who undertakes it would have to understand and accept that risk."

This sobering message brought silence to the room for a moment. Then Joe cleared his throat and asked, "Now, about this assault on the tower . . ."

They plunged into the discussion of the details of the campaign. William and Joe carried most of the dialogue, talking of troop placement and terrain passability in the universal jargon of battle strategists everywhere. Even the colonel, whose suspicion of strategies in general and Imperial strategy in particular was yet obvious, was caught up in the discussion, asking intelligent questions and even making good suggestions from time to time. William was in his element, pondering ways of modifying his strategy to accommodate the limitations of the Rebel army. He quickly saw that while he had thought himself a trained strategist, this real-life planning was far better training than five strategy classes. It was one thing to draw up a strategy with theoretical access to the resources of the entire Imperial Army but quite another to tailor one to fit the capabilities of a real army in the field. It was by far the greatest challenge he had ever undertaken. Sergeant Joe was a tremendous help, with his thorough knowledge of the state of the Rebel army and his limitless enthusiasm, but his lack of formal training restricted his usefulness, so in the end it was William who actually adapted the strategy for the Rebels. Joe advised, and from time to time other sergeants were summoned for more precise reports on the state of certain units or the availability of some supply, but it was William who did the thinking. He was intrigued to notice that all the critical officers were noncoms. If there was anyone other than the colonel who held a commission, William never saw him. He also noticed that they introduced him as "Mr. de Rowan", making no mention of where he had come from.

The sun climbed toward noon and past while the men planned the assault. William was grateful that he had already constructed the basic strategy and knew it well enough to recite it in his sleep. If he hadn't, the task would have taken days, if not weeks. He became so caught up in the strategy that he completely forgot his mission, as well as the fact that these people had captured him and treated him like a criminal not six hours before. He even ceased to notice the color of their uniforms or the occasional odd turn of phrase that marked them as Rebels. The battle became his, and the plan became the most important thing in his life on that hot afternoon.

One issue that repeatedly cropped up during the planning was that of supply, especially food. The archers could make the long outland trek to come up on the south bank of the river—if they had the supplies for it. The force to hide in the hills to the north of the road could trace their way through the narrow paths—if their supplies lasted that long. If the supplies . . . , if the supplies . . . It quickly became obvious to William that this campaign would stand or fall on the question of supply. The colonel and Joe made light of the issue, stressing repeatedly the stamina and determination of their men. William never doubted that, but he remembered the meager grain gruel and pruning hooks that he had seen on his way through camp and recalled the axioms he had learned at the Academy. A fully packed soldier of average stamina and high determination could make twelve miles a day over rough terrain on full rations. One on short rations could make only eight miles no matter how hard he tried, and that figure dropped by a mile per day for every day he remained on short rations. A soldier who had marched on short rations for a week had less fighting strength and stamina than a well-fed one who had lost two nights of sleep in a row. These factors were critically important to this campaign, since just positioning the men for the action was going to take more than a week. Then there was the question of equipment. The Rebel infantry was certainly strong and brave, but they could not take their pitchforks and pruning hooks against cavalry. The archers might draw long and shoot true, but it would do small good if the fletching fell off their arrows in midflight. No amount of rhetoric or enthusiasm could negate those hard facts. If the campaign was to succeed, or indeed begin at all, something was going to have to be done about the supplies.

But what? William pondered the question more and more as the strategic discussion moved through the major questions and into the more trivial issues of the campaign. At times he would withdraw from the table, leaving the colonel and Joe discussing some point while he paced in the background, mulling the options. He could think of few, for supply was something he had never studied. He now regretted that deeply and repented of every sneer he had ever directed toward the quartermaster corps, whom he had always treated as something less than real soldiery. What he would give for a good quartermaster now! Some were true magicians, able to whistle up supplies from a seemingly barren countryside. He had never appreciated that skill, much less thought to learn it. The only thing that had mattered to him was that the supply trains kept coming . . .

The supply trains! With a start William stood straight, suddenly remembering the mission. Had he missed his rendezvous? In a panic he grabbed his saddlebags off the floor and rummaged through them until he found his orders. A quick reading relieved him of concern—he was to meet the convoy along the nearby road at some time today, which to a supply train meant late in the day if not tomorrow, since the muleteers could never be hurried.

William looked at the cargo manifest in his other hand and thought. The thick sheaf was a detailed list of the supplies on the train—bolts of cloth, ash spear handles, barrels of molasses, cordage, arrows, jerky, dried peas—thousands of pounds of material destined for the already overstuffed supply tents of the Imperial camp. He stared at it for a full minute, pretending to think, but in his heart he knew the decision had already been made.

Stuffing the papers back in the saddlebag, William turned to where the Rebels were standing and found that they were looking at him. The small commotion he had made with his saddlebags had been enough to distract them from their work. Now they looked at him silently, sensing his tension and excitement.

"Just checking some paperwork", he said casually. They seemed satisfied with that but did not return to their conversation. It seemed an appropriate time for a break, since it was now well past lunchtime, and they had not eaten since before dawn. William stepped over to the table where his field rations still lay, only slightly eaten, and carved himself a slice of cheese. Noticing how hungrily the Rebels were looking at the food, he motioned for them to join him, for there was certainly enough for three men by the standards that held in the Rebel camp. Soon they were chatting merrily about various minor points of the battle plan, which was essentially complete. William's mind was only partly attentive, however, for through it all he was thinking furiously and waiting for an opportune moment. When they were just finishing the last of the apples, he decided to make his move.

"Well, sirs," he said, standing, "I had a mission I was pursuing when I was distracted by your little project. I beg your leave for a few hours in order to complete it."

It was a bold stroke, though not the boldest William intended to attempt that day. What he had intended to bargain for he was now simply demanding, on no firmer basis than the goodwill he had developed with the Rebels throughout that morning. He forced himself to breathe while he waited for the Rebels' response. The success of his whole plan, and indeed the entire campaign, hinged on how they responded to this request. The Rebels looked at one another with tense discomfort, partially because he had mentioned the embarrassing matter of how he had been apprehended and partially because he had raised the even touchier issue of what was to be done with him.

"A few hours, you say?" asked Joe.

"I'm hoping", responded William. "Though it could be nightfall before I'm back." He hoped they would not press him on the nature of his mission. The colonel rose to his feet awkwardly, clearly in acute discomfort.

"Can we, er", he stammered. "Are—may we be assured, Lieutenant, of your honorable parole?"

Even though he had anticipated such a response, William's cheeks suddenly flushed with anger, and his response came more sharply than he intended.

"A parole is given to a prisoner of war, sir." His clipped words struck the colonel like blows. "I am unaware of any state of war between the Empire and any Rebel force—unless you have chosen to declare one." The colonel withered under William's icy gaze, but Joe quickly stepped in.

"Of course we haven't, Lieutenant", he said. "It's just that—well, we're unsure of how to handle you."

"What's to handle?" William replied, seizing the opportunity to create a path of least resistance. "As far as I'm concerned, I've just helped some fellow soldiers work out some strategy. You haven't maltreated me—aside from the minor difficulty about my arrival, which I'm as willing to forget as you are—and you have given me no cause to consider a complaint against you. My mission is specified to be completed 'today'; if it is, my superiors will not ask what I did with my time, and I see no reason to tell them." The Rebels looked as if ten stone had been lifted from each shoulder, but William hurried along lest they begin questioning him about his mission. "If it is not completed, however, or if I do not return on time, there will be many difficult questions with few satisfactory answers." He let the threat of that possibility hang in the air while smiling inwardly—he was getting plenty of opportunity to use that ploy on Rebel officers recently.

"Let's do it your way", said Joe after a brief pause.

"Certainly", the colonel added. "You've already been more help than you know, Lieutenant, and words cannot thank you enough."

"Oh, that's nothing", replied William. "Happy to help. Now, I should only be gone a couple of hours, but . . ."

"Why come back at all?" asked Joe. "You're free to leave."

"For one thing, to pick up my maps, which I intend to leave with you for a while yet", said William. "For another, to return the supplies I hope to borrow from you."

"Borrow?" asked the colonel.

"A pen. Some ink. A writing board. A candle." William listed them, smiling at the Rebels' mystification.

"Planning to write a letter?" asked Joe.

"Something like that."

Since William showed no intention of further elaboration, the Rebels quickly went about meeting his request. The supplies were produced in short order, and soon he was riding back toward the road through the Rebel camp. Despite the midday sun he kept his riding cloak over his uniform and returned none of the inquisitive glances directed at him. Horses were not common among the Rebels.

Once clear of the encampment, William turned aside from the path that led back to the road and found a clearing in which to work. Locating a stump of suitable height, he set up the writing board and arranged the writing materials about. Then he studied the cargo manifest carefully for some time before he spread a clean piece of parchment on the writing board, dipped the pen in the ink, and began writing in the universal copperplate hand used by scribes throughout the Empire. He had in his youth detested the tedious sessions in which his father had forced him and his brother to learn the formal writing style, despising it as suitable only for clerks, but he was grateful later in his life when his ability to "scribe" had kept him warm and dry indoors while other cadets had been out parading in the rain. Never had he been more grateful for the skill than he was in that clearing as he drew up a document that could be the key to freedom for a city. The Rebel ink was, as to be expected, thinner and less pure than Imperial ink, but William hoped that the convoy master would notice only the parchment, Ceremonial script, and seal.

After the document was finished came the most delicate operation of all. Striking a small fire with his tinderbox, William lit the candle and began heating his knife blade. Then he spread his orders on the board and began carefully easing the wax seal off the parchment with the hot blade. Though convoy masters were always supposed to examine the orders of officers who came to escort them, they rarely did. William hoped this one would not break the pattern, for without the official seal his orders were void. He worked delicately, reheating his blade often, for the slightest false move would crack the brittle wax or disfigure the seal. Hardly breathing during the procedure, he finally eased the last corner loose and removed the seal, intact, from the orders. Gently lifting it over to an appropriate place on the counterfeit document, he once again used the hot knife blade, this time from the underside of the parchment, to heat the area until the wax melted just enough to fuse onto the surface.

William leaned back and stretched his cramped muscles. His critical eye could spot every flaw in the document he had created, but examining it as objectively as possible, he had to admit that it looked authentic. It would have to do. Looking around the clearing, he was suddenly alarmed at the length of the shadows. The operation had taken far longer than he had thought it would. A chill of panic shot through him—perhaps he had missed the supply train! He hastily repacked his gear and mounted Coney, turning him toward the road. Soon they were cantering along the dusty road through the lengthening shadows.

Surrounded by the late afternoon silence as he rode along by himself, William busily pondered the plan for the taking of Numaris. Had he accounted for and weighed all the factors? Would the Rebel soldiers perform as Joe and the colonel said they would? Would these supplies be adequate? He weighed these questions over and over again, only dimly aware of a desperate edge to his deliberations. Something deep down inside him, a part that he didn't want to listen to, was asking if he knew what he was doing and if he had really considered all the consequences of what he was contemplating. But he successfully buried those questions under an avalanche of minutiae regarding the strategy. The plan was the important thing. The successful retaking of the city was the issue; everything else could be handled as things went along. They would have to be. They would have to be.

So William rode along, wavering between taut anxiety and desperate self-reassurance. Not helping his apprehensive state was a suspicion that grew with every bend in the road that he had lingered too long and the convoy had already passed by. He did not want to think of the consequences if he had missed the convoy—that would make his plan so complicated as to be nearly impossible. He debated turning around to see if he could catch up to it, but if he did that and it hadn't yet passed, he wouldn't locate it until too late. Furious at the circumstances that had rendered him so impotent, he gritted his teeth and rode on, hoping for the best.

Finally, when the shadows were truly lengthening toward evening and an edge of cold despair was just creeping into his thoughts, William rounded a bend and nearly ran over a scruffy man riding a scruffy donkey at the head of a trail of mules that stretched back into the twilight. Both the man and William reined back, startled. William, accustomed to armored cavalry columns, had forgotten how quietly a mule train could travel. He was so lost in thought and relieved by the appearance of the convoy that before he could think he cried out, "So here you are!"

"Er, yessir, yessir." The man fumbled to calm the startled mule. His tone was whining and apologetic; he clearly thought himself in deep trouble. "Lost some packs about lunchtime, had to repack, difficult mules—came as fast as we could, sir, just as fast as we could." The residual ale on his breath told William that the packs had been lost near a good inn and the difficulty had not been with the mules alone, but that did not bother him now. He was so glad to see the muleteers that he could have kissed them all and their mules too, but he thought a tone of impatient indignation would be particularly useful at this point.

"Dolt! Bumbler!" he replied. "What do I care about your packs? All day I have kept to this road waiting for you, all because you cannot tie a load on an ass!" The man wilted beneath William's tongue as the convoy came to a halt behind him. It was sooner than William had intended, but he decided to set his hook now, while the man was flustered and easily cowed. "Had you taken any longer, the field detachment would have had to move on without their supplies, and you would have felt the wrath of the commandant himself."

"Field detachment?" the man muttered in confusion. "But . . ."

"Yes, fool, field detachment", William interrupted. "That should have moved out this afternoon, had their supplies been on time! I only hope we can yet reach them."

"My orders say nothing about a field detachment." The man fumbled in a saddlebag and produced a sheaf of papers. "See? Right here it says, 'Delivered to the Fifth Battalion headquarters encampment'. Nothing about any field detachment . . ."

"Of course it doesn't!" William shot back, hoping he could maintain the scathing outrage act long enough. "They were dispatched just two days ago—on short supply, I might add, since they were supposed to meet up with a supply train sometime today."

"This is most irregular", the convoy master spluttered, waving the papers. "Most irregular indeed. I should have received a manifest modification—regulations are quite strict on this— 'All deliveries are to be made intact to the receiving authorities . . .'" The man began reciting supply code, but William cut him short.

"I wouldn't start quoting regulations too loudly", he said with an ominous tone. "You've never had to deal with Commandant Lloyd, have you?"

"Er, no, I haven't", the man replied, which instantly proved the fact. The commandant, though not a lover of administration, always ensured that the proper procedures were followed.

"Well, then, you can either fulfill this supply order he wrote or get a chance to know him personally—without any supply officers present to speak for you!" With the threat of such an unpleasant encounter hanging in the air, William produced his forged document. The man examined it carefully with the exasperation of a lover of order and efficiency who had just received another complication in an already difficult day. With great relief William realized that the authenticity of the document was not even being questioned. The man compared the list and his manifest for some minutes before speaking.

"This will be quite difficult. We'll have to do substantial repacking to construct the loads as specified. It could take quite a while." William knew this to be an exaggeration, for he had carefully constructed the list from the manifest in such a way as to minimize repacking delays. But the convoy master was struggling to regain some control of the situation, so William said nothing. The man examined the papers in silence for some minutes more, then turned to William.

"How far ahead is the encampment?"

"About a mile and a half. East of the road."

"All right", the man said with a nod. "It doesn't look too bad after all. We're stopped now, so we might as well repack. Shouldn't take much more than four dozen mules—you gonna want to keep them, too?"

William breathed another silent sigh of relief. Some convoy masters would have used the unusual request as an opportunity to gripe and make life difficult for the requester; this one had resigned himself to the situation and was going to make the best of it.

"For a little while", William replied.

The master then turned the waiting muleteers to the task of repacking the loads to match the specifications William had counterfeited. About two dozen mules needed no repacking and were sent on ahead with four muleteers. Twenty minutes of load shuffling had the rest of the mules packed, and they moved on up the road while the master reordered his convoy and William galloped ahead to catch up to the first group of mules. He caught up to them near the turnoff he wanted them to take.

"Just ahead here there's a trail leading off to the left", William explained to the lead muleteer, who nodded silent assent. It was deep dusk when they reached the trail, but the slow yet sure-footed mules followed it as truly as if it had been full daylight. The evening was so quiet that sounds could be heard from the Rebel encampment up ahead, and the pungent smell of the campfires hung in the evening mist.

"Right into camp?" asked the muleteer.

"No—they're packing to move out. There's a clearing up ahead—we'll park 'em there and let the quartermasters sort it all out." Again the muleteer nodded, obviously not one to question the doings of his superiors, for which William was grateful. The little mules, looking minuscule under the bulky loads on their backs, filed obediently into the clearing and stood about in small groups, twitching their ears and nibbling the knee-high grass. The muleteers staked them all on loose pickets, then headed back to the road to intercept the next group of mules. It wasn't long before they came along and were arrayed beside their brethren. Then without a word the muleteers all disappeared back up the trail to rejoin the convoy, which could barely be heard passing by on the main road above.

Dismounting, William examined a few of the packs, here and there untying one just enough to remove one or two objects. When he had all he wished he remounted Coney and turned his head back to camp, making sure to retrieve the writing board, which he had hidden under a bush.

It was fully dark by the time William rode back through the Rebel camp, and in the light of the campfires it looked just the same as an Imperial bivouac. Though the flickering shadows misled him a couple of times, he finally found the command tent. The flaps were closed again, and yellow lamplight shone through the gaps in the canvas. Tying Coney to the same tree where he had spent the entire morning, William clutched his small load with one hand and slapped the tent flap with the other. Joe poked his head out a moment later.

"Lieutenant?" Joe asked quietly. "Come in, please." An odd note in his voice indicated to William that, despite his assurances, the Rebels had not really expected him to return. He smiled to think of the surprise they were in for. He ducked under the flap into the brightness of the tent, where the colonel was standing by the table with two other sergeants. They looked at him with wonder, the two sergeants with curiosity and the colonel with a smile of true delight.

"Mr. de Rowan!" he said. "How good to have you back!" He obviously was truly glad to see William, which seemed odd, since William had gotten the impression that his Imperial identity made the colonel uncomfortable.

"Indeed, sir", he responded. "As I mentioned, I wanted to return the supplies I borrowed. I also brought you a present." With that he dropped his little armload onto the table—a couple of arrows, some food ration packets, a small length of rope, and a small roll of leather. The Rebels looked in confusion at the items.

"What's all this?" asked Joe, picking up a ration packet to examine it. The others also picked up the objects, passing them from one to another.

"Supplies. There are four dozen mules in the clearing up the trail loaded with these items and some other things. Not enough to outfit your army the way it should be, but hopefully enough to keep this campaign going."

The Rebels stared at him, dumbfounded. Predictably, it was Joe who reacted first.

"Are you kidding?" he yelled, nearly crushing the ration pack in his excitement. "Are you kidding?" The others also began chattering.

"How comes this?" asked the colonel, fingering the leather.

"Best not to inquire too closely, sir", William replied. "Just a little diversionary activity. It'll never be noticed."

"What else is there?" asked Joe, his enthusiasm bubbling all over the tent.

"Oh, some beans, molasses, and bacon, as well as a good number of ration packs. Pike handles and heads. Bows and strings, and a few hundred arrows. Leather, both soft and hard tanned. Some other provisions—like I said, enough to get you by." The men gaped at him as he recited the list. Then one of the unknown sergeants ducked swiftly out of the tent into the darkness. Joe sank onto a stool, silent at last, with only the shining of his eyes betraying his amazement at the unbelievable fortune that day had brought.

"Wait a minute." The harsh voice of the remaining sergeant broke into William's thoughts. "What's all this?" He had been examining an arrow and now held it out to the colonel, pointing at the shaft near the head. He was scowling, and his voice was thick with suspicion.

"I'm not sure", the colonel replied after a moment's examination. "Mr. de Rowan?"

William knew what it was without even looking at the arrow. It was a custom among Imperial fletchers, blacksmiths, and other weapon makers to engrave brief maxims on their weapons that called down curses on the Black forces or blessings on the Imperial troops that wielded the weapons. "May this shaft swiftly find the eye of the enemy" and "Strength to the arm that wields this spear" were the sort of thing that could be found. William had never considered them either harmful or beneficial. The difficulty was that the sayings were written in Imperial Ceremonial, which the Rebel sergeant had recognized.

"Just harmless sayings, wishes for success in battle", William explained. "They aren't carved deeply enough to affect the strength of the shaft."

"This is the Imperial Ceremonial tongue", the sergeant, not to be mollified, said to the colonel. He ignored William entirely.

"Who cares what it is?" interrupted Joe. "The point is that it's an arrow, straight and well made. Look at this gluing! Our men are tying on feathers with twine, while this . . ."

"The question, Colonel, is do we want to equip our men with weapons from some Imperial source inscribed with something unknown in an Imperial tongue? Are we a Freeman's army or an Imperial regiment?" the suspicious man asked, spitting the word *Imperial* as if it were a curse. He still ignored William, which was too much for Joe. He exploded off his stool, eyes blazing with fury.

"Then scrape it off, you bloody fool!" he thundered. "Are you really so asinine that you can't appreciate a gift when it's freely given? Didn't you hear? We have the supplies to complete the mission! Without them we fail—but you in your spiteful bigotry don't care about that, do you?" The sergeant, taken off guard, was stammering and backing away in the face of Joe's bristling wrath. Joe was so angry that for a moment it looked as if he would strike the man, but Colonel Cole intervened.

"Sergeant Jacobs! Sergeant Wilder!" he cried, stepping between the two men. "No grievance is worth this dissension within the ranks. Sergeant Wilder, come outside with me immediately." With that the colonel bustled the suspicious sergeant from the tent, as much to protect him as anything, leaving Joe alone with William.

William was stunned. He had been anticipating a hero's welcome when he reappeared with the supplies. He had been expecting to prove that even though he was an Imperial soldier, he was a King's man first and willing to help anyone who fought for the King. He had even hoped to soften the colonel's suspicious attitude toward the Empire. He was dismayed to find that the colonel had, if anything, a relatively tolerant attitude toward things Imperial, and that the mentality that had burned Imperial villages to the ground just one generation ago was still alive among some of the Rebels. He got a cold, sick feeling in the pit of his stomach and sank onto the stool as he gazed without seeing at a knot on a pole across the tent. He was amazed at how much he hurt. Why did they treat him like that, after all he had done—after all he had risked—for them?

". . . like that, Lieutenant. Honest, you gotta believe me—please." He became slowly aware that Joe was talking to him in a plaintive tone that sounded near to tears. William gazed at him for a moment.

"Why, Joe?" he asked quietly. "Why do they treat me like this? What have I done to earn this? Why?"

Joe hung his head and chewed his lip for some time, clearly

struggling to maintain his composure. When he finally spoke it was through halting, ragged breaths.

"I—I don't know what to say. I don't know how to apologize for how we've treated you, after all you've done for us. I'd wring Wilder's neck with my bare hands if I thought it would help, and Harold's too, for that thong this morning. But please, please believe me", he raised his eyes to meet William's. "We aren't all like that. Mostly we just want to fight for the King and don't care about the color of the uniform of anyone who'll fight beside us. Please believe me." William said nothing but reached out and firmly grasped the earnest little man's hand.

They stayed like that for some minutes before a sound that had started quietly but grew steadily finally intruded on them. It was a wild, enthusiastic sound, that of many men yelling and cheering. The mules were being led into camp.

"Think I'd better go", said William quietly, standing up.

"Can't you stay just a little longer? Just a couple more minutes?" Joe asked. William smiled faintly.

"So I can get what's coming to me? No—you've done a good deal of that already, Joe. I'd best get going. Good luck." With that William ducked out into the dark, leaving Joe open-mouthed inside. There was truly nothing more that words could do. What was done was done, and William still had challenges ahead that could yet overwhelm him. He untied Coney, quietly mounted him, and turned toward the road. Ahead of him were torches and the excited cries of the men greeting the unexpected supply convoy. He steered clear of that, choosing instead the shadowed paths of anonymity. As he rode away he heard from within the command another sound, barely audible above the hubbub—the low, steady thumping of someone hammering angrily on tent fabric with hard fists.

William had meant what he said to Joe—the little sergeant's sincerity had done much to purge the hurt and bitterness from William's heart. Perhaps there were only a handful of the mean, suspicious types around. Joe was certainly decent enough, as had been Clarke. Even the colonel was at least courteous. He had to admit that it was difficult to overcome the attitudes of a lifetime in a single day, even a very extraordinary day. Things took time.

The random cheering and shouting off to William's right had died down, replaced by someone speaking in a loud voice, interrupted from time to time by enthusiastic applause. Though he could not hear the words, he recognized the voice as that of Colonel Cole. The perennial optimist in William welled up. He was certainly encouraging the troops in their ambitious undertaking—perhaps he would also give due credit for the assistance received. After all, explanation would have to be made and some thanks given for the unexpected windfall of supplies that made it all possible. William turned Coney's head toward the torchlight so that he might hear the colonel and leave the camp with at least some satisfaction that his work had not gone completely unappreciated. As he drew closer to the torchlight he could catch an occasional word, but the words were not important. William could now understand more of what gave Colonel Cole his command: the man's voice could inspire beyond anything William had ever heard. Even without hearing the words, William's spirit was ignited by the powerful oratory. The men, their faces illuminated by the flickering torchlight, were riveted by the impassioned speech, the fire in their eyes reflecting the fire in their hearts. They were determined warriors with a firm purpose—they would retake Numaris.

Suddenly William found himself among mules. The small convoy had been clustered behind the impromptu speaking platform and was being swiftly unloaded by dark figures working in silence. Still desiring to get closer to the colonel, William began paying closer attention to where he was going so he wouldn't run over a mule or one of the men. In doing so, he noticed an unusual activity off to his left, apart from the quiet unloading. Steering that way in curiosity, he saw that whatever it was did entail some unpacking, as men were unstrapping large bundles of straight sticklike things that William immediately recognized as arrows. But rather than being carted off as the other supplies were, these were being stacked on the ground near some other men, who were busily engaged in some urgent task in the midst of the piles. Wondering what could so occupy these men while their fellows were so busy unpacking, William nudged Coney until he had a better view.

The men were busily scraping at the shafts, just below the heads.

William wheeled and, darkness notwithstanding, galloped from the camp.

The ride back to the Imperial camp was a cyclone of turmoil for William. At first his rage choked and blinded him as he galloped headlong through the night. The fools! The ingrates! Whatever had possessed him to aid such hateful fanatics? He should have said nothing at all and let them go out to die under the hooves and battle-axes of the Black Army as just repayment for their thankless bigotry. Curse them, curse them all for a lot of spiteful, ignorant peasants! May they all perish with their pitchforks, led to defeat by the strategic ignorance of their petty leaders.

But the heat of such a rage could not be maintained forever, not least because Coney was picking up on it and becoming unmanageable. William slowed to a trot and comforted the beast, trying to calm his troubled heart as well. Why? Why did they return suspicion for assistance and slander for generosity? William brushed away hot tears of bitterness and resentment. A rational part of his mind kept trying to resurrect mitigating images—Joe's touching and sincere apology, the thought of the pitiful slaves of Numaris sweating under their oppressors—but no matter what he did, he could not erase the harsh accusation in Sergeant Wilder's voice or the memory of those dark figures working furiously to erase any trace of the ones who had provided for the Rebels.

The stars wheeled in the night sky as William rode along, alone with his internal struggle. He rode for some hours before the hunger and exhaustion that had been hovering on the edge of his consciousness finally overwhelmed him. He had been up since well before dawn and had had an intense day. Even so, he would have kept riding had he not recognized that Coney could not keep up such a pace all night. Reluctantly he found a clearing by the side of the road and turned into it. Tending to Coney and making a small camp kept him distracted for short while, but when it came time to turn in—hungry, for he had left his rations in the Rebel command tent—his mind reengaged the argument. Futilely he gnawed at the happenings of the day, turning them over and over in his mind, imagining things he should have said and done while with the Rebels. Sleep was very long in coming.

The bright dawn found William stiff and unrested from his fitful night. Coney was contentedly munching grass, which made William hungrier, but he ignored that. He had to put the matter of the Rebels behind him—there was nothing he could do about those fools anyway. More imminent was the much more delicate issue of the explanation for the missing supplies. In the light of a new day he saw clearly what a foolish and impulsive thing it had been to do. The Imperial supply network was tight as a drumhead—not even a button slipped through without being accounted for. Whatever insanity had made him think he could divert fifty mules' worth of supplies without a shred of authorization? And he had committed forgery to do it! A deep gloom settled over William as he struck his little camp and returned to the road. He could imagine the court-martial now—standing before the somber-faced tribunal, the charges being read . . . Yesterday he had imagined the scintillating speeches and stirring appeals he would make to convince all questioners of the propriety of his actions. Yes, first the Rebels and then his own army would rise to acclaim him for having the courage to do what he did! But the Rebels had spit in his face, and now he realized that he had no explanation to give to his own command. Slowly the realization dawned on him that he was finished. Officers had been cashiered and even imprisoned for siphoning off supplies to sell, and he didn't even have that poor excuse. He had given them away—to *Rebels*. What rationale could he possibly give for that? He would be lucky to get away with being stripped of his commission.

Lost in depression, William rode along through the bright morning light. His optimistic side struggled to suggest one scheme after the other to salvage the situation, but the realist in him crushed them all. He finally came to a grim conclusion: he would not wait for the charges to be filed. He would resign first thing when he returned to camp and hope that would satisfy the service. It only meant that he had to arrive before the supply train, which would be no trouble because he was taking a shorter route that was impossible for a mule convoy and also because muleteers were never in a hurry.

The day wore on slowly, a churning mass of anxiety. What would his father say? Would they allow him simply to resign, or would they want more? What on earth would he do? The army was William's entire world—he knew no other livelihood. All these worries boiled inside him as he rode along and so affected his thinking that by the time he cleared the last rise at dusk and looked down on the fires of the Imperial encampment, it was with the eyes of one resigned to exile. He was a stranger to the service now; all that remained were a few formalities.

William rode down into camp unchallenged and indeed unnoticed, which surprised him a bit until he realized that despite the weight of his crime, it could not be seen by those he was passing. All they saw was a dusty lieutenant, no different from any other. That would soon change, he thought, when the conditions of his resignation became known. Slowly he rode toward his tent, drinking in the familiar sensations of the camp. What he especially noticed were the smells—the acrid smoke of the campfires, the musty smell of the sun-heated canvas, the tar on the ropes. He felt as if he were smelling all these for the first time. He cherished them all the more for knowing that it was the last.

William hardly stopped at his tent, ducking inside only long enough to fetch the item he came for. From there he rode to the stables to see after Coney's care. Only after the horse was stabled and fed did he square his shoulders for the short march to the commandant's tent.

"Show him in", he heard the Commandant say. The orderly, after making clear his opinion of mere lieutenants who appeared after hours in dusty uniforms asking to see the commandant but refusing to state their business, had condescended to announce him. Having received the summons, the man stepped outside again and held the door open for William to pass through.

Inside he found the commandant wrapped in a comfortable-looking smoking jacket seated on a chair next to a small fire in a brazier. He had been reading a book, but now he laid that book aside on a table at his elbow and gazed without speaking at William. The nature of William's visit made him somewhat uncomfortable with the informal tone that the colorful smoking jacket set. He would have far preferred to resign to a man in uniform, but the commandant did not seem to mind, so there was nothing that he could do. He stood stiffly at attention for some moments before he realized that the commandant was still watching silently, following his usual habit of not initiating conversation. Swallowing hard, William drew his sword and held its hilt out to the commandant.

"I beg permission to submit the resignation of my commission, sir", he said in as level a voice as he could manage. For some time the commandant continued to gaze at him, neither speaking nor moving, showing no surprise or relief or any other emotion. Finally, in a move that tore William's heart despite his preparing himself for it all day, the commandant rose from his chair and took the sword. After examining it silently for a moment, he calmly walked over to a desk nearby and laid the sword down on it. Then, still without saying a word, he returned to his seat and looked at William for a while longer. At last, when William's nerves were near to breaking, he spoke.

"Report."

With something like relief William poured out the tale of the prior days, from the time he received his orders to when he left the Rebel camp for good. Not one fact was left out except the treatment he had received at the hands of the Rebels. He made no attempt to hide or rationalize his crimes, even the forging of an official document. Through it all the commandant listened without interruption, calmly gazing at William and occasionally sipping from a glass of brandy that stood on the table beside his forgotten book. When William finished the commandant still did not respond but rose and walked back over to where the sword lay. He picked it up and examined it for a minute.

"This was your father's sword, was it not?" he asked.

"Yes, sir, it was", replied William. "It's been in the family for several generations." The commandant put it down and returned to his chair.

"How did the Rebels receive the supplies?" he asked sharply. William blinked—this was not the question he had been expecting.

"Sir?"

"The Rebels. Were they grateful for the supplies?" the commandant rephrased his question with careful patience. William swallowed hard—he had not wanted to get into this part of the matter, but the commandant left him no choice. He began explaining what he could of the Rebels' reactions and attitudes toward him as an Imperial officer. It was not so easy to be dispassionate this time, and soon he found himself pouring out his anger and frustration. The commandant still did not interrupt the narrative, but the manner in which he listened was slightly different. William felt less like a subordinate reporting to his superior and more like he was talking to his own father. He found it easier to recount the shame and rejection he had felt at Colonel Cole's unspoken suspicions and his hot fury at the final insult of defacing the arrows. When William finished, the commandant nodded, then turned to gaze into the flickering fire, musing. He muttered into his hand as he thought, and once William thought he could catch the muted word *Numaris*. But the commandant did not seem inclined to ask any more questions, which was fine with William. He had not wanted to dredge up those barely covered emotions of disappointment and embarrassment and was still surprised that he had been asked.

Abruptly the commandant rose and walked over to William. Taking one of his hands, he examined the raw abrasions where the overtightened thong had cut into his wrist. The cuts had scabbed over, but the whole wrist was still red and angry from the abrasion.

"What did this?" he asked, so William was forced to explain about the sadistic Sergeant Harold. When he finished the commandant grumbled something inaudible and turned to walk to the other side of the room again. He paced for a while; then, stopping behind the brazier so the glow cast eerie shadows on his face, he turned to William and quietly asked; "Would you do it again?"

William was stunned. This was the last question he had expected. He thought the answer obvious—after all, wasn't he turning in his resignation over the criminal nature of his activities? Hadn't he just recited the tale of the humiliation he had received at the hands of the Rebels after all the assistance he had given? He opened his mouth for a swift reply, then shut it again. Despite all those factors, he realized that he was not certain of the answer.

"I—I don't know, sir", he stammered. To his surprise, the commandant also gave the slightest hint of a smile.

"How so?"

"Part of me wants to give the obvious answer, sir. Of course I wouldn't do it again, especially if the Rebels are going to take that attitude, et cetera, et cetera. But another part of me says that the Rebels' response never was a factor from the beginning. You had to be in the Rebel camp to understand, sir—it was unlike anything I'd ever experienced. Bigoted and narrow-minded though some of them are, these people are fighters, in a different way than we are. For us fighting is more of an abstraction than anything. We spend far more time discussing it, theorizing about it, examining it, writing it up, critiquing it, and evaluating it than we ever spend doing it. These people live to fight. Unsophisticated as it was, their dedication to the King was right on the surface. So was their compassion for the captives. Commandant, we were defeated at Numaris thirty-three years ago. The critiques of the battle are still classified. Only now are alternative strategies beginning to be explored—mine was one of the first. We'd probably spend twenty-five more years in committee before attempting another assault. All that while the citizens of Numaris—once free Kingdom citizens—would be living and dying in slavery. These Rebels saw that, decided to rectify it, and launched their campaign."

"And yet without your strategic assistance would have failed as miserably as we did", the commandant added.

"True", replied William. "Which is another thing. It seemed odd to me that we should be so inverse in strengths. Here they are willing and anxious to fight, while we can't seem to move out of our strategy sessions. Yet they couldn't plan a battle to save their lives and are abysmal at supply, while we've got so many battle plans that we've had to create a special library branch to track them all, and our warehouses are so full of supplies that we have to erect temporary tents just to hold them—supplies that hardly ever see battle! I spent all day trying to get them to see that it takes more than zeal and determination and 'attack, attack, attack' to really do damage to the enemy—you also have to have a good solid plan and stable supply lines. At the same time, I couldn't help wondering if we aren't a little too concerned with our strategies and supplies, that perhaps we could use a little infusion of that zeal to do a little more 'attack, attack, attacking' of our own. That's what went through my mind when I made that decision—I thought of all our tents and tents full of beans and spears just sitting there while these soldiers were getting ready to march off to die with empty bellies and pitchforks. I thought that fifty mules' worth of supplies would never be missed against all our stock. I know it was illegal and foolish, but that's what I was thinking. So to answer your question, sir—I'm not sure."

The commandant nodded silently. He turned to pace again, the fire casting an immense shadow against the far tent wall.

"That your actions were illegal is without question. How foolish they were remains to be seen." He turned to face William. "The greatest danger, of course, is that these supplies will someday be used against our own army." William gasped—this possibility was not one he had considered. "Independent forces such as this are the most prone to that sort of activity, but from the sounds of it this Colonel Cole, thought not grateful enough for the help he received, would probably not be so treacherous as to attack those who supplied him." The commandant turned his back to William again, lost in thought. This time William distinctly heard him mutter "Numaris" as he pondered. Finally he strolled over to the sword and picked it up again.

"You are a sentimental and impulsive man, Lieutenant," the

commandant said. "Watch those tendencies. They can harm you."

"Yes, sir", William responded, not knowing what to make of that comment. The commandant continued examining the fine sword. Silence reigned in the room.

"Sergeant Beauchamp!" the commandant bellowed abruptly. William stiffened to attention again as a cold claw seized his heart. This was it. No amount of mental anticipation could completely prepare him. He had never seen the inside of a brig before. He thought it a cruel irony that it was to be Beauchamp who took him there.

"Yes, sir?" came Beauchamp's voice from behind William. He didn't turn around to look.

"This impetuous young man", the commandant gestured toward William with the sword, "needs guarding. You are to be that guard. Since he seemingly cannot be trusted more than five miles from camp without getting into dire trouble, you are to stay near him at all times to keep him out of it. Take special care to keep him away from Rebels. I will draw up the papers tomorrow, but, effective immediately, you are his bodyguard. Your first task is to take this sword and give it a fine edge, for it needs one badly." He held out the hilt to Beauchamp, who came and took it. William just gaped as if the commandant had gone out of his mind.

"And you, Lieutenant", he continued, turning to William. "Much as I appreciate your earlier request, I cannot entertain it now. Submit it again in a few months, if you wish. In the meantime, when the medics certify you for full duty again, you will be transferred to my staff. In light of your recent activities, I cannot inflict you on any of my officers, so I must take responsibility for you myself. I will draw up the orders tomorrow and take care of some other matters of paperwork as well. You are dismissed." With that he turned his back on them. They saluted and left. Still pensive, he walked over to where his brandy stood by the brazier.

"Numaris", murmured the old commander. "Numaris." He thought about a desperate Rebel commander and an army willing to march in bare feet to fight a battle. He thought about an impulsive young officer who had risked his career to help that army. He thought about his own army, carefully supplied right down to the fine brandy that he was sipping. He thought about these things for a long time; then he reached out and deliberately dumped the brandy into the fire. It flared briefly, then died down again.

"Numaris", he muttered.

Meanwhile the two friends were walking back to William's tent.

"What was that all about, sir?" asked Beauchamp, completely mystified. William, who was feeling alternately dizzy and giddy, looked at him and giggled.

"That, Beauchamp," he replied, "is a long story."

Five weeks later, William's arm was completely healed, and he was back on active duty assigned to the commandant's staff. He still needed to exercise back to full strength, however, and since the commandant's remark about his sword edge was equally applicable to his sword skills, he made saber drill a regular part of his routine. He found that the shield work strengthened his arm wonderfully.

Thus it was that after supper one evening he and Beauchamp were stomping out a few rounds beside William's tent when a messenger boy ran up, panting as all messenger boys do.

"Lieutenant de Rowan?" the boy asked.

"Yes?" replied William, removing his helmet.

"Visitor for you at the east gate, sir."

"Visitor?" William looked at Beauchamp in mystification.

"Yes, sir. Says he has a message for you, sir." Then the boy hesitated, as if reluctant to deliver the rest of the news. "He's—he's a muleteer, sir."

"A muleteer?" asked Beauchamp, incredulous. Muleteers generally remained near Imperial encampments only long enough to deliver their loads. The thought of one staying to deliver a message was very unusual. Beauchamp wasn't sure what was going on, but he decided to come along to investigate. William laid down his arms and armor to follow the boy. Beauchamp did likewise, except that he forgot to leave behind his sword.

The muleteer was impossible to miss when they arrived at the gate: he was cloaked and hooded in the coarse black fabric common to his trade, and all his mules were clustered behind him, moving quietly and snuffling in the dark. The circumstances were so unusual that the guard was standing outside his gatehouse, watching the mysterious figure closely. The messenger boy ran right to the guard's side and stood watching while William strode right up to the figure.

"I'm Lieutenant de Rowan", he said.

"I know", replied the figure, turning so the torchlight fell on his hooded face. There William saw the curly black hair, broad smile, and dancing eyes of Staff Sergeant Joseph Jacobs.

"Joe!" cried William in delight. The guard, misinterpreting his tone, picked up his halberd to approach the stranger. Beauchamp also took a step closer, but William waved them both off. "It's all right. Just a message from my brother." That satisfied the guard, who then retired to his post. Beauchamp stood where he was. William turned back to the Rebel sergeant.

"Numaris?"

"Taken!" Joe replied with a grin that nearly split his face. He grasped William's arm in excitement. "Taken—and all thanks to you!"

"Tell me about it", William said.

"The battle was letter-perfect, exactly as planned . . ."

"Exactly?" William was astounded. He knew enough to know that battles never went according to plan.

"Exactly", Joe confirmed. "There was only one field improvement we added, and it wasn't really necessary. The weather was perfect except for a little drizzle one day, which was annoying but didn't prevent anyone from getting into position on time. It was great—it was just great! Our decoy force marched right up the road, bold as you please, and made a very dramatic showing when they encountered the field garrison. Then when the Black cavalry from Numaris showed up . . ."

"Did they retreat in good order?" William interrupted. One of their greatest worries had been that the decoy force would not understand the importance of the appearance of a rout and would continue to fight when they should run, thus ruining the whole strategy.

"They were fantastic! All of 'em." Joe was nearly hopping in his enthusiasm. "They all should've been actors. Once the colonel and I explained their role, they played it to the hilt! You have never seen such a boastful attack. The Black garrison was so overwhelmed by all our shouting and posturing that they never noticed that we were hardly hitting at all. Then when it was time to flee, they were so hoodwinked that they ran after us stripping off their armor so they could chase us better. Can you believe it? Stripping off their armor—right in the middle of the battle! They paid for that."

"You mentioned a field improvement—what was that?" William asked.

"Oh, that", Joe replied. "Well, there was so much cloth in the supplies you gave us that we were able to sew dozens of new uniforms for the worst clad of our men. Then we had all the old clothing at hand, so we stitched 'em together and stuffed 'em with straw like scarecrows to make mock soldiers. When our decoy force went trooping up the road in close file, every two men carried between them a straw soldier . . ."

"Giving the impression of a greater force!" William interrupted in his excitement. "Great idea!"

"Wait, wait—it gets better", Joe said. "When we retreated, we carried the straw men along as far as the west neck of the gap, where we threw them all down. The Black Army rode right over them in the haste of their pursuit, but when our trapping force came down from the hills to close off the gap from the west, they piled the straw corpses up and lit them, closing the gap with flame. The force at the east end of the gap had already piled up brushwood, and they fired it when the Black Army was entrapped."

"That was a bold stroke", William said with as much censure as amazement. Flame on a battlefield was dangerous and unpredictable, so quick to turn upon the forces using it that no prudent strategist included it in a battle plan. "But risky. The smoke could have obscured the targets from the archers."

"We knew that and were prepared to abandon the tactic at

any time if the conditions weren't right. But they were perfect—dry, virtually windless—and it worked beautifully. With the fire and steel closing both ends of the gap, the Black Army went mad when the arrows began cutting them down. It was complete carnage! They were so panicked that in their terror they began slaughtering each other. The cavalry started trampling the infantry, who in turn began stabbing the cavalry in their rage. Meanwhile our archers, calm as judges, kept firing into their ranks, dropping scores with each volley. Toward the end, when the worst of the flames had died down, some of those still standing tried to charge through the coals. Those that made it died on our steel. It was an absolute, total triumph!"

"Casualties?" asked William.

"Again, incredible. A dozen or so wounds, three lost. The wounds were mostly sprains and the like, and the deaths were accidental."

"How so?"

"When our decoy force began its retreat, one of the men broke his ankle on a stone. Two of his comrades stayed with him, though he urged them to go on. Together they holed up in a rock crevice near the road to make their last stand. The Black Army killed them, of course, but even in death they were victorious—those three took eight of the enemy with them," Joe explained.

"Did you attempt the overmountain assault on the city itself?" William asked.

"Certainly did!" Joe exclaimed. "There was enough rope for two dozen men, so we took the best of the volunteers—there were many—and sent them the long way 'round behind the mountain. They were magnificent! They force-marched under full pack, then scaled the mountain with all their gear, then rappelled down into the rear quarters of the city. That would have been better attempted at night, but we had no choice about that. Nobody was watching anyway—the token force left in the city was clustered in the gate towers, watching the cavalry ride off and drinking—"

"Drinking?" asked William with amazement.

"Drinking!" Joe confirmed. "The entire company was so certain of a Black Army victory that they began celebrating a little early. They paid for that arrogance. Our mountaineers mixed their blood with their wine and secured the city within an hour. When our main force came marching down the valley road after destroying the Black Army, they found the gates standing open for them. A complete liberation with essentially no loss of life."

"Unbelievable", William murmured, amazed by the totality of the victory. Only a handful of battles in all history had been won as quickly and thoroughly at such small cost. The two soldiers stood silently together, savoring the sweet taste of the campaign's complete success.

"So," said William at last, "Numaris is free again."

"Yes, and all thanks to you", Joe replied.

"Oh, I wouldn't say that", William said. "After all, I didn't . . ."

"Nonsense", interrupted Joe firmly. "It was your advice that warned us off our original strategy. It was your strategy that paved the way for the victory. And it was your supplies that allowed us to see it through. You, more than anyone else, are responsible for the liberation of Numaris. There was never a more fortunate day for any army than that morning when you were brought handcuffed into our camp."

"Well, I . . ." began William, at once flattered by the credit being given him and disturbed by the reminder of how he had been treated by the Rebels.

"Which reminds me", Joe hurried on, as if anxious to get a message out. "I've been asked by Colonel Cole to convey our formal apologies for how we treated you that day in our camp. It would have been a shame and disgrace to deal with anyone that way, and it was a complete scandal considering how much aid you gave us. We acted worse than barbarians—the Black Army itself couldn't have heaped more insults on you than we did. Please forgive us." The small man, who had avoided William's gaze during the entire apology, now looked full into William's face. William could see the tears standing in his eyes.

"Oh, Joe," replied William, not knowing what to say, "you certainly never . . ."

"Please", the sergeant whispered, "forgive us."

"I forgive you", William quietly replied.

Joe closed his eyes briefly upon hearing the words, visibly relaxing. Then he continued, "Colonel Cole would have come himself to beg your forgiveness except that administering Numaris is proving to be quite a task. He was beside himself when he came back that night to find you gone. In his speech to the troops he kept talking about how the King had provided for the campaign, which got him thinking about the person the King had used for that and how shamefully that person had been dealt with. He stayed up all that night, anguishing over whether to ride after you or not. In the end he figured he couldn't, but that didn't stop him from making no secret of where the strategy and supplies had come from. Not that it was ever a secret—regardless of foolishness like scraping those inscriptions off the arrows, it was obvious to everyone that they were Imperial supplies. And at the end, in his victory address before the gates of Numaris, the colonel publicly acknowledged our debt to the Empire for the assistance."

"He didn't say my name, did he?" asked William in alarm. The retaking of Numaris would draw considerable attention all over the Empire, and careful note of all details would be made at the capital command posts.

"No, no", reassured Joe. "The whole camp knew you by sight, but only a couple of us actually knew your name. The credit infuriated a couple of jackasses like Wilder, who stormed off before we even got marching, but the rest of us just accepted the help thankfully. In fact, many of us—including the colonel— spent a lot of time examining our attitudes about the Empire and what we've always been taught about it. Lots of us who had always considered you Imperials just another enemy like the Black Army got to wondering if maybe our perceptions didn't need some adjusting."

"We've got our share of jackasses in the Imperial Army", said William quietly. "And I think all of our perceptions need some adjusting."

"True", replied Joe. Silence fell on them for another minute before he spoke again.

"At any rate, the colonel also asked if there was one more thing you could supply us." William looked at him with intense curiosity. "The Black Army flag has been torn down, and the ensign of the First Freeman's Army now flies over Numaris. But in recognition of the assistance rendered by the Empire, and also to acknowledge the city's long heritage as an Imperial outpost, the colonel asks if you can provide an Imperial ensign for him to hoist on the ramparts." Then the sergeant, who had delivered his unusual request with uncharacteristic solemnity, broke into an impish grin. "We seem to be a little short on those."

William simply stared for some moments before responding. The gesture was so unusual and so bold that he had no idea how to handle it. He didn't know where to find an Imperial ensign, especially that late in the evening, but as he looked around in his confusion he spotted Beauchamp. Summoning him over, he introduced the two sergeants, then communicated the Rebel's request to the Imperial veteran. Beauchamp, who knew all the tricks of acquiring such goods, vanished silently.

"Another thing", Joe continued when Beauchamp had left. "In recognition of and thanks for your help, Colonel Cole respectfully requests that you accept this small token of gratitude." He held out something that looked like a roll of parchment, which William took. It seemed heavier than it should be and was somewhat lumpy to the touch. This was explained when William unrolled it and a small medal dropped into his hand.

"It's the Legion of Valor—our highest award", Joe explained. William examined the decoration—it was plain, as Rebel artifacts were wont to be, a small square suspended from a blue ribbon with a sword and spear crossed on its front. There was no legend or inscription other than the single word *Numaris* engraved on the back. The parchment was the official citation awarding him the medal, sealed by Colonel Cole. "We hope you'll accept it with our thanks."

"Certainly", said William. "Thank you for allowing me to

be part of such an important victory." He shook the sergeant's hand firmly.

"Oh, yes", said Joe, as if remembering something. "I've brought your mules back as well." He swept his hand over the herd behind him. "They were quite helpful." That got them into more discussion of the battle details, which lasted until Beauchamp returned with a cloth bundle under his arm. Joe took it and prepared to depart.

"Thank you again, Lieutenant", he said, shaking William's hand again. "I hope we meet again, and under happier circumstances than we did the first time."

"Ah, but this has ended far better than we could have hoped. Perhaps it portends even greater things to come", replied William. Then Joe shook Beauchamp's hand and, giving another of his broad smiles, vanished into the night.

"Beauchamp, do you think you could find someone to get all these mules back to the quartermasters?" asked William.

"Our quartermasters, sir?" said Beauchamp, surprised.

"Yes—they're our mules", replied William.

"Very well, sir. Beggin' your pardon, sir—what's that?" said Beauchamp, indicating the parchment in William's hand.

"A medal", said William, handing both items to him for inspection. "The Legion of Valor for my assistance with the assault on Numaris—though what valorous thing I did they don't make clear." Beauchamp, having examined the medal, handed it back to William and proceeded to read the citation.

"Well, they certainly think highly of you, for all that, sir", said Beauchamp as he finished reading.

"Seems that way", replied William as he examined the simple decoration. "Though for the life of me I can't imagine where they expect me to wear this thing."

The Purging

THE CLOUDS OVERHEAD WERE A SLATE GRAY that thinned to a heavy white as they stretched out over the valley. Down there it was lighter; the valley floor bore the look of a meadow that had just been rained on, and the river almost sparkled as it wound through the lush green grass. The slopes on the far side of the valley looked brighter yet, all but fully illuminated by direct light. It had the appearance of sunlight trying to break through after a heavy rain—yes, that was it. Either that, or . . .

Jack clutched his filthy shirt close around his throat as he turned his back to the piercing cold wind. To his left now, behind him as he had scowled across the valley, the grim rocks rose to cruel peaks. Above those peaks towered fuming black storm clouds from which blew a bitter cold wind that swept down across the face of the range he was standing on. The wind easily cut through the thin rags that hung about him for clothes. Maybe the light in the valley was the final light before this storm came crashing down from the mountains. Perhaps that light would soon be darkened.

Jack. That was his name. No, it was more—John. John William. But they called him Jack. Jack. He spat the name as if it were a bitter chew. Jack. What a name. He hated it. "Get the pot, Jack." They had called him Jack, and he hated it, and them. "Get the broom, Jack." Bastards. He crouched down by the rock, seeking shelter from the biting wind, shelter that he did not find, mumbling curses against those who had called him Jack. He chewed the words, and his mouth seemed to want something else to chew on, something bitter, but there was nothing but the words.

He did not know where this place was or how he had gotten here. He did not know where the filthy rags he wore had come from, or what it was that his jaws kept craving. He knew he was Jack, and Jack was cold, and Jack hated them. They would like that valley, Jack was sure. Perhaps they lived there. Now their afternoon sun was going to be blotted out by the storm, and then they'd be cold and miserable, too.

He really didn't care about the valley or care to move at all again. He would be content to crouch there, cold and miserable, muttering his litany of curses, but the prospect of seeing the sun snuffed out by the boiling black clouds piqued in him just enough desire to look down once more. Not rising, but rather half-squatting, half-walking, he crawled to a spot where he could peer around the rock to see the catastrophe descend on the valley. But it looked just the same, neither brighter nor darker. The same just-rained-upon grass, the same near-sparkling river, the same almost-lit far slope. He snarled. Well, at least the light didn't appear to be gaining. Perhaps the storm was just slow in coming. After all, the grass at the foot of this slope was dark enough.

Then he saw the house, down there on the hillside. It was well below him, about a third of the way up from the bottom of the rock slope. The house was low, built into the slope, and the roof was broad, so slightly slanted as to be nearly flat. The roof was white, he could tell, though it looked flat gray under the wings of those clouds. He could see nothing of the building but the roof, and the rocks clustering close around it.

Suddenly he was aware of his hunger. Jack was hungry— not the growling, aggressive hunger of one who has not eaten for days but the hollow emptiness that immediately precedes that state. Jack licked his lips as he looked down at the white roof, and he was aware now that his lips were dry, as was his whole mouth. Jack was hungry and thirsty. Perhaps down at the house . . .

Jack whipped his head about, snarling and brutally thrusting the thought down. Oh, they'd have food there, all right. They'd even give him some. "Oh, it's Jack." "Get some food for Jack. Hungry, Jack?" Water, too. "Get the cup, Jack. I'll get you some water." "Another drink, Jack?" Jack, Jack, Jack. He made a spitting noise but spat nothing, for his mouth was too dry.

"Damnation", he muttered. They were down there, in that house. He would not go down there. He would go away from them. He cast his eye up to the grim peaks that loomed above him, dark under the threatening clouds. They would not go there, so he would, where no one would call him Jack. Slowly, stiffly he rose. Hoping in vain for relief from the chill wind, he pulled the sparse rag-shirt closer around himself. It tore. He cursed the shirt, and the house below, and the wind, and the cold, sharp rocks under his bare feet. He staggered away from the smaller rock behind which he had been sheltered, trying to go around the end of a larger boulder behind him. He tripped and fell, cutting his knee painfully through his rag trousers and grinding his palms into the dirt. He could feel the cinders under the skin, but he picked himself up. Seizing the great rock with his bleeding hands, he began his climb up to the dark clouds.

Martin. That was his name. Martin de Porres. Was that all? No, there was more. Martin de Porres something. That wasn't enough. Or perhaps—he had the curious feeling that the name was sufficient—indeed ample—while it was he who was insufficient.

"I'm Martin de Porres someone, though I am insufficient for my name", he announced to the air. "Though not", he added, looking down at himself, "as insufficient as these clothes, if clothes they are." The rags that hung on him bore only a passing resemblance to a shirt and trousers. He tugged experimentally at his left sleeve, which tore off in his hand, laying bare the well-muscled ebony skin beneath. Well, that was no great loss, he thought as the icy wind whipped the rag in his hand. I could tear this whole shirt off for all the good it's doing. Where is this place, anyway? He let the rag go, and the wind whipped it away among the rocks. His eyes followed it for a minute. It hung up briefly on an outcropping, flapped futilely for a moment, then was swept away into the darkness.

Martin stood gazing uphill at a barren range of irregular boulders and sharp outcroppings that mounted up to brutal-looking peaks. The rocks were all ugly brown and dingy gray with no beauty in them anywhere. Even the peaks were uninspiring—rather than soaring above the grotesque rock formations, they seemed instead to be lumpish aggregations of the rest of the drab landscape, bleak ugliness on a larger scale. The awkward range stretched as far as he could see to his left and his right, varying nowhere, forbidding everywhere.

"Perhaps it's just those clouds", said Martin, again to nobody at all, as if making an excuse for the gruesomeness of the mountains. The storm clouds piling up behind the bleak range certainly did not cast a flattering light. They were high and black, and no light penetrated them. They seemed to be the source of the cold wind that cut down from the rocky ridge through the boulder field in which he was standing. He wondered when that storm was going to break over those mountains, and whether it wouldn't be better for him to be somewhere else when it did. That in turn led him to wonder where else there might be to go, which led him to turn around.

"Ah," he said, smiling, "now that is something like!" Below him swept a spacious valley that was carpeted in a light yellowish green and through which threaded a silvery river. The light was brighter there, though not open sunlight, and it grew brighter as it climbed the opposite side of the valley. That valley wall was especially lovely, as luscious and fruitful as this side was bleak and barren. He could see scintillating streams ribboning the slope, weaving their way through wooded thickets and ordered plantings of trees that had to be orchards. It had to be warm over there, or at least warmer than it was here, and the grass looked like it would be wonderfully soft to walk on.

That brought his own feet to his attention, and Martin was suddenly aware that they hurt. Looking down, he saw that he was standing barefoot on sharp pebbles and rough cinders. Small wonder his feet hurt—he lifted one foot and saw blood spots on the sole from half a dozen little cuts. Wherever this land was, it was no place to stay. Stepping around the rock behind which he had been standing, he began cautiously picking his way down the slope. The rocks were sharp and the pebbles cruel on his bare feet, but he fixed his eyes on the grass below and kept moving. He had descended a hundred yards or so when he spied the white rooftop below and to his right. He didn't know what kind of building that might be, or who would live in this forsaken place, but it was something to aim for. He altered his course to begin angling toward the roof.

Gasping and coughing, Jack leaned back against the boulder and tried to catch his breath. He cursed the thin air silently, having no breath to speak with. It seemed that he could not get enough air no matter how hard he breathed. The bitter air filled his lungs but brought no relief. It was cold, too, and dirty—he could feel the grit in his mouth when he coughed, and a dull pain in his upper chest gnawed with each breath. The rock he was crouching behind offered some shelter from the wind, but precious little. He was out of the main blast, but small eddies of cold curled around the rock from time to time, throwing more dust in his face and chilling him anew.

Jack had no idea how long he had climbed or how far he had come. He had not even counted the number of rests like this that he had taken, not that any of them had done any good. He'd risen from each one more cold and tired than when he had sat down. The peaks above seemed no closer, and the storm seemed neither to build nor to abate but hung threatening over the barren slopes just as it always had. The only thing that could be said was that the valley seemed further away. It too remained unchanged—the same grass, the same river, the same near-sunlight on the far slope. He couldn't see it from where he sat, but he could dimly picture it in his mind. He did not think of it or look back at it as he climbed. He had for a while, but he gave it up because each time he looked, an urge welled up from deep within him to descend to that valley, to walk on that soft grass instead of these cruel rocks—How hard they were! his legs and arms were bloody from climbing—to wash the grit from his mouth in the shining river. But no! He clenched his teeth to suppress the ache that rose inside him even now. That was getting easier each time. Once the pull had been almost irresistible, and he had nearly gone plunging headlong down the slope toward the valley. But he had resisted. He would not retreat now, not after all this climbing. He was no quitter, and he certainly would not give them the satisfaction. "Come wash your feet, Jack", they would say. "Look at those cuts, Jack! Let us bind them." Not for him, no indeed.

With a sharp shove of his legs Jack pushed himself up, and the rock he had been leaning against shredded what remained of his shirt back as well as most of the skin beneath it. He grimaced and swore but at the same time wondered again why it did not hurt more. A massive abrasion like that should sting much more than it did, as should the cuts on his feet. But they didn't, instead settling down to a dull, nagging ache that gnawed at his strength and stamina. The cuts didn't bleed much, either, though neither did they clot, instead oozing constantly, staining the rocks where he walked and gripped. For some reason he knew wounds shouldn't behave that way.

That was the end of the shirt-rag, though. Jack cursed again and, momentarily overcome by rage, savagely ripped the rest of the rag from his shoulders and made to throw it away into the wind. But he stopped, then desperately clutched the rags around himself again. They might be nothing, or worse than nothing, but they were all he had on his grim journey. It was time to begin again, unrested as his brief halt had left him. His bones ached, and his cuts ached, and his chest ached, but he had to keep climbing. He did not know why—perhaps only to get away from the valley—but climb he must. His mouth worked again in that chewing motion, gnawing at nothing, as he gazed up the slope at the grim, pathless waste.

"Damnation", he muttered again and began his climb anew.

The curious thing, thought Martin, was that the valley appeared no closer. The lumpish peaks did seem a bit farther away, but that was hard to gauge while he was still almost directly below them. At any rate he knew he was making progress, for the flat white roof was just below him. He had come that far at least.

Looking down at himself, Martin was suddenly seized by an urge to run back up into the rocks. Whoever lived in the house would surely want nothing to do with him, bruised and filthy from the difficult descent as he was. His pants were in tatters, and he was cut in a number of places, a couple of times quite seriously. (Odd things, those cuts. Shouldn't they bleed more? They should certainly hurt more than they did.) But the urge to turn and run came from a source deeper than concern for his appearance. He was ashamed to present himself to the inhabitants of the building. (He knew they were there, though he had as yet seen no sign of them.) They would see him and know him. Perhaps he could return to the rocks, where they could not find him. He could hide there, for a little while at least. Or forever—then they would never see him, never know him.

The urging welled so strong within Martin that he half-turned, and his feet were almost stepping back toward the bleak boulder field. He was ready to return there, hateful though it was, for at least he knew the rocks and the wind and the grit. But no. He shook his head suddenly, dispelling like a mist the curious and irrational urge. Return to the rocks? What was there? He was already trying to forget the grim descent—the stumbling weariness, the cold wind blowing dirt into his eyes and mouth, the sharp stones underfoot, the falling, the aching, the hunger. Why would he want to go back to that? Even if these inhabitants didn't want to deal with him, he could always proceed down to the valley, which was his destination in the first place. He began climbing down the last few rocks to the little hollow that was flattened in front of the building. He could see nothing yet, not even the open space, but he knew there was one because no rocks thrust up from there. The rocks surrounding the hollow, though not as sharp, were harder to cross, and it was a long time before he found himself stepping down from them into the level area in front of the building with the low roof.

It was hard to call it a building, since it appeared to have been carved from the rock of the slope. The building face was the same color as the rocks surrounding it, and carved into it were a doorway and two windows that opened into an interior blackness. The face was recessed deeply beneath the edge of the white roof, which also appeared to have been carved out of stone and placed there by some unknown force. In the midst of the flattened courtyard in front of the building blazed a bright bonfire. Martin wondered why he had seen no smoke from the fire until he noticed that the fire appeared to produce no smoke at all. Between the fire and the building stood a sturdy but simple wooden table with two benches.

All this Martin took in at a glance, which was all he gave it, for what caught his attention and riveted it was the woman. She had been leaning over placing something on the table when the slight noise of his descent caught her attention. She turned to look at Martin, and he saw that she was unquestionably the most beautiful woman he had ever seen. It wasn't because she fulfilled all his ideals of beauty but rather because she redefined them. He knew as he looked at her that he had never seen true beauty before, and everything he had thought of as beauty was burned up and blown away as quickly as a leaf would be consumed on the bonfire before him.

They stood looking at one another for a long minute. Her perfectly featured face contained a deeper quality to which Martin could only apply the term *open*. Her skin was deep olive, and her face was framed by raven-black hair that curled down from beneath a white headdress that seemed half warrior's helmet and half veil. Her hair cascaded down over her shoulders, which were covered by a long white cape that was fastened about her throat and draped to the ground. Her eyes were deep black, and she looked neither young nor old but wore a timeless freshness that bespoke the vitality of youth and the grace of years.

She wore nothing other than the headdress and cape, which disturbed Martin, causing him to think for a brief moment that the woman should be ashamed and that he should be ashamed of looking at her. But this thought lasted only a moment, being swiftly replaced (as his definition of beauty had been) by a deep certainty that it was not the woman who should be ashamed, but himself. Here again he felt the same curious feeling of inadequacy that he had felt when he had remembered his name: that somehow he, though clothed, was insufficient, and the woman, though unclad, was sufficient. Her nudity, or that which lay beneath it, was decent and proper, even for this place, while his clothed state was indecent. The tattered rags were a part of it, but it went deeper: a void that no clothing could conceal. He would have covered himself if he could.

All this flashed through Martin's mind while he stood silent, gazing at her. It was she who broke the silence. In a deep but very feminine voice she spoke a phrase in a language that Martin could not understand, though from its inflection Martin took it to be a question. His puzzlement must have shown on his face, for she nodded and smiled kindly, apparently accustomed to strangers unable to speak the language.

"Er, I'm Martin", he stammered. "I was up in the cliffs, and I—ah—came down." He felt foolish, unsure of what to say. His voice sounded dry and weak after hers, partly because of the shyness he felt and partly because his mouth was parched. It didn't seem to matter—she still smiled and stepped toward him with outstretched arms. She spoke another brief phrase in her strange tongue while taking his hands in hers and kissing him lightly on the cheek. Her smile was dazzling. She seemed over-joyed to see him, and he would have been equally glad of the welcome had he not felt all the more naked and exposed for her nearness. As beautiful as she was, he would have gladly crawled behind a rock to hide from her and cover his shame.

She seemed to sense his discomfort and stepped back. Her face grew serious, etched with compassion, though her eyes still danced with joy. She called over her shoulder toward the building, then laid her hand on his elbow and guided him toward the table. As he came with her, a man stepped out of the doorway holding what looked like a water flask and a wooden goblet. His face was ageless like the woman's, untouched by wrinkle or blemish but crowned with silver hair and set with deep brown eyes. His face also was open, and like her he was completely nude except for a white cape and a headdress that was truly a warrior's helm. His body was young and strong, and just as Martin had felt naked and ashamed before the woman, so before this man he felt embarrassed that he had ever considered himself a man. He stopped dead, though the woman kept walking.

The white-haired man smiled at Martin, then stepped forward and poured something into the goblet. He offered it to Martin, who took it with a nod of thanks. He was glad for the water, not just because of his thirst but also because it allowed him to gather his thoughts. He was being buffeted by such a storm of emotions that his head was spinning. Surprise, shame, relief, awe, curiosity, and dozens of other feelings made it difficult to think. His host seemed to understand, simply smiling at him and motioning for him to drink. The water was cool and refreshing, but the dust in his mouth prevented him from swallowing, so he rinsed it out and spat it on the ground. That embarrassed him as well, but his hosts didn't seem to mind. They didn't seem to expect anything of him, so he let them lead him where they would. Shortly afterward he found himself seated on one of the benches, which had been brought over near the fire, warming himself while he drank deep draughts of cool water from the goblet and devoured some delicious fruit that his hosts had given him.

Martin was still not completely comfortable with these beautiful but strange people, but he was glad for their help, and they seemed even more glad to help him. They were kind and understanding, even of the mysterious shame that he felt in their presence. But they also seemed expectant, and their quiet conversations together were punctuated with searching glances at the rocks. Martin got the impression that they were expecting someone else besides him.

When Martin was finished with his fruit (or fruits—in his hunger he had consumed far more than one, and since they had neither pit nor stem he had eaten each one entirely) and had slaked his thirst, his host and hostess approached again, this time bearing a small pot and some strips of cloth. Gently they began washing and binding the cuts he had received from the rocks, daubing them with a clear, sweet-smelling salve that eased the pain marvelously. These folk sure knew how to help travelers, and Martin got the impression that they did it frequently. He found himself again wondering who they were, and why they were here—and just where "here" was.

"Hell and damnation!" Jack swore as a swirl of wind threw more grit into his eyes. He crouched down, rubbing them with his filthy hands, which only worked more dirt in. Tears streamed down his face until he gave up and ground his forehead into the rock.

Jack had never thought he could be so cold and tired. He was sure that he had been climbing forever. But no, once there had been a valley. He dimly remembered it. They had called him Jack, and he hated them. There had been water, too, but they had taken it from him and made him climb these cruel rocks. "No water for you, Jack." Now he had nothing to rinse the dirt away, and his tongue was swollen and stuck to the roof of his mouth. His fingers were stiff and numb with cold, and those fingernails he still had were cracked and torn. What was that sticky stuff on his hands? He could not see well—the darkness was nearly complete. The wind screamed through the rocks, cursing with him the hard land in which they both wandered.

Jack was near the top now; he had to be. He could not see the peaks any more, for in the deep shadows of the storm clouds they blended into the sky until all was one dark mass. Perhaps he had reached the top already—but no, he was still ascending, more by touch than anything else. The climb had become much steeper and more treacherous. Rocks slid beneath his feet, and black crevasses yawned suddenly where he did not expect them. He had nearly fallen into one, twisting his leg severely in the process—his knee was still not working quite right.

Why had they made him climb this gruesome cliff? Why did he keep climbing? He had stopped a few times, seeking rest but finding none. Despite his sickening weariness he could not sleep. He had tried once, finding a large enough flat surface to stretch out upon (they were few, and none were sheltered from the wind's fury), but no matter how long he lay still, sleep would not come. What had come was a painful awareness of every cut and bruise on his body as well as a redoubled ache in all his limbs from the piercing cold and weariness. He had also been made aware of every knob and ridge in the rock which he was lying on and the brutal sharpness of the wind-whipped cinders that lashed his skin. There was no resting on this forsaken

149

slope, only climbing and thirsting and falling and freezing and aching, all against a backdrop of stumbling exhaustion.

Neither did this boulder, behind which he now crouched, provide a place of respite from his tortures. The rocks beneath his knees still bruised; the cold wind still stung his face. A distant corner of his mind, like the dream of a dream, suggested that the grass of the valley would not be so cruel to bruised knees, nor would any wind that swayed grass so gently be likely to bite as this one did. But no, he could not go to the valley. They had forbidden him and made him climb these mountains without water. At least Jack had. They had told him to—"Get him out, Jack"—and Jack had sent him. He cursed Jack, bitter tears biting his cheeks as he wept at their cruelty. His groping hand found a flat shard of rock, and gritting his teeth he gouged at the cinders embedded in his palm, hoping to work them out. Even though nothing mattered now but the agony of the climb, he nonetheless idly wondered why even the coarse self-surgery didn't hurt more than it did. It was as if nothing was sharp here. Everything was dull and rough and ache and abrasion; nothing was piercing; nothing was extreme. But he was too exhausted to wonder much, too cold even to think. Muttering curses that came out as mere whispers, he wedged himself against the boulder in hope of finding some sleep, or even rest, though he knew that neither would come. The wind gusted more furiously as if enraged that he would seek to escape it.

Would he ever find a drink of water?

With every fresh breath he took of the clean air, Martin grew more amazed that a place this mild and beautiful could exist so close to the harsh and barren cliffs. He was not yet on the valley floor, but the wind had long since receded to a mere whisper, and a warm one at that. He was walking along a slender trail that wound through terrain that was still rocky but was dotted here and there with small plants that shot up between the rocks, giving promise of more verdant land farther down the slope. Even the rocks themselves seemed more hospitable. Instead of being merely ugly brown with harsh edges, these held flecks of mica that scintillated in the semilight and were painted with streaks of varied color that teased the eye. They were delightful to look at. They were also rounded and looked like they could be climbed upon. Wouldn't it be fun to climb these and go leaping on them, rock to rock, like he had when . . . Martin's brow furrowed briefly. When had he gone leaping from rock to rock like that? He couldn't remember. In fact, he couldn't remember a lot of things—he still didn't know where this place was, or how he had gotten here, or where he had come from. Something in the back of his mind whispered that this ignorance should bother him, that he should know more answers to all these questions, but the whisper was small and easy to ignore. He would find out all that in good time. For now it was enough to be away from the dirt, darkness, and bitter winds of the cliff.

Martin was feeling very refreshed. He had not slept at the rock house with the curious, noncommunicative hosts, but they had helped him rest. When his weariness had become more obvious after he had eaten and drunk, they had come to him, laid their hands on his head and shoulders, and sung a quiet, melodic song in their unintelligible language. As this went on, he had found himself slipping into a quiet, trance-like state that wasn't quite sleep but seemed to refresh just as much. In time he came out of the trance, and his hosts gave him another fruit and more water. Then they made him understand by signs and drawings in the dirt that he was to proceed down a trail through the rocks until he came to some other place, presumably a building or shelter of some type. They had not seemed concerned that he would miss this other place; it was apparently quite obvious. So he had set off, glad to have a destination for which to aim and even more grateful to depart the horrid mountain range. For some time the trail offered no advantage over his journey down the cliffs except for better footing—it had the same cold wind and harsh grit—but as he descended the conditions had gradually gotten milder until at last they reached this pleasant springlike state. Now he didn't know if he wanted to reach his destination, if traveling could be this enjoyable.

But reach his destination he did. Coming around a large boulder, he saw on a level space below a low building made of stone and surrounded by treelike plants. It was indeed impossible to miss, for though it was made of the same stone as the surrounding terrain, it was set in the midst of the first truly green space he had yet seen. In addition to the trees shading the building there were bushes and grass all about it, making it an inviting oasis amidst the rock. The trail seemed to lead directly to the building, so Martin stayed on it.

As he approached the building, Martin noticed that what had appeared to be walls was in fact a staggered arrangement of thick pillars that were placed so as to obscure the interior as effectively as a wall while allowing air to move freely through the building. The pillars were spaced far enough apart that they could be easily walked between. As he walked across the thick grass, the dappled shadows cast by the trees in the demilight of the valley edge reminded him of something else that he could not quite recall. He knew that somewhere, sometime he had walked through a similar glade of trees in light like this. It was quiet, too—the trees blocked the noise of what little wind remained this far down the slope, and Martin realized that for the first time in this mysterious land he was walking in the midst of true silence.

It was this silence that allowed Martin to hear voices from within the structure as he approached. This neither surprised nor alarmed him; he had assumed it would be inhabited, even if he could not communicate with the inhabitants. Nonetheless, as he came upon the pillars he felt a resurgence of the irrational urge to turn from this place and run, run back to the rocks, where he could not be found. Something akin to homesickness slowed his steps, finally causing him to stop with his hand on one of the pillars. It seemed so reasonable, so desirable, to turn from this strange place with its curious, unintelligible residents and return to the cliffs, where he could go where he pleased and did not need to be seen by anyone. Who were these people to tell him where to go and what to do?

Martin bowed his head, then shook it sharply and drew a deep breath. What madness was this? Return to the cliffs? Go back to that bitter, lashing horror? Why would he ever want to do that? He wondered if something could be seriously wrong with him that he should fall prey to such spells. Shaking his head again, he lifted his chin and squared his shoulders. Whether he could talk to the occupants or not, he was going in.

Passing between the pillars, he found the building interior to be one large space that seemed more like a courtyard than a room. The floor was grass, though shorter than the grass that surrounded the building. The room was long, he judged about fifty yards, and at the far end was a raised dais on which were set three simple chairs and before which flickered two standing torches. He wondered what their purpose might be—surely not light, for the room was well lit by an arrangement of open skylights. He noticed that the torches seemed to smoke very little.

Martin observed all this swiftly, giving it little attention, for what most interested him were the people. There were few in the building, and most of them seemed to be occupied with some business that left them disinclined to investigate visitors at their gate. None were hurrying, but those who were moving did so with a subdued determination that indicated their business was serious. They walked quietly in and out through the pillars at his left, the side of the building that had been hidden from his approach, and some were passing to and from the darkened area behind the dais. None of these spoke, and though none of them smiled or laughed, their faces were all marked by a serene openness that assured Martin that whatever else they were, they were not hostile. There were three who were not moving but rather standing together near the dais in a little knot. They seemed to be talking, but in very low tones, since Martin could hear no speech, understandable or not, in that quiet place.

All this Martin observed while standing still beside a pillar. Again he was seized by the curious feeling of inadequacy and embarrassment that he had felt when he first saw the inhabitants of the house among the rocks. For all those in the building were unclothed, but they carried themselves with such strength and confidence that he felt exposed and shamed before them.

He was still wearing the pair of battered trousers as well as a long white cape that his hosts among the rocks had given him when they sent him down the trail to this place. Yet once again, though he was clothed and they were not, he knew that he was the naked one; it was they who belonged, and he who was the intruder.

Martin's embarrassment did not affect what he had to do. He had already shaken off the perverse urge to turn back to the cliffs, so he was not going to resort to that again. He had been sent here, and he would endeavor to discover why before he traveled any further.

Martin squared his shoulders. He decided to approach the three talking men and began walking toward them, his feet making no noise on the grass. Now it seemed he was noticed for the first time, and any who were walking through stopped to watch his progress. None approached him or said anything, instead seeming content to watch him approach the three men. He focused his attention on them and forced his feet to keep walking.

He had to cover nearly the entire length of the building to reach the three men, but his stride was so muffled by the grass underfoot that he was nearly upon them before they became aware of him. He was already slowing down, wondering how he was going to intrude on such a private conversation, when one of the three noticed his approach and motioned to the other two, whose backs had been turned. Together they turned to face him, and he stopped abruptly and stared. The man on the left, one of the two who had turned to face him, was black, as Martin was. His frame was trim and strong, and he stood a good two inches taller than Martin. His hair was shot with gray, especially about the temples, but his face was not old, instead bearing the unwrinkled agelessness that marked all those whom Martin had seen in this place. The man's skin was smooth and his beard full, befitting a young man in the prime of his strength, but his eyes were deep and calm, reflecting years of wisdom and experience. But all this was incidental, for there was something that set this face apart from all the others Martin had seen.

This face he recognized.

The calm eyes watched with quiet expectation as Martin's mind raced to recall who this man was and why he should be familiar. Images, blurred and unrecognizable, danced just beyond his mind's grasp, swirling and joining and melding as if defying him to bring them into focus. The muscles of his face and throat seemed frozen, and he realized that in the intensity of his concentration he had stopped breathing. Forcing control, he expelled the breath he had been holding and drew another. His lips seemed to act on their own as his throat released just enough air for a faint, ragged gasp.

"Uncle Leon?"

Once the words were out, the images that had eluded him came rocketing through his mind with crystalline, if only momentary, clarity. That close, curly beard being used as a scrubbing pad on his cheeks and neck, turning a tender hug into a fit of convulsive giggles. Those lips smiling gently at some achievement being presented for approval. Those brows clouded with righteous fury at some transgression that Martin had knowingly committed. Those eyes gazing down upon him with deep pride after some significant accomplishment.

All these pictures and more flooded Martin's mind, each claiming but a moment of attention before passing, yet each carrying with it the full potency of all the emotions that had marked that particular incident. He was caught up in the surge of all the feelings, tossed by their strength and their often conflicting natures. He was buried in an avalanche of emotions, losing all touch with his surroundings, only dimly aware that he had again ceased breathing.

At last, after what seemed like a long siege but Martin knew must have been less than two minutes, the crowd of images tapered away to just a few and then were no more, save for a shadow or two hovering about the edge of his mind. His vision cleared, and he drew a deep breath. He was spent and would have stumbled where he stood had one of the men not reached out to steady him. Shaking his head, Martin raised his eyes to the face that had triggered the rush of images. The man was still watching Martin closely, a gentle smile tugging at the corners of his mouth, his deep eyes hiding some secret amusement. Martin couldn't help but think that he was fully aware of the effect that recognition had had upon Martin. They gazed at each other for some time before the man finally spoke.

"Yes, I am your Uncle Leon, though you shall know me more deeply soon. We rejoice that you've come." With this last statement he spread his arms slightly to encompass all those in the building. Looking about, Martin saw that some number of people, presumably those who had been passing through the building, had stopped to watch the meeting. He recognized none of them, but from their faces he judged that Uncle Leon was right; they did indeed rejoice that he was here. Martin looked at Uncle Leon again and stumbled for words.

"I'm happy to be here myself—sir . . . I'm also glad to be able to talk to you. Those people in the rocks couldn't understand me, so they couldn't tell me where this place is. Can you?" Martin finished lamely, feeling slightly embarrassed because something about Uncle Leon indicated that he was an important man with important concerns who shouldn't be troubled by trivial questions from ignorant travelers, relatives or not. But Uncle Leon didn't seem to mind.

"I can tell you", he replied. "But the full tale must wait for another time. Meanwhile, there are matters to attend to. We have been awaiting your arrival." Here Uncle Leon took Martin by the arm and began gently leading him toward the dais. The sincerity of this last statement caused Martin to realize with a shock that he was one of the 'important concerns' with which Uncle Leon was charged. "But there were to be two of you. Did another come as well?"

Martin was puzzled. "No, sir", he replied. "It's been only me—except for the two people in the house among the rocks, and we couldn't talk. I didn't see anyone else."

For a minute Martin feared he had failed some task, for Uncle Leon stopped, and his face was momentarily shadowed by something like grief. His smile disappeared, his eyes grew sad, and he sighed the sigh of one who has received terrible news, much feared yet more than half expected. He dropped his head, his eyes closed.

"Sir, I—I didn't know! Should I have looked for someone?" Martin cried, alarmed to see that noble face clouded.

"No", replied Uncle Leon, lifting his head. His smile was reassuring, though Martin saw that tears stood in his eyes. "No—you did well. Come, we must see you rested before your journey begins."

Soon afterward Martin found himself alone with Uncle Leon in a small chamber behind the dais. The walls were hung draperies, and a skylight above provided light for them. There were a simple cot along one of the drapery walls and a table with two chairs in the center of the room. Martin and Uncle Leon were seated at this, and some fruit and a container of water had been placed on it for Martin. Like the people on the cliff, Uncle Leon seemed disinclined to eat or drink.

"All who come to this country", he was explaining, "are free to go wherever they will. But in order for this freedom to be granted, they must first come before the King of the land. You are on the beginning of the road to his palace."

"Please, sir", interrupted Martin. "Can you tell me how I got here, and where I was before? I know that you were there." Uncle Leon smiled.

"All these questions will be answered in time. In the meantime you will be told all you need to know for the task before you.

"Everyone begins his journey among the accursed cliffs, as you did. To assist him along his way to the throne, the King has established outposts along the range such as this one, and stations farther up in the hills. You found one of these, though you could not understand the attendants. By such aid, newcomers are assisted along the way and soon come to the King's gates.

"There are those, however, who do not choose to serve the King, preferring instead their own paths. The law allows this; the King has no unwilling subjects, but the law also states that all must first present themselves before they go their own way. All are welcomed, none are forced—but the King's authority is acknowledged uniformly.

"But even this simple law is despised by some. They would

spurn his invitation and ignore his command, choosing instead to remain among the cliffs, unsubjected."

"Excuse me, sir," interrupted Martin, "but are you sure of that? I've just been there, and I can't imagine anyone wanting to stay there any longer than he had to."

"Can't you?" asked Uncle Leon, fixing him with a knowing gaze. Then Martin remembered those inexplicable spells when the urge to flee back to the cliffs had almost overpowered him, and he fell silent.

"As you well know," continued Uncle Leon, "the issue is not as simple as it may seem. There are those, like you, who hate the cliffs, but unlike you, they do not find it easy to summon the courage to descend. They may wander among them for years, until their fear of descent is overcome by their weariness and hatred of the barren range, and they come to the King at last. But then there are those who will never come."

"Do they like the cliffs?" asked Martin, incredulous. His own memory of that hateful place was too fresh for him to comprehend that.

"All hate the cliffs", Uncle Leon replied. "But those who stay there do so because they more deeply hate the alternative, which is to acknowledge the King's lordship over this land. But the King's law must be obeyed. If there is one who will not come, another must be sent to bring him down.

"This has become your task. There was another who was to come down from the hills with you. He has not come, and we know he bears the marks of one who will not come unless he is brought. You are the one who must fetch him down and bring him before the King."

Uncle Leon was looking at Martin with deep compassion as he said this, and though Martin did not relish even the thought of returning to the cliffs, he could not help thinking that Uncle Leon was even more reluctant to be sending him. They sat silently for a moment, each with his own thoughts.

"Perhaps", began Martin hesitantly, "he's only lost. Maybe he can't find his way down and just needs someone to help him find the way." The idea that someone could be lost among the hills seemed both more reasonable and more palatable to Martin. Not only was a lost person more understandable than one who stayed there deliberately, but it also changed his imminent role from marshal to rescuer. Uncle Leon smiled and patted Martin's arm.

"That may be hoped, Martin", he said in a voice that indicated that he himself had hoped it before. "But it is of no matter. Lost or rebellious, he must be fetched down." Again they both fell silent, Martin pondering this new development, Uncle Leon waiting for Martin's questions. For some reason the journey back to the cliffs to locate this mysterious person didn't seem to be in question—if it had to be done, he would go. But he did want to understand more.

"Sir, if these people want to stay in the hills so badly, what harm is there in leaving them? If they're going to be allowed to go there if they wish, why not just let them stay up there? Why must they be brought before the King?"

"The King's law stands!" Uncle Leon replied with a hint of fire and an edge to his voice that spoke of hidden authority that could be wielded if required. "The law is just, for the land is the King's, and all who come here are rightfully subject." Then his voice softened. "But the law is also a mercy. I have seen those who would wander hungry among the cliffs brought snarling before him, wanting only to curse his face and be gone. Yet when they saw his might and majesty and heard the mercy of his offer of peace, they accepted it." He sighed. "But those are very few—most choose their own way and are allowed to go upon it. No, lad—the law is reasonable. All get their way in the end. They only must give the King his due."

"All right", said Martin after another pause. "It seems it must be done, and I'm willing. But why must it be me? I'm new to this country. Surely you, or one of these others, would do a better job. I'm so—so . . ." He struggled for words to express the nakedness and inadequacy he felt before everyone he had met in this land. He found none, but it didn't seem to matter. Uncle Leon gripped his arm reassuringly.

"I understand", he said. "This also will be explained in time. For now you must believe me that neither I nor any of those you have met can ascend the cliffs. The station you found was as high as any of us can go. The task must be done, and it is you who must do it."

This satisfied Martin, though a small corner of his mind wondered. Somehow he felt that in another time, another place—perhaps where he had been before this—he would have asked many more questions before undertaking such a mission. But here, now, it was so simple to believe Uncle Leon, and to trust his authority. Martin still wished to go to the valley, and he would. But before doing that he had a job to do, so he must return to the hills.

"I'll go look for him, Uncle Leon", Martin replied. "Can I take along some water, though? It's thirsty traveling up there."

"We'll give you a good bit more than water." Uncle Leon smiled.

Some time later Martin found himself ready to embark. After agreeing to undertake the journey, he and Uncle Leon had talked a bit more while he ate and drank. Then Uncle Leon had called someone else, and they had Martin lie down on the cot by the drapery wall. Then they had sung the same sort of chanting song over him that the man and woman at the station had sung, and he had slipped into the mysterious trance again. When he had come "awake", Uncle Leon and a woman had been there with something he had not expected: clothing. It seemed that, although those who lived here did not wear clothes, they were kept available for those who needed them. Martin, recalling the harshness of the rocks, was grateful for the garments: heavy boots, trousers of some sturdy material with a smooth lining, a thick tunic with a high collar and the same smooth lining, and a headdress/scarf affair that Martin knew would prove invaluable against the windborne grit. A thick belt went around the tunic, and he was given a water bottle to hang on one side of the belt and a small satchel containing some fruit to hang on the other. Completing his outfit were a small knife that hung by the water bottle, a length of rope that he fit bandolier-style over his shoulder and across his chest, and a sturdy walking staff. When this was complete Uncle Leon led him out to the grassy area outside the building and they both stood looking up at the dark slopes and the clouds massing above them. Uncle Leon pointed out a trail that led up into the cliffs, a different one than the one which Martin had come down.

"Your search should not take long", Uncle Leon explained. "You should find him among the higher rocks above where that trail ends. I do not know if you will be able to talk to him or not, but if you cannot, you must bring him along as best you can."

"But, sir," asked Martin, "what if I cannot find him?"

"I don't think that will be a problem", replied Uncle Leon with a confidence that Martin couldn't understand. "But if the search takes overlong, return to one of the stations or to this outpost for refreshment."

A moment of silence followed as they both gazed up at the mountain range, and Martin wondered about this curious fugitive he was supposed to find. Who was he, and why had he chosen to stay among the rocks? Then Uncle Leon turned and grasped Martin's arm firmly.

"Be off now", he said; then, stretching his other hand out over Martin's head, he spoke some sentences in the language of that land, which Martin could not understand. A curious feeling shot through him, like a cold shiver that passes as soon as it is known. Then Uncle Leon smiled at him, clasped his shoulders again, and he was off, face set toward the barren cliffs, ascending the trail before him. He strode on steadily for some time, turning only once to look back at the outpost. It had grown much smaller already, and Uncle Leon still stood before it, watching Martin's ascent. Seeing him turn, Uncle Leon raised his hand and waved. Martin waved in response and turned back to his path. As he did, an image that had held back when all the others had cascaded through his mind suddenly became clear for just an instant before vanishing.

It was of Uncle Leon's face lying quiet and serene and very, very still.

"Nooooo!" With the desperate strength of frustrated fury Jack hurled the rock against the cliff face as his scream of anguish mounted higher and higher into the dark clouds. The rock shattered, pieces flying, some striking him on the face and chest. He did not notice; he knew only the mounting scream of agony that was existence in this land.

The land answered. As if to scream with him, the howling wind gusted to a roar that took Jack's cry and dashed it against the clouds as he had dashed the rock against the cliff. But like the cliff, the clouds proved unyielding, and his fury fell upon the barren land to die there unfruitful, as did all else in this brutal desolation. Curse them! They had sent him here, away from—from some other place, to this place of unceasing ache and thirst and exhaustion. How long had he wandered? He did not know—all now had run together into a featureless blur of torment. All was crawling and stumbling and aching and cold. Both his legs were hurt now, but there was no help for it. There was no rest here, no shelter, no water, no good thing. Finally his frustration had boiled over as this brief venting of fury.

Yet he was mocked even in this. Taking the last expression of strength and will he could make, the land swallowed it whole and spat it back at him. Defeated, Jack sank to his face among the sharp stones. Blackness engulfed him, and he was still, but in this place stillness brought neither peace nor rest, only an alteration in the form of his suffering. It was either scrambling and climbing and bruising or aching and hardness and the nagging of a hundred little cuts and scrapes. Behind it all threaded the common tapestry of exhaustion and thirst and hunger and bitter cold. He could stay still or keep moving; it did not matter any more. He hugged himself against the cold, rocking slightly to and fro, an occasional whimper escaping his cracked lips. Overhead the wind gusted and screamed through the crags.

The blast of wind caught Martin by surprise, nearly blowing him back between the two boulders through which he had just come. Grasping one of the boulders to steady himself, with his free hand he threw his scarf around to shelter his mouth from the grit being hurled in his face. The path was growing fiercer now.

The climb had gone well for some time. Well fed and rested

as he was, Martin had found the initial stretch of the trail into the rocks nearly pleasant. Even when the trail had begun leading up into the harder rocks, he had still made good time. But by the time the trail had petered out among the rocks, he was quite glad of the sturdy boots and thick tunic. He had made a cross-sling from a length of the rope to tie his walking staff across his back so he could use both hands for climbing. Continuing his ascent, he progressed in short order from leaping to scrambling to hand-over-hand crawling up the increasingly difficult grade. As he climbed, he was dumbfounded at how swiftly the climate changed from that of the almost balmy clearing to the cold brutality of the rocks. The wind increased steadily as he made his way up through the rocks, and the light failed just as predictably. He had not paid much attention to the cliffs when he had first found himself among them, but now, as he climbed toward the towering black clouds, he found himself wondering about them. There seemed something unnatural about their evenly predictable violence. It struck him as odd that the wind should gust and bluster across the face of the range without ever either invading the valley or receding over the mountains. It also seemed strange that the cloud line that loomed above the cliff tops should just stay there boiling, neither descending in fury nor being tattered and blown away by the winds that battered them. But as with so many things that didn't quite fit in this curious place, he didn't know why it should seem odd; it just did.

Now Martin had reached a point that he was certain was higher than he had ever been, and the climate was deteriorating quickly. He was certain of something else as well; if anyone was wandering around up here, it had to be because he was lost. Martin could not conceive of someone choosing this place over the valley that lay below. Whoever he was looking for had to be lost up here somewhere. Had to be.

Martin's growing certitude that he was rescuing a misdirected traveler rather than capturing a rebellious refugee lent an additional motivation to his trek. He had to find, to help, this poor man. The only problem lay in that he did not know where to look for him. He couldn't very well comb the entire range for one person. Uncle Leon hadn't seemed concerned about how the missing man was to be found, concentrating instead on what was to be done when he was.

Originally, Martin had thought of climbing as high as he could in order to gain a vantage point from which he could look down among the rocks, but it was quickly becoming obvious that this plan would not work. The light was failing so rapidly that he was already climbing in a thick twilight, and the swirling clouds of grit obscured most of the cuts and gullies in which a lost person would most certainly seek shelter. The grit was also cruel to the eyes when it got in—he'd already had a bout of stinging agony when an errant gust had thrown some directly into his face. He was doubly thankful for the scarf he'd been given, but even that would not be much help against the more furious winds that raged near the tops of the cliffs.

Well, if he couldn't climb much farther up, it was time to begin working sideways. Standing on the narrow ledge he had just gained, Martin could see little latitude to start. Away to his left and right the ledge crumbled and failed against the cliff face. Above on his left, however, lay a steep but climbable rock-laden slope that would bring him to the mouth of a gully or wash that cut the slope above it. The gully seemed to lead up to a space among the rocks that appeared to be more level and to allow at least some lateral movement. He would try climbing to there and then see what was possible.

Before proceeding up toward the gully mouth Martin took a small sip of water. He was trying to conserve it, since he knew neither how long he would be here nor what the condition of the lost man would be when he was found. Fortunately this conservation was not difficult since Martin did not seem to need much. This puzzled him; he felt that he should need more water, with all the climbing he had been doing. But what puzzled him more was that stopping brought no rest. Not that he was all that tired yet, but for some reason he seemed to expect that stopping to sit would restore his strength somewhat, and he was surprised when it didn't. He thought for a while and realized that the only times he had found rest in this place were when Uncle Leon or his people had sung that curious chant over him and put him into a trance. The effect of that seemed to last for quite a while, but the realization that this was the only way to get rested affected how Martin looked at his search. He could only continue for so long before he would have to return.

But that didn't matter now. He could go for quite a while on what he had. The most immediate problem he faced was getting up that rock slope and into the gully. Tying his scarf a little tighter so it would stay on while he climbed, he leaped up on the lower rocks and began his ascent.

Jack heard the climber's approach first. The noises had initially been indistinguishable from the howl of the wind and the other sounds among the cruel rocks. But when they remained steady and grew louder, he began to pay attention. Coming out around the boulder which he was squatting behind, Jack crawled over in the direction of the noise. He soon found himself at the edge of one of the too-common gullies that slashed through the barren landscape. The noise was coming up the gully.

Even in the dim light Jack could see the figure scrabbling up the grade below. He was clothed—clothed!—in white or some other light-colored garments, and he was concentrating on his climbing instead of the rocks above. Jack quickly pulled back from the edge and curled against a rock to ponder this unknown visitor.

Jack knew that they had sent this climber. They were looking for him! They were going to make him come down and go where they wanted him to. Without thinking he began edging farther from the gully—back toward the rock heights, back toward the isolation, back to where he could hide and never be found.

But wait! He was tired and hungry and thirsty—perhaps this traveler had some food, or even a flask of water. He was but one and could be overcome.

For a long while Jack battled within himself, gnawing hunger and thirst against smothering fear of the unknown traveler and those who had sent him. He had finally decided to retreat once again to the safety of the cliffs and their hidden crags, when he became aware that the climbing noises were now very much louder. Venturing cautiously around the boulder, he cast a quick glance into the gully below.

The climber was almost directly below Jack. His head was down, his attention focused on the small rocks and scrabble beneath him. Jack could see a staff tied across his back, and by his right hip swung something that had to be a flask of water.

The choice was made without thinking. Jack crouched, reaching for a hand sized rock nearby.

The impact was so swift and unexpected that all Martin knew at first was confusion. One minute he was carefully watching the treacherous slide of loose rocks at his feet, panting with the exertion of his climb; the next minute he was smashed brutally against the rocks, the breath driven from his lungs, his head numb and his vision dark from the blow that landed so heavily on his back. His body, however, reacted instinctively even while his mind was still groping. Whatever had struck him had also rolled him a bit to the left; he continued rolling that way with a swift twist of his torso. Dimly his mind registered that the twist seemed to have dislodged something. He struggled, trying to use the force of the roll to twist into a sitting position, but his lungs didn't want to work properly. His eyes cleared slightly; he could see dim circles at the ends of long black tunnels. He shook his head and quickly discovered the fierce pain that the blow against the rocks had brought.

Abruptly Martin's assailant was upon him again. The realization that he was under attack was even more startling than being knocked down had been. That corner of his mind that was still functioning had been wondering about the size of the rock that had fallen on him; suddenly he was fighting that "rock" as it clung to his back and rained blows on his head and sides. He turned and tried to rise, pushing the attacker away as best he could and catching a sharp blow on the shoulder in the process. The pain helped clear his thinking; all in a rush he realized the severity of his circumstances. With a roar he threw the man off his back, rose, and wheeled to face the assault.

For two or three long breaths Martin stared at the one who

had attacked him. Crouched among the stones where Martin's mighty shove had thrown him was a battered, scrawny man in tattered clothes. The man's intent was clear; he glared at Martin with undisguised hatred, and his mouth was drawn back in a snarl of contempt and anger. He was a small man, thin and gangly, and his bare arms and legs were bruised and bleeding from numerous gashes. His cheeks were hollow, and his eyes, though fiery, were red and sunken. His ribs showed through his skin, and his lips were cracked and blackened. Had circumstances been otherwise, Martin would have been concerned for the man's health.

All this passed in an instant. Bruised or not, the man was attacking him. He still showed ample agility as he scrambled to recover from the toss Martin had given him. His left hand still clutched the rock that had bruised Martin's shoulder, while his right scrabbled among the dust and pebbles in which he lay. Martin understood this just in time to shield his eyes from the spray of grit and sharp pebbles that was hurled in his face; then the attack was resumed.

Braced as he was, Martin was far less damaged this time. His assailant seemed more to be lashing out in blind fury than to be pursuing a planned attack. The man hurled himself at Martin, all kicks and random blows, snarling and gibbering with rage. Martin blocked these easily, taking extra care to avoid the large rock in the man's hand. Martin did not fight back, since the man seemed hardly to know what he was doing. Indeed, his attack was very disjointed, seemingly split between blows to Martin's head and shoulders and clutching grabs at the vicinity of his belt. Mystified by this, Martin allowed himself to be forced back. Then he realized, even as his foot caught a stone and he began falling backward to the ground, what the man was grasping for. His water flask!

"Hey!" he croaked, neither his lungs nor his throat obeying properly. The man was on top of him, pummeling him with blows that were astoundingly weak for all their fury.

Martin put both hands to the man's chest and shoved. He was light and would have been thrown well clear had he not been clutching at Martin even as he fell away. Martin shoved himself to his knees, shook his head (catching his breath as a wave of pain and nausea swept over him), and tried to speak again.

"If you wanted water, you didn't have to jump me. I've got plenty—here, take what you need." To prove his sincerity Martin unhooked the flask from his belt and held it out to the man, who lay there sprawled amidst the dust. The man stared at Martin, his mouth working silently and his chest heaving with exertion, and Martin could see in his eyes the titanic internal struggle between the ache and thirst for what was offered and the fear and hatred of the offerer. Caught in the web of this tension, the two gazed at each other for a long minute: Martin steadily proffering the flask, the man gazing back with burning thirst and deep suspicion. Keeping a steady eye on the man while still holding out the flask, Martin struggled to his feet amid the sliding rocks and gravel. Panic flared in the man's eyes, and he shoved himself away from Martin back up the dusty slope. But his thirst still held him, so he did not go far. Cautiously Martin stepped toward him; one step, then two, then he was within reach. Slowly he bent over, stretching to hold the flask as close as possible. The man's eyes flickered to and fro: now to the flask with trembling longing, now to Martin's face with fear and burning hatred. Suddenly his lean arms shot out with astounding speed, snatching the flask from Martin's hand and knocking him off balance in the process. As Martin recovered himself, a task made more difficult by the sharp throbbing pain in his head, the man crabbed backward up the slope using only his legs, his hands working furiously at the stopper to the flask. He opened it after some difficulty and immediately began gulping great swallows of water. He drank so frantically that he seemed to be biting or gnawing at the neck of the flask, as if trying to swallow it in his desperation. So great was his urgency that much of the water wasn't even being swallowed, flowing instead around his mouth and down his chest, streaking the dust and grime that covered him.

"Look," said Martin, holding up a cautioning hand, "you don't have to drink it all right now. We'll need some for the trip down, and there's plenty more where we're headed." Martin had quickly come to the conclusion that this dirty, emaciated man was the one he had been sent here to find and bring back. Seeing him now, Martin understood why he had been sent on the mission. Nobody in that condition could survive long in one place among these cliffs, much less survive the difficult descent from these heights unaided. How fortunate that they had found each other so quickly, even though their introduction had been rather unorthodox.

The man had apparently not heard Martin's warning, for he was still gulping at the water with the same frantic abandon that had most of it flowing down his chest. Martin looked up at the black clouds and felt the bitter, furious wind that whipped the severe gray rocks. This was no place to linger. He stepped toward the man.

"You've probably about finished that by now", Martin said, holding out his hand for the flask. "It doesn't matter, though— the way isn't far if we walk directly. Come on, let's get moving."

The man now noticed his approach. With wary and suspicious eyes he watched Martin while still gulping as much as he could from the flask. Martin could see the struggle surfacing within the man once again: fear against need, suspicion battling hunger and thirst. He stepped closer yet, almost within reach of the man.

Without warning the man twisted and hurled the flask at him with a shriek of fury. Martin ducked, barely in time, the flask glancing off his head and flying off to his left. Bracing for another attack, Martin was surprised when it did not come. The man was running away, scrabbling and climbing up the slope back toward the brutal rocks.

"No, wait!" cried Martin, starting after the man. "There's no water up there! The stations are down below! This way!"

In answer the man stopped long enough to hurl a handful of sharp gravel at Martin and then resumed his frantic ascent. The pebbles stopped Martin momentarily, since one of them struck perilously close to his eye, but they did not damage him. He watched the retreating figure for a moment. It would not be easy to stop him, frantic as he was, and fairly dangerous to try with just bare hands. Martin unslung the staff from his back and began running after the retreating man.

The man was in full and desperate flight up the gravelly slope, but in his exhausted state he was no match for the well-fed and rested Martin. It was the work of a minute to bound up close behind the man, who was snarling as he climbed, too intent on escape to turn and fight again. Martin thrust the staff between the man's feet, which brought him down sharply. The man twisted as he fell, trying to grab the staff, but it was snatched away too quickly. He writhed in an attempt to escape, but Martin wasn't allowing that. Casting the staff aside, he fell on the man, pinning him against the rocks. With his torso he weighed down the man's legs and after a moment's struggle managed to stretch his arms straight out, immobilizing them. Six inches separated Martin's face from the man's, which was contorted in a grimace as he snapped his head from side to side, seeking an escape that he would never find while held by those strong arms. For a minute or two he struggled until his position became obvious, and he quieted enough to lie still, glaring at Martin with naked hatred.

"I don't know what you're fighting so hard about", Martin said. "I've come to take you down from here. Out to water, and food, away from this cold wind." The wind was howling so fiercely above them that Martin nearly had to howl himself.

In response, the man growled back in some unintelligible language, though not the same one that the people of the valley had used. His tone, however, was unmistakable—it was so full of venom that Martin drew back in surprise. Then the man spat full in Martin's face—or rather made spitting motions, for his mouth was still too dry for spittle. Something flared deep within Martin but died too quickly to be recognized, leaving him with the curious feeling that he should feel more upset about the man's behavior than he was. What Martin felt instead was a curious mixture of compassion for this wretched creature and frustration that he continued to struggle against the very one sent to help him. Martin then remembered Uncle Leon's words that there were those who would remain among the cliffs if they could. He looked hard at the man's face, full of agony and bitterness, and wondered.

Then he realized—of course! His language! He spoke some unknown tongue and probably could not understand that he was being helped. Grasping eagerly at this straw of hope, Martin's mind worked desperately, searching for a means of communication. All the while the man glared at him with stead-fast hatred, his mouth working constantly, an occasional snarl escaping his cracked lips. Once or twice he tried pulling his arms away, but Martin's powerful grasp stifled these attempts effortlessly. After some minutes of this Martin finally sighed and looked hard at the pathetic figure.

"Well," he said, "if I can't explain it to you, I guess I'll have to show you." With that he eased his grip on the man's arms and started to rise.

What followed was a frantic, tiring repetition of the sequence that Martin had endured when tackling the man the first time. At the first hint of relaxation of Martin's vigilance the man exploded into a snarling, scratching bundle of desperation and wiry strength. The struggle lasted several minutes, until Martin finally subdued the man by brute force—which was barely enough—slamming the man's face into the rocks with a shoulder hold that nearly broke his arm. As he lay there, momentarily stunned, Martin quickly looped an end of the rope around the man's hands and cinched it tight. He cut that off, and then another length for a hobble, though applying that was more difficult, since the man had recovered enough to realize what was happening and kicked furiously to prevent it. Martin succeeded in the end, however, rising to look on the bound and strug-gling figure with a mixture of satisfaction and sorrow. Reaching down to lift the man by both arms—making sure to keep his hands out of reach of the man's teeth—he steadied his captive on the uneven rock-and-gravel slope. Looking about quickly, he spotted a suitable point on the far side of the gully. To this spot he half-led, half-dragged the man and then turned him to face down the cut of the gully.

At this height up the face of the cliffs it was difficult to find an unobstructed view down to the valley below, so dark was the overcast and so deep the ravines between the jagged boulders. But the wash of the gully provided enough break in the rocks to afford such a view, or at least part of one. A jutting ledge obscured some of it, but beyond that Martin could dimly make out the brighter plains of the valley floor and perhaps a bit of the silvery ribbon that was the river. With fierce determination Martin grasped the man's shoulders, squared him down the gully toward the valley, and pointed to it.

"There", he said, loudly so as to outshout the wind. "The valley. I am going to take you down to the valley." He tapped his chest twice, then the man's, then jabbed his finger emphatically toward the valley, hoping to convey by gestures what he could not by words.

He succeeded, but the result was not what he had expected. Perceiving Martin's intent, the man burst into another raging fury that surpassed anything he had yet demonstrated—something Martin didn't think possible. Shrieking with fear and outrage, the man wheeled and rammed Martin full force, sending him sprawling backward on the rocks. Martin rolled away as he fell, sheltering his head with his arms in anticipation of another attack. None came, for once again the man seemed more concerned with escape than with combat. He did not get far. Denied his arms for balance and his feet for climbing, he reeled for twenty to thirty yards up the slope before stumbling and falling hard on his face. He struck the ground with such force, and without arms to break his fall, that Martin jumped up and ran to him, fearing he had seriously damaged himself. The man lay still and quiet where he had fallen, and Martin turned him over to see a face brutally torn and bruised along one side where it had struck the rocks. Amazingly, the man was still conscious. Dazed as he was by the fall, he still glared back with that singular hatred that assured Martin that the only thing protecting him from another assault was the man's inability to move. Martin sighed.

"Well, mister, even if you don't like it, you've got to go down there", Martin said to himself, since the man could not understand him. "Though I know you just don't understand. It's better down there, better than up here. You'll like it once you get there. Besides, it doesn't matter if you do or not. I've got to take you back with me. You've got to see the King—everybody does—and I'm the one that's been sent to bring you."

All at once, even as he said these words, the realization came to Martin that this was exactly what he must do. He saw now that this had not been certain in his mind before.

It was certain now. Martin knew nothing of this King or why he had such a law. He had even questioned Uncle Leon about it, and had left on the mission convinced that he was going to rescue the lost. He had not even thought about what he would do if the lost were to refuse rescue. Here, now, that very thing was happening. By his actions this man was turning Martin from rescuer to jailer, and Martin was accepting the role—if not for the sake of the man, then for the sake of the King of whom he knew nothing. With astonishing clarity the words of Uncle Leon and an image of his face flashed through Martin's head—"The King's law stands!"—and the decision was made. He would bring this poor wretch to the valley, where it could be hoped he would overcome his irrational fear but where in any event he would be taken before the King.

"Come on", Martin said, pulling the man to his feet. He was still struggling weakly, even to the point of snapping at Martin's hand, but Martin had his measure and held him firmly by one arm and a shoulder. They marched over to where the staff lay, and Martin ran it behind the man's back and between his elbows. Then, lashing his elbows to the staff with one short length of rope and his wrists to his sides with another that went around his waist, Martin secured the man in a manner that was both more secure and less harsh on his wrists. The staff also made it easier to control the man's movements. Using this, he guided the man over to where the water flask lay. It had fallen so as to drain completely into the dust, and not even the smallest mouthful remained. As Martin looked at it and the damp patch where it had lain, he fully realized how hungry, thirsty, and exhausted he was. Reaching for the satchel at his side, he found that it had been torn off, and the fruit it had contained trampled underfoot in the struggling. There was nothing to eat or drink, and the descent of the harsh cliffs lay before them.

"Well, you've made a rougher trip back for the both of us," said Martin, looking from the flask to the man's face, "but the sooner we get moving, the sooner we'll be finished. Let's go." He firmly turned the man and began walking him down the gully, one hand firmly gripping the staff that secured his arms.

The second descent of the cliffs was the most difficult trial that Martin had yet known in that curious land. He was sore in joint and limb and exhausted beyond anything he could have ever imagined. His eyes ached with weariness, and his arms and legs were heavy as he walked. The bitter wind pierced his clothing and chilled him to the bone, making his every movement sluggish. The fighting had taken its toll as well—he had been scratched and bruised in many places, and one ankle had been badly twisted, making each step difficult. The blow on his head had given him a throbbing headache that shot flashes of pain behind his eyes every time he moved his head. Fierce thirst accompanied all this: a rasping, grating torment that was less painful than any of his wounds yet more burdensome than all of them. His throat felt so dry that each breath seemed to have to force it open, and his lips and tongue were cracked and parched. A dull ache in his stomach reminded him of his hunger, but that was the least of his sufferings on that horrible journey.

As great as these burdens were, they were not the heaviest that Martin had to bear. The prisoner, even bound and defeated, was the sorest trial of all. Martin did not expect that he would come along willingly, but neither did he expect the sullen peevishness that became the man's attitude for the descent. He would walk only when propelled in some manner, either by a hand on his shoulder or by Martin's holding the staff. He would lash out in any petty way he could: biting if Martin's hand got too close, kicking, ramming him to knock him off balance. Martin quickly learned that he could not precede his captive down even a small slope, for the man would seize the opportunity to kick free a painful shower of rocks onto Martin's head. These trivial but persistent expressions of resistance wore away at Martin as time went on, amplifying his exhaustion. This behavior made it clear that he could not even think of loosening the man's bonds even though they made travel more difficult. The cliffs offered few stretches of descending terrain that could be walked, which meant that Martin spent much time easing the bound man down steep grades or through narrow gaps in the rocks. Once or twice Martin had to carry his captive bodily across especially hazardous stretches, which would have been excellent opportunities for the man to damage Martin or himself seriously with a substantial attempt at resistance. But here the man's own condition worked against him; as exhausted as Martin was, the man was more so, and his waning strength limited both his efforts and his imagination to the petty shows of resistance that he performed whenever possible. Even these came less frequently as the journey progressed, until the most he could manage was a steady, hate-filled glare that Martin was able to ignore.

So they proceeded down those dismal cliffs—bound and free, captive and captor—toward a destination that neither understood. To Martin the journey seemed endless; overhead the dark clouds still boiled, ever brooding, neither advancing nor receding, cursing all that barren land with bleak twilight. Before and behind and all round them the land was gashed deep and piled high into great folds that seemed designed to hinder their progress. Among these the wind screamed and lashed, angrily hurling clouds of black grit against the rocks, whirling along the cliffs for a moment in an impotent dance of rage, then sweeping up another burden of dust with which to punish some other corner of the tormented range. Through all this the travelers struggled, now blinded by wind-borne dirt, now turned aside by an unperceived chasm astride their path.

To Martin it seemed that the land itself was seeking to hinder their progress, as if the cliffs were enraged by this attempt to take their prey from their hands. He could not remember the upward journey taking this long, though he no longer trusted his own judgment, clouded as it was by weariness. There was no tracking in this dismal place, so for all he knew they could be lost on the great cliff face, wandering aimlessly among the brutal rocks. He shuddered at the thought but knew there was nothing to be done about it. They could only struggle on, seeking always the downward path, thirsting, hungering, ever weary, never resting, chilled to the bone by the fury of the wind, chilled to the heart by the bleak emptiness that surrounded them. Martin no longer looked upward or even far ahead, focusing instead on his feet, watching them intently as they lifted and fell, step after weary step, as if by concentration of sight he could assist them in their thankless task.

For how long they trudged on this way Martin could never tell. There was no coming or going of days in that place, only the semilight that shrouded the cliffs; there were no rest periods to punctuate their trek. Dulled as his senses were by the gray veil of exhaustion, Martin did not perceive the gradual easing of the slope or the lessening of the wind's violence. But eventually there came a point—just when Martin was beginning to feel that he could not walk another ten steps—when he thought the terrain around him seemed brighter than he had remembered it being. Even as his fatigue-numbed mind began to ponder the significance of this, he was interrupted by something that both confused and excited him: the cry of voices.

Martin stopped short, yanking lightly on the staff that bound his captive to signal him to stop. The man had long since ceased even token efforts of resistance, settling down to a mindless plodding in whichever direction Martin steered him. He stopped short, head hanging, making no movement except to cast a sidelong glance with eyes creased with more weariness than Martin had thought any man could endure—but not yet too tired to hate.

Hearing the cries again, Martin looked about in a daze, seeking the source of the voices. He had a bit of trouble focusing his eyes, but when he did he spotted movement amidst the rocks above him. A closer look revealed a low white roof nestled in the cliff a few hundred yards back up the slope they had just descended and two figures scrambling down toward them, waving and calling as they came. Martin stared dumbly for some time, trying to piece together the significance of all this, as the figures got closer and closer. When they finally reached terrain that was unbroken enough they began to run toward Martin and his captive. The sight of them running—

two strong men, nude except for the white capes that flew out behind them, calling in clear but unintelligible speech—finally jogged Martin's memory. Uncle Leon, the woman, the fire—rest, food! In their stumbling weariness Martin and his captive had walked right past a station, and now the custodians were coming for them.

Martin did not try to move, instead standing and waiting for the men to come to them. Indeed, he seemed unable to do anything regardless—the surge of relief that flooded over him seemed to wash away the last of his perseverance, and he felt he could not take another step no matter how hard he tried.

The two men finally reached them. So strong and vibrant were they, so full of life and power, that Martin felt all the weaker by comparison and wondered if he would be able to remain standing. He must have begun falling, since one of the men caught him suddenly with a cry of alarm and propped him up with strong arms. Their speech, of course, could not be understood, but Martin knew enough to know that the station meant rest, warmth, and comfort, so he did not object when the shining men began leading them back up the slope toward the station. He was too fatigued to watch closely, but he did register that his captive objected even more to these new arrivals than he had to Martin, and he struggled against them. It was no use, of course—the spark of resistance within the man had already been burning dimly when he fought Martin and had since been even more thoroughly crushed by the brutal miles and buried beneath overwhelming exhaustion. His struggle was a token one, and in the end he allowed himself to be led off. Martin came more willingly, leaning so heavily on his benefactor's arm that he was almost being carried up the hill.

They soon reached the clearing in front of the station, which was just like the last one Martin had seen—the same deep-set building beneath the same low overhanging roof, the same table and benches, and the same roaring bonfire. His host led him to the fire, sitting him down close by it on the ground. Martin sat for a moment, reveling in the warmth and stretching his chilled and stiff limbs in the heat. Then one of the men brought him a little water in a goblet, urging him with signs to drink it slowly. A bit at a time was all he could handle, so piercing was the ecstasy of that cool water in his parched throat. When Martin had finished the goblet, a little more was given him, and when he had finished that, more again, until at last his thirst was slaked. Then he signaled for water with which to wash, and a bowl of warm water was brought to him. By now he was beginning to feel truly warm, and the combined relief of feeling both warm and clean again was almost too delightful to contain. Then his stomach reminded him of its existence, and he made signs requesting food. The one serving him smiled, nodded, and went off to find some.

While he waited, Martin looked about the clearing. Off to one side he saw the captive, outside the circle of warmth cast by the fire, still bound and seated on a rock with his head hanging down. This puzzled Martin, for he could not imagine such hospitable hosts treating anyone with callousness. When his attendant returned, Martin made signs to inquire if the captive had been cared for. In response the man spread his hands in a gesture of resignation and, taking a flask he had brought with Martin's food, walked over to where the captive was seated. He poured a little water into a goblet and held it out to the man. At first the captive turned away from the goblet but then seemed to change his mind and took a drink from the cup. This encouraged Martin, but his hopes were dashed when the man lifted his head and spat the mouthful of water full in the face of his host. It was obvious from the fury in the man's eyes that he intended to accept nothing from these people, no matter how much he might need it. With a sigh the custodian turned from where the captive sat, bound more by his hatred than by any ropes, and returned to Martin wearing an expression of deep grief, the stain of the man's bitter rejection dripping from his beard and falling like tears on his chest. Martin sighed as well, while the man sat down beside him and began giving him fruit and bread from a tray he had brought, once again a little at a time. The food on his empty stomach was the most delicious thing he had ever tasted, and it was some time before he stopped motioning for more. He had a little more water after that, stretched himself luxuriously in the warmth of the fire, and heaved a great sigh of satisfaction. He was almost completely content.

His thirst and hunger assuaged, Martin's weariness now came back to him full force. With relief he remembered that these people had the power to impose by their singing the trancelike state that provided rest here. He motioned to the custodian that he would like to stretch out on one of the benches and be allowed to rest. To his surprise and dismay the man indicated that this would not happen but rather that Martin and his captive should return to the road.

"No, no, no", Martin said, lapsing into speech in his astonishment, even though he knew it could not be understood. "You don't understand. We cannot go farther. We must rest first. Then we can go. Rest first." He tried to make his motions as clear as possible to convey the point that he was too exhausted to move even from this clearing, much less farther along a lengthy journey. In response his host rose and went into the building, leaving Martin muttering, "We can't. We just can't. We must rest", as if to assure himself that things would turn out that way. In a moment both of the men emerged from the hut, each holding a small cup and one holding a staff of some sort as well. Martin waited as they came to him and offered one of the cups to him. He took it, sniffed the contents, and took a little sip. The liquid, which looked like water and had no scent, turned out to be a most amazing beverage. It had a very slight spicy taste and felt warm in his mouth but cool in his throat. He took another sip, then drank the whole cup. As it went down he had the most curious sensation of strength being poured into him. It did not banish his exhaustion but rather buried it beneath a flood of new strength that filled his whole frame. His weariness was still there in the form of a dull ache behind his eyes and a slowness in his perceptions, but his limbs were alive with a new vigor that he knew would carry him many hard miles. Whatever the liquid was, it was certainly good stuff to travel on. As he handed the cup back to the man Martin felt as if he had just finished a draught of liquid light.

The men grew slightly grim as they addressed their next task.

179

They walked over to where the bound man still sat sullenly on his rock, coming toward him from opposite sides. Espying their approach, the man sought to dodge away, but they were ready for him. One caught and held him fast while the other quickly did something about his head with the staff he carried. Then the one holding the man tightened his grip, immobilizing the man, and with his elbow tipped the man's chin back. It was obvious what they intended, and it was equally obvious that they were accustomed to doing it. The man struggled in vain against the strong arms that held him and forced his jaws open. The other approached warily and, when signaled, poured the contents of the other cup down the prisoner's open throat.

The response was predictable and violent. The man coughed and spluttered and spat, but it was quickly obvious that most of the liquid had made it inside him. His struggles immediately became more vigorous, and he began bellowing and kicking in defiance. The one who had been holding him stepped away but quickly picked up the staff, giving Martin a chance to see clearly what it was. At the end of the staff was a noose that had been tied about the captive's neck, loose enough not to be uncomfortable yet tight enough not to be slipped by even the most vigorous struggle. The effectiveness of this device was demonstrated conclusively as the custodian controlled the captive's struggles with a minimum of effort, and the captive learned his limitations quickly. When he ceased struggling, the man holding the staff motioned for him to walk over to the bonfire, where Martin stood. When the prisoner planted his feet and stared back in defiance, his captor simply walked over to Martin regardless, dragging the bound man stumbling behind him. Facing Martin, the custodian made signs that he and the captive were to take to the road immediately and then held out the staff for Martin to take.

Martin just looked at the man, and at the staff he offered. Here again, more clearly than ever, he was being forced into the role of captor by circumstances he didn't like and couldn't control. On the cliff face, when faced with the option of binding the man to bring him down, Martin had first consoled himself with the thought that the man didn't understand that he was being taken to comfort and safety. But here, in the midst of reasonable comfort and safety, he had refused help and spat provision back in the face of those who would assist him. There was no other possibility; if he refused water here, he would not take it anywhere else. As impossible as it seemed, the man truly did seem to prefer the cliffs, and though Martin could not understand that, something deep within him bridled at the thought of forcing this man to go somewhere he didn't want to go. Martin did not want to take the staff.

Once again welling up from deep within him came the knowledge that decided the issue. The man must come before the King. Uncle Leon had said that some who refused to come at first changed their minds when brought to the King. Martin had not understood why anyone would not come when the option was the cliffs, but now that he had seen that, he drew hope from the possibility that this man could be cured of his insanity by the mercy of the King. Besides, the men who staffed the station, obviously compassionate and helpful people, did not hesitate in taking action to ensure that the captive went where he had to go. They were never cruel, though they were firm when necessary, and they were obviously at least as concerned for the captive's welfare as Martin was. Perhaps they hoped, as Martin did, that before the King's throne the man would turn from his self-destruction. At any rate, he would be offered the option, and if he chose to return to the cliffs, that would be allowed. Martin took the staff.

This station was downrange from the first one Martin had found, and the path from it led more directly toward the valley floor. As they walked, the captive learned quickly to pace his stride to match Martin's in order to avoid a prod from the stick or a tightening of the noose. Martin learned quickly always to be wary, for after they had reached reasonably smooth ground and walked uneventfully for a pace the man suddenly leaped to one side, yanking the staff from Martin's hands, and ran off across a field. He didn't get far, since the staff trailing behind him flapped about his legs and soon tripped him. The fall was brutal, made all the worse by his arms being bound by his sides and useless for breaking the impact. The man's face was again badly bloodied, and though the glare of hatred was undiminished, he made no more escape attempts. Nevertheless, after that Martin always ensured that his grip was tight on the staff.

The trip was otherwise delightful. The custodians had indicated no further directions other than that they should proceed down to the valley floor and up the far slope. The path that led down from the station went that direction, so Martin followed it. They were soon out of the worst of the rocks and found themselves surrounded by greenery. The air grew milder and milder, and the light grew brighter as they went along. Martin looked up and saw that they were passing out from under the grayest clouds that overshadowed the cliffs and into the land that lay under the whitening clouds that stretched out over the valley. Instead of biting sand, soft and pleasant scents came on the breezes, and Martin breathed deeply of them. The clean air strengthened him almost as much as the draught of liquid had, though in different ways.

Presently the path joined a larger path, which was more like a road. This ran parallel to the cliff face, and Martin decided to follow it. It meandered for a while, joined here and there by other paths that descended from the rocks on the right, finally turning left to head down across the valley. Martin stayed on it, guessing that it would take them to their destination—wherever that was.

Crossing the valley was a sheer delight for Martin. It was every bit as mild and beautiful as he had imagined and more so. Lush yellow-green meadows streaked with pungent patches of wildflowers spread away on both sides of the road. The grass bowed gently before the mild breezes, which carried from the flowers delightful fragrances that pierced his mind with colorful and ecstatic images. The richness of the colors was both exciting and soothing, for even while his heart beat faster while looking at the meadows, a deep inner calm seemed to flow from them, draining away the tension within him. The sounds were soothing as well, primarily because there were so few of them, and they were gentle. All the time spent among the cliffs had been accompanied by the constant howling of the wind, and that background cacophony had cost Martin more stamina than he had realized. Here the only sounds were those of meadow grasses and wildflowers rustling quietly beneath the gentle breeze, and Martin could feel something inside him relaxing now that he did not have to contend with the unending roar of the wind among the cliffs. He delighted in this and wished his fatigue-dulled senses were more awake so he could appreciate it more fully.

Wonderful as all these sensations were, they were not what most held Martin's attention. What enraptured him most, what surrounded and filled and lifted him with every forward step, what penetrated and brought him new strength even as he walked, what was all around him and grew with intensity as they traveled on, was the light, the light that barely reached the gray rocks but flooded the valley with muted iridescence. Martin had never known such light, which could not only be seen but felt as well. How it affected him could not be easily described, for it seemed not just to surround him but also to penetrate him and do things to him under his skin. It was a prickly-tingling feeling that swept through his body, at times reaching an almost uncomfortable intensity that was nonetheless exhilarating when it happened. Martin knew it was the light that did this, for he could feel the gentle penetration more intensely on his exposed skin than under his clothing, though it never completely shut out the sensation. He realized that light as light was something he had never thought much about before, being interested only in whatever it illuminated.

But this light could not be ignored, for it not only illuminated but also enfolded, bringing vigor and life directly where it fell. Quite a few times Martin craned his neck to look upward for the source, which seemed to be hidden by the clouds, for he wondered what heavenly body could cast such vibrant rays. But each time he was frustrated, for the light, instead of concentrating around a central source, as would seem expectable, remained diffused across a wide stretch of the clouds. This confused Martin, for the source of the light should have become visible, or at least more discernible, as the clouds thinned, yet he could see nothing. But he did not concern himself much with this, for the light itself, wherever it came from, was delight enough for now. He did find himself wondering that if the intensity of the diffused light had this effect, what could be expected of the rays directly from the source?

Through all this beauty the bound man stumped along sullenly, his face grim and his eyes fastened firmly on the road in front of him. Martin could not understand how anyone could travel through this land and remain unaffected by the beauty all around, but then again neither could he understand someone wishing to remain among the cliffs. It was obvious from the man's behavior that either he was not aware of the surroundings, or he was aware but was ignoring them, or he was affected by them differently than Martin was. None of this mattered to Martin, except that the man's subdued state seemed to make him less inclined to try running away. Martin still kept a grip on the staff, but it seemed that the man so disliked the valley that he would not think of willingly taking any route that would carry him through the grassy fields.

So they traveled, Martin amid a delightfulworld shot through with tingling sensations and delicious smells all bathed in warmth and murmuring quiet, the man stalking along locked within a sullen prison of his own making. Martin didn't know for how long they journeyed across the valley—the far slope looked no nearer regardless of how long they walked, and the black cliffs, which initially had faded quickly to a dark mist in the distance, seemed to recede no farther. They saw no other living thing save the meadow plants around them. There was nothing to time their progress except the imperceptibly increasing intensity of the light and the nearly imperceptible waning of their strength as the effect of the liquid they had been given wore off. This didn't affect Martin as much, since he seemed to be drawing strength from the air and the light, but the captive was clearly suffering, his footsteps falling leaden and heavy on the road and his head hanging low.

After traveling for some time they found the road descending slightly, this time to reach the bed of the river, which splashed and sparkled across their path. There was no bridge, so the road ran down to the water's edge and out the far side as if it ran right under the river. Martin could see that the water, never very deep, seemed shallow enough here to be waded. It was a ford, and looking across the river Martin could see that on the other side the road began to ascend. After walking so far with no apparent progress, they had finally reached the base of the valley wall. The water sparkled and babbled over the shallows, refreshing and inviting. Martin was eager to get down to it, so he began the descent quickly.

Just as quickly Martin discovered that the captive did not share his enthusiasm for the water. The man stopped and stood fast, nearly yanking the staff from Martin's hand. Turning to see what the problem was, Martin saw the man staring at the river below with a mixture of shock and horror that seemed far out of proportion to the circumstances. Martin laughed.

"Oh, come on", he said, trying to make his tone of voice reassuring. "It's not all that deep and probably not a bit cold. If you trip, I'll pick you right up, and if it's too deep, I can carry you." Martin motioned for the man to step down. "Besides, I'd think someone in your condition would be glad to see water."

But the man remained still, bracing his feet and pulling back on the noose with his head. He clearly had no intention of descending to that river. Martin, however, had no intention of staying on the bank and did not hesitate to use the advantage he had. Pulling gently but firmly on the staff, Martin's superior strength quickly overcame the resistance, bringing the man stumbling down the slope. He tried to stop at points along the way, digging in his heels in attempts to make a stand, but Martin was having none of it.

"I don't know what you're so afraid of", Martin said after one particularly difficult struggle. "The water's not going to kill you, and it could do you some good." But the man only intensified his resistance as they approached the river, crying out in his strange tongue what sounded like pleas intermixed with curses. But Martin remained adamant, dragging the man on until both of them splashed into the shallows.

The river was colder than Martin had expected it to be considering the climate, but it was not unbearable. After a minute's adaptation he found it refreshing and began splashing about. He even let the staff slip from his hands, reasoning that the prisoner could not run either fast or far while standing knee deep in water. He was correct in that guess; with eyes closed the man stood stock still as the water foamed and swirled about his legs, a look of total horror etching his face. He looked as if he were standing in burning oil. Martin shook his head—whatever was wrong with the man was beyond his reckoning. The water was a little chilly at first, but one got used to it. It also seemed to Martin that the water had some of the qualities that the light did. It seemed as if it not only wet the surface of the skin but also penetrated to bring refreshment. He had never known such a bath as this—even though he was fully clothed, he felt like much of the grime and stain of travel was being washed away. He reveled in it, splashing his head and arms and even opening his shirt to wet his chest thoroughly. He had a good many deep drinks as well and would have stripped his clothes off entirely had he not felt pressed to move on. He also didn't think he could do that to the captive, who through it all stood as he had first entered the river: quiet, still, and horrified.

After some minutes of this delightful diversion Martin picked up the staff and urged the man forward again. He came along with obvious hesitation but fewer struggles, which Martin guessed was to reduce the likelihood of falling and getting thoroughly drenched. The cries and curses had quieted to faint whimpers now, which grew louder as they waded deeper and deeper into the water. The ford had more depth than Martin had estimated, wetting them both to the chest at the deepest point. This invigorated Martin, who took a moment to submerge himself completely, but it petrified the prisoner. From that point the water got shallower with each step, until they finally reached the other side and stood dripping on the roadway that led upward from the riverbank.

As with most slopes, this one appeared less steep looking up from the base than it had seemed from across the valley. Not that Martin minded; he didn't think he could handle a steep ascent at this point. The upward trail looked like a delightful walk, for the slope was dotted with copses and thickets of flowering shrubs watered by streams that danced and splashed down to meet the river. Through these the road wound to the top, where Martin thought he could see a few larger trees against the skyline.

The two began making their way up the road. The cool breezes against Martin's wet skin and clothes helped keep him alert and moving. Despite the refreshment brought by the river water, his fatigue was returning in earnest now, and he found himself having to force his feet to move up the road. He regretted that his senses were so dulled by his exhaustion, for the ground cover on both sides of them was a spreading aromatic shrub that filled the air with a warm, spicy scent that he found tantalizing and wished he could appreciate more. What the captive thought of it Martin could not tell. The man still plodded along, oblivious to all around him.

As they trudged along, Martin found himself thinking more about their destination. Presumably the road took them on to the King, but now that the prospect of facing this mysterious monarch was looming larger, Martin found he was afraid. It was a curious type of fear, a clean, quivering tingling that had elements of shyness mixed into it. The prospect of scaling the cliffs had made his stomach hurt; the prospect of standing before the King turned his blood to water and made all his joints weak. It wasn't that he feared what the King would do to him, it was just . . . it was . . . he did not know what it was. For one thing, he had no idea what to say. He couldn't speak this country's language, and the only person who could understand him was presumably back across the valley at the outpost near the foot of the cliffs. Why, he didn't even know the way to where the King was! Martin wondered at himself that he had taken on and worked so hard at a mission that he did not know how to conclude.

Thus he pondered as he walked, the captive stumbling along behind. Their clothes dried soon in the fresh breeze, and the light was again bathing Martin in that lilting sensation that he had felt along the valley floor. It was stronger than ever here, and again he searched the clouds for whatever was casting those potent rays but found nothing. The diffusing clouds were still hiding the source of the light.

After they had walked for some time, and Martin had long

since ceased looking up toward the top of the slope to see if they were drawing any closer (they never were), his thoughts were interrupted by a noise that he certainly hadn't expected to hear in that place: the clear sound of a horn ringing down from the ridge ahead. Looking up in surprise, he saw that they were very close to the top, and that two objects that from a distance he had taken for two odd-shaped trees standing close together were in fact twin towers, standing one on either side of the road. But what caught his attention most quickly were the two figures galloping down from those towers, descending toward them rapidly on swift horses. Mystified by this, Martin stopped and awaited the arrival of the riders, which would be shortly at the rate they were coming on. The captive did not like this, for he appeared at least as terrified of the riders as he had been of the water, and he tugged and pulled at the noose in an attempt to get away. Martin, being in no mood to put up with this nonsense, merely tightened his grip and waited.

With a thunder of hooves and a flurry of snorting and whinnying, the riders descended upon them, reining in just a dozen yards or so away. They were clothed in riding trousers, boots, and neatly cut tunics of rich-looking blue cloth. It appeared that they were in uniform, an effect that was enhanced by small bits of metallic-looking embroidery that trimmed their sleeves and shoulders. They looked tall, strong, and valiant, with open faces marked by kindness and keen authority. Before them Martin felt weak and dirty and ragged.

The rider who had stopped in front of Martin gracefully dismounted and stepped forward. Raising his hand, he said in his clear voice something that sounded for all the world like a salute. The rider was addressing Martin, and though Martin couldn't understand a word that was said, he nevertheless felt vaguely embarrassed by the greeting.

"Uh, hello", he responded, wishing he had something grander or more dramatic to say. "We're going up there, to see the King, I guess." Here Martin pointed to the crest of the ridge. "Is that the way?"

The rider didn't understand his words but seemed to grasp his meaning clearly. Indicating that they would escort the travelers to the top, the rider then signed to Martin that he could ride the horse if he wished. But Martin, overwhelmed by the size and high spirits of the creature, shook his head to indicate he'd rather walk. The man smiled at this but made no attempt to remount himself, instead choosing to walk beside Martin. The other rider also dismounted and took the staff from Martin's hand, something the prisoner did not like in the least, and together they began walking up the hill. The horses came walking behind as they ascended.

As they approached the crest, Martin could see more people clustered about the base of the towers, perhaps a dozen all together, clad in the same blue tunics as the riders wore. He also saw that between the two towers stretched a simple gate that barred the road. Beyond the gate the road passed along a level place for a while before plunging into a forest of tall trees. Martin thought there was something strange looking about the trees and was trying to figure out what it was when they came to the gate.

At close inspection the gate turned out to be two gates, one attached to each tower, that met in the middle of the road. They were simply but gracefully carved of wood and joined with a blue cord. They stopped just before the gate, while two of the blue-clad attendants stepped out, untied the cord, and swung the gates wide. Then the two riders who had escorted them up the last stretch of road did a strange thing. Rather than proceeding through the open gate, the rider who had been walking beside Martin signed to him that he should stand where he was. Then the rider stepped across the line that had been marked by the gates, turned, and signaled that Martin should step over to him. Martin wondered at this and looked about for some clue as to what this might signify. The rider only smiled reassuringly and motioned to him again. Martin shrugged and stepped over next to the man. This greatly excited those standing about, and they smiled and laughed and talked excitedly to each other. This mystified Martin, for if there was some great effect that was supposed to result from this, he had no idea what it might be. He couldn't see what was so exciting about taking a step down a road; he'd certainly done enough of that recently.

Now the people in the blue tunics did something else strange. The rider who had been leading the captive by the noose staff untied it from the man's neck and handed the staff to one of two others who were stepping up behind the man. The rider then stepped across the gate line while the others untied the captive and stood behind him. The rider stood waiting until the man's bonds were off and then, with compassion and deep sorrow etched across his handsome face, beckoned for the man to step after him.

The man stood still for a moment, suspiciously evaluating his surroundings. He was still clad in the torn and filthy rags in which Martin had found him on the cliff face. He was bruised and bloody in many places from scrapes and falls, and his face was pinched from thirst and exhaustion. His eyes were sunken red circles rimmed with dirt and tears where they had been punished by the dust whirls of the cliffs. His shoulders were stooped, and his breath came raggedly through his cracked and swollen lips. He looked thoroughly wretched, and Martin pitied him, even though he knew that the man had brought these conditions on himself. Yet despite all the trouble and abuse that his willfulness had brought down upon his own head, the man was obviously still intent on going his own way. His eyes, glazed as they were by exhaustion, flicked to and fro seeking a path by which to escape. His jaws worked with the chewing motion that Martin had seen him do so often. He obviously wanted nothing to do with this place or these people. The rider beckoned to him again, and in response the man half-turned and rammed into the two who stood behind him, seeking to shove his way between them and escape back down the road.

He had no chance against the solidly built man and the lithe woman who guarded him. They caught him before he could harm himself or them and planted him squarely back in the road before them. Again the rider motioned the captive to come to him.

Frustrated once, the man wasted little time before making another attempt. He tried turning and running around the woman, who was behind and to his right. She caught him effortlessly and returned him to his place as he snarled and spat his defiance. The rider beckoned to him once again, watching him closely. But the captive could clearly see that both fight and flight were useless and simply stood, staring sullenly around him, ignoring the invitation being offered. The rider gestured once more, waited a long minute for a response that did not come, then sighed and nodded to the two standing behind the captive. Swiftly and firmly they grasped him and tied his hands. His struggles availed nothing against their strength. Then the horses were brought forward, and the rider who had beckoned to the captive remounted. The rider standing beside Martin showed no inclination to ride again, so another of the gate wardens mounted the other horse. A small coil of rope was given to each of the horsemen, with which they did something that rather shocked Martin—each took the loop that was at the end of one rope and fastened it loosely about the captive's neck. The man stood frozen in terror during this procedure, and while they brought their steeds around to either side of him, but he need not have worried about their skill. They were very careful, as well as solemn and a little sad, but they went about their business with the deliberate air of those who must perform a task whether they liked it or not.

When they were ready to move on, the wretched man stood dwarfed between the huge beasts, each one about an armspan away on either side of him, his hands bound behind him and the two nooses resting loosely around his neck. A controlling rope from each noose stretched to the hand of each rider, making it obvious that when the riders chose to move, the captive would have no choice but to move as well. It occurred to Martin that he was seeing a man who had been as completely subjected as any man could be.

Martin, in contrast, was perfectly free, walking beside the blue-clad rider. The man was both delightful and delighted in Martin despite their inability to communicate. They started off down the road toward the forest together, the two horsemen leading the captive along behind them. Martin's escort strode along in grand style, breathing deeply and laughing for sheer joy of heart. It invigorated Martin to walk beside him. Presently he began singing in his strange tongue, and the men on the horses would join in from time to time. Martin could tell from the tone and beat that they were triumph songs, wherein every beat and measure spoke of great victories against impossible odds, or joyous parades returning home after vanquishing a tremendous and powerful foe. Martin's blood raced to hear them, and he held his head higher as he walked. Then one song became a two-part affair, with the walking rider chanting out a verse in his strong, clear voice and the two mounted ones responding with a refrain sung out with a vigor that shook the very air about them. The strength in the song was both exciting and a little frightening. Martin wondered what the captive thought of it, but he did not look back to see. In this manner they proceeded toward the forest, the miles going by much more quickly than when it had been just Martin and the captive by themselves.

As they approached the trees, Martin had a chance to examine them more closely to see if he could discern why they looked so odd. It was something about the light among them, a strange effect that seemed vaguely familiar, though he couldn't quite remember from where. He stared and stared, searching his mind for the connection, when suddenly it came to him: the light was coming through the trees! It was like a sunset or sunrise, with the light angling among the trees, illuminating one side of the trunk and casting the other in shadow. Except that the light wasn't right—it was too white, not like sunset light, which should have been redder. But if it were sunset or sunrise, the light in the sky should—here Martin looked up, puzzled. The light in the sky was as bright as ever, in fact brighter, and still diffusing across half the sky. Now he was thoroughly confused. His escort caught sight of his puzzled skywatching and smiled, giving Martin the impression that his questions would soon be answered.

Shortly afterward they came to the edge of the forest and stopped there for a minute. Here the walking rider indicated that Martin should stay back a little as he stepped forward, raised his hand with his palm toward the forest, and sang a couple of lines in a melodic chanting that was different from the voice he had been using. The two riders on the horses answered this with a similar chant. This went back and forth a couple of times, and Martin got the clear impression that this was no longer just songs while walking along the road but an actual ceremony that was being performed. After a while they began moving again, deliberately marching this time, with the walking rider in front chanting his pieces, followed by Martin, followed by the two horsemen chanting the responses and leading the captive between them.

The forest itself consisted of younger trees, thin and medium thickness, without much underbrush or ground cover. The overall coloring was a light, translucent green, enhanced by the clear white light streaming through the trees. The road cut cleanly through the forest and was overhung by thin-leaved boughs that formed a natural arch, which echoed back the deep-chested chanting of the riders magnificently.

Not far into the forest the road made a slight turn, at which point Martin became aware of three things. One was that the forest was not very thick, for ahead he could see the far side, where the road went out of the trees. Another was that the light source had to be far brighter than any sunrise, for the trees near the forest edge were illuminated with a brilliance that would have done justice to a midday sun. The third was a resurgence of the feeling of insufficiency that he had felt a couple of times before in this land. Whatever destination these horsemen were escorting him toward, which apparently lay on the other side of the belt of trees, he did not feel in the least confident about going there. He wished he were walking the road unescorted, so he could at least tarry along the way to delay the arrival at the end of the wood. But he kept on regardless—the riders made sure of that—for there was certainly no other place to go, and his feet were so accustomed by now to walking that they seemed able to take him whether he willed it or not.

Martin's feeling of inadequacy grew as they approached the end of the trees. The light grew as well and once again had the same tingling, invigorating effect that it always had, only more pronounced, since it was so much brighter. This produced a fascinating contrast of sensations within him that he could not reconcile. His hesitation battled his exhilaration, and at one point he laughed to realize that he felt just like slinking off to hide in a hole as long as he could go singing and dancing along the way.

They finally came to the end of the forest, after stopping just inside the edge for a stirring sequence of chanting that sent thrills up his spine, and Martin knew that there was no way he could avoid it. He had to face whatever lay beyond the trees. As if knowing Martin's thoughts, the leading rider stopped at the edge of the forest, where the clear light fell unshadowed on his face, and turned to him, beckoning him to come and look. Hesitating only a moment, Martin stepped forward into the light and gazed down in amazement.

When his eyes adapted, he saw that the road dropped away down a moderately straight slope that formed a little valley with a matching slope that came down from about two miles across from where they stood. The road ran straight, ending at the bottom of the valley about three-quarters of a mile away, where stood the thing that so fascinated and frightened Martin. The bottom of the valley was dominated by a vast hall. It was by far the largest structure Martin had ever seen, so great were its length and breadth and height. It was beautiful as well, set about with spires and soaring arches. It was all crafted in a milky white translucent material that reminded Martin of alabaster. But as beautiful and awesome as the structure was, that was not the most astonishing thing about it. The astonishing thing—which riveted and terrified and exhilarated Martin all at once—was the light that welled forth through the building's walls. The building was not illuminated by a source of light; it was the source of light. There was no rising or setting sun. The building itself, or that which resided within it, was what bathed this whole valley in the brilliant white light—and not just the valley but the forest through which they had just traveled, and even the sky overhead. That was why the diffused light among the clouds never revealed a heavenly source! Because it wasn't transmitted from above; it was reflected from below, from this iridescent structure in the valley. He marveled to think that the mere reflection of this brilliance off the clouds was ample to give light and life to most of the valley through which he had traveled, even to shining so far up the barren cliffs. He wondered at the smoothness of the walls and longed to touch them, to see up close how it was that they shone so brilliantly yet could still be gazed upon directly. With a thrill Martin realized that he would have the opportunity to do that, for there was no doubt in his mind that this was the King's house, and the very place that he desired so greatly to see was the very place toward which he had been traveling.

Then suddenly within him rose a titanic struggle that tore at his heart. As two giant waves will meet and, neither yielding to the other, throw themselves together with such force as to send tons of water hurtling high and thunderous echoes for miles across the sea, so in Martin's mind two brutal realizations collided, leaving him stunned and breathless. One was the pure knowledge that he must come into that glowing hall, and the other was that he could never come there. When he looked upon the light shining from the building, he knew that this was what he had been seeking from the moment he stood on the barren cliffs and chose to descend into the valley. This was what had called to him. The light in the valley was only a reflection of this light, literally and figuratively. This was what he had sought, and this was what he must have.

Against this came the realization that he could not come into that pure place. Martin looked down at himself—dusty, stained, clothes torn, beaten up from travel. He could not come there. The people who lived here—like these riders, or those who worked the stations—they were the type to enter glowing halls and serve great kings. Battered travelers like himself—well, perhaps he deserved to wander among the bleak hills, fetching down renegades and occasionally resting at the stations. But not to come inside this great hall, no, never that.

For what felt like an eternity these two sensations battled within him: the fierce hunger to come that was an ecstasy in itself against the bitter, leaden realization that he was totally unworthy to come. Martin could not reason these out. He could not even grasp the arguments; indeed, it was the arguments that were grasping him, grasping and shaking like quarreling dogs will shake a rag which they contend for. He was having trouble breathing, and he looked desperately at the rider standing beside him. The rider smiled back, his eyes full of sympathy, as if he knew just what Martin was feeling.

Then, as if the rider's smile had jarred it loose, there flashed through his mind a clear image of Uncle Leon giving his instructions. "All who come to this country . . . first must come before the King."

The King's law! He must come before the King—it did not matter whether he desired it or despised it; he would come into the building because he had to! It was the law. Martin grasped hold of that and clung to it as a man being swept by a torrent will cling to an overhanging log. The emotions within him subsided a bit. They were still there, only tamed by the firm reality of the King's command. Martin laughed aloud at himself. How quickly he had forgotten! After all, wasn't this command the very reason he had gone up into the cliffs to bring down the man who stood tied behind him? How ironic it was that the very command from which the captive had fought and cursed and fled was now for Martin refuge and freedom. He did not have to worry about whether he was worthy. He had only to obey.

Martin looked at the rider and grinned. He would go before the King, for the King commanded it. The rider, clearly understanding him, let out a fierce whoop of joy and leaped into the air. Then he grasped the horn that hung at his belt and blew such a call that Martin's ears hurt. From the hall below came an answering call, and the lead rider gestured to the mounted riders. Together they began the descent to the house of the King.

To Martin it all seemed like a dream. His exhaustion, the tingling effervescence of the light, the opposing tugs of desire and shame warring within him, and the aftermath of the relief he felt when he found refuge in the King's law—all these combined to make him feel giddy and light-headed. On top of all that, shortly after the answering horn was heard from the hall, he spotted a crowd of people coming up the road toward them. Scores—no, hundreds—of people were coming out to line the road for their approach. There were all sorts of people—men and women, nude and clothed, all clapping and shouting for—him? Martin didn't understand, so he just kept on walking as the crowd closed in behind the travelers, singing and cheering as they followed.

After walking through all this in a dreamlike state for what seemed like both an unbelievably short and an unbearably long time, they came to the building itself. It was huge, and the light was so bright near it that Martin didn't understand how he could bear it, but he could. The road led to what seemed like a side door, around which many people were clustered. Only one, however, stood before the door, and the rider stood aside for Martin to approach him. The cheering and singing died down, and the atmosphere grew very somber around the place where Martin faced the man. They looked at each other for some minutes before Martin finally spoke.

"I've brought the man down like you said, sir", he said. Martin thought of apologizing for taking so long, or asking why the man had to be tied, but none of that seemed to matter. Uncle Leon seemed to understand and just nodded in acknowledgment, his eyes telling Martin that he had done well. Then he responded.

"Since you are the one who has brought him under the law, you will be the one to bring him before the court. Take him to the King."

At this the two riders who had been escorting the man, both of whom had dismounted when they reached the door, brought the captive forward and removed the ropes from his neck. The man offered no resistance. Martin took his arm. Uncle Leon swung open the great door, and Martin passed through, leading the prisoner before him.

As Martin walked through the door into the vestibule that opened onto the great hall, fear welled up within him. Now was the time to come before the King, now was the time to give account of his work, and he couldn't make his knees work. It took all his effort just to continue placing one foot before the other. He was afraid; no, he was terrified to come before the King. He wasn't scared of what would be done to him or even that he would do something wrong. He was simply trembling with fear at the thought of the King, of his might and majesty and awe-full-ness. That was what he felt—awe. He stood in awe of the King. Except that so much awe felt much like sheer terror. Well, there wasn't much to be done about it— already they were coming out of the vestibule into the great hall. Martin forced his feet to keep moving, pushing down the rising flood of panic that clamored for his attention.

Martin and the prisoner passed into the main hall. Martin did not need to be told where the King's throne was. He could tell, even with his eyes firmly fixed on the floor. He could have told where it was with his eyes tight shut and his back turned. It was to his left and up a bit, not forty yards away. The place where the light was coming from. Martin's terror redoubled. What kind of King was this? Step after step, he forced himself to keep walking. Out to the center of the hall. He could feel the intensity of the light on his left side. Had the King seen them? He must have—they seemed to be the only ones moving in the whole hall, and they were walking right out in front of the throne. Martin's knees almost gave out at that thought, but he stiffened them and concentrated on each step. Had they walked too far? How far was far enough? Would someone tell them when to stop, or was he expected to know?

Suddenly Martin's nerve gave out, and he couldn't walk another step. He found himself sinking to his knees, and as he did so he pushed down on the captive's arm to make him kneel as well. To his shock, the man refused to kneel! Martin could feel him trembling in every limb, barely strong enough to stand, but nonetheless using his last shred of willpower to stand in defiance before the King. Stunned that anyone could be so foolish, Martin grasped the man by the back of the neck and forced him down by main strength. Under Martin's powerful hand the man finally collapsed on the floor, and Martin sank to his knees beside him, turning them both toward the light as they fell. He hoped he had come far enough, but even as he knelt he knew it didn't matter. He didn't know what to do next. At times in his journey he had thought about what he would say to the King. Usually he imagined something forthright and courageous about how he had brought this captive in obedience to the law or something similar. But now that he was in front of the King, he found it was all he could do to breathe, much less talk. So he crouched there, trembling, staring at the gray floor, and hoping this would end soon.

After some moments of terrifying silence, there came from the direction of the throne a deep rumble that sounded like thunder but that clearly contained a command. Martin's heart nearly failed at the sound, yet he knew that regardless of how petrified he was, if that command were issued to him, it would be obeyed. But somehow Martin understood that this command was not for him, though he could guess who it was for. He lifted his head a bit and indeed, the captive man was kneeling straight up, his hands still tied behind him, and looking directly into the light. There was another rumble from the throne, and then, to Martin's horror, the man began to glow. Beginning with his eyes, a bright white glow quickly engulfed his head and spread down his shoulders and the rest of his torso. The man writhed and twisted and, just before the white glow covered his whole body, opened his glowing mouth to scream an unintelligible phrase that ended with a brief shriek that was quickly cut short. Then the man's body collapsed in a quickly disintegrating pile of ash, and it seemed to Martin that a small gray shadow went flitting up from it and through the roof back in the direction of the dark cliffs.

Silence reigned again for some minutes, while Martin quivered in terror on the floor. Then came another thunderous rumble, and this time the command was for him. He had no strength to obey, and no will, but his limbs responded to the command regardless. He knelt up straight, lifted his head, and fixed his eyes on the throne.

Then, as the fire pierced his eyes, Martin understood. It all became clear, even as the white heat consumed his brain and licked down his shoulders. The images flashed by lightning fast. Uncle Leon! Of course! How necessary it had been, even this! The flames were licking his arms, and he raised them to surrender more fully. Let it all go—it didn't matter now! All the dirt and grime of travel, and all the other dirt and grime as well.

The agony was excruciating, but it was all being burned away, which made it worthwhile. It was going to be all right, now that he understood, and now that all that was taken care of. It was going to be all right.

As the fire died, Martin found the will and the strength to speak. He lifted his hands toward the throne, and the words came easily to his lips.

I Have Slaved for You

D RAWING A DEEP BREATH, he buried his face in his arms and sighed. Idly kicking the dust into a small pile with his toe, he faced the bleak reality: he could wait no longer. The cattle were in the corrals, the men off to the bunkhouse, his own saddle hung up, and his horse combed and stabled. He'd even paid off the temporary help and seen them on their way. He had delayed as long as he could; it was time to go in. His stomach tightened at the thought, and weariness washed over him like a cold wave as he shoved himself away from the fence. How could he explain it? How would Dad take the news? How tired he was! He slapped his hat a few sharp blows against the fencepost and jammed it on his head. He'd faced tougher situations before; he'd weather this one as well. His head hung with exhaustion and discouragement; he did not see the scurrying figure coming from the house toward him until it was almost upon him. When he glanced up and noticed the other for the first time, they were within speaking distance. He tightened his lips momentarily, drew another short breath, and spoke.

"Hi, Dad."

"Son!" boomed the figure in response, his arms spreading out as wide as his smile. "One of the hands told me you were back. It's so good to see you again!" The son endured his father's hearty embrace with a weak smile. "I told Jimmy to hold supper for you, but then you took so long that I thought I'd run out to see if everything was all right."

Something inside him tightened in anger at those words. That was Dad for you: always checking up, never trusting a guy to do his job without being watched. Of course, he mused glumly, his news wouldn't help convince Dad that he could be trusted—perhaps he really couldn't.

They were walking toward the ranch house now, Dad prattling on about some trivial happenings about the ranch that day. "Uh, Dad—" he said nervously, interrupting his father's cheery monologue as his anxiety overcame his dread.

The father stopped talking and looked at him. "Yes, son?"

"I—uh—I've got some bad news about the drive. There was a—I mean, I made a mistake", he stammered, searching for just the right words. Dad just looked at him, waiting, causing him to feel even more keenly the weight of his failure. "Dad, I lost six head crossing the North Ford", he blurted out, surprised to find himself fighting back tears at the bitterness of his admission. "I—I knew the South Ford was safer, especially with the rains in the mountains recently, but I didn't want to take the extra two days. I—"

"Son," his father interrupted gently, "six head from a herd of fifteen hundred is nothing. Don't worry about it. Things like this happen on drives."

"But—but Dad," the son continued, "I tried to send too many across at once, and they jostled each other out of the shallows. I should have known better—I did know better, but I—"

"Don't worry about it, son", his father interrupted again, even more gently than before. "It's nothing at all." They were at the ranch house now, and the father opened the door for his son to enter. "With your fine management I've so many cattle that I don't know what to do with 'em all. The important thing is that you're home safe from another successful drive."

Fine management indeed. Much more fine management like that and they'd all be looking for a new home. The son wrung his hat in his hands. Dad always talked like that—if he really knew how inept . . .

"I've had Jimmy cook up your favorite supper." Dad was speaking again. "Though the biscuits may be a little hard by now—but that's okay. It's just good to have you home again, son!" This earned another of Dad's wide grins and hearty backslaps as they sat down at the table.

The savory stew was indeed his favorite, and the biscuits

were still fresh, but he just didn't seem hungry. He picked at his food as Dad chattered cheerfully about something. "I know . . ." he suddenly exclaimed, startling his father. "Tomorrow's auction day, isn't it? I can run into town and get six more head—out of my own money, of course. I can get an early start and be back . . ."

"Son," his father said gently but firmly, fixing him with a steady gaze, "forget the animals. Just forget about them. They mean nothing."

"Yes, Dad", the son whispered and dropped his eyes, stung by his father's disapproval.

"You did a fine job on the drive", Dad continued. "But now that you're back, I thought we might take a day or so to spend together, just you and me. Get an early start tomorrow and go for a ride. Ask Jimmy to pack us a lunch and just head out like we used to. Maybe go inspect the back fences on the summer range, or whatever. Make a day of it, just the two of us—a long, lazy day. How does that sound?"

How did that sound? The son didn't respond, instead tightening his jaw and staring blankly at his plate. The back fences! They were in terrible shape! How many times in the past months had he reminded himself to get out there and fix them? But had he done it? No, not him—he'd let a thousand details distract him, and hundreds of petty tasks demand his attention, all the while letting the back fences go to ruin. And now Dad was going to see them! His insides churned at the prospect of displaying for Dad—again—such clear evidence of his incompetence.

But Dad was talking again: ". . . get to see you any more, what with the ranchwork and all." Then he stopped, and a note of concern crept into his voice. "Are you all right, son? You look a bit peaked. Coming down with something?"

"Er, no, Dad—I'm fine", the son replied. "Just tired from the drive, that's all."

"Of course, lad", his father said. "You just need a chance to rest. Say, if tomorrow's too soon to go riding together, we could always . . ."

"No, no, Dad—that's okay. Don't change your plans for my

sake", the son said, rising from the table. "I'll be fine—just need a little rest, that's all. Think I'll turn in now, though."

"Sure thing, son. See you in the morning", his father said gently. He gave a little sigh and shook his head as he watched his son trudge off to his room. Then he turned to the cook, who was standing in the kitchen door. "Jimmy," he said, "could we have two early breakfasts tomorrow? And that pack lunch I talked to you about earlier? Please have it ready to go immediately afterward."

"Sure thing, Boss", the cook replied.

The eastern sky was just beginning to turn rose as the father buttoned his vest and smiled in anticipation of the day to come. He could hear Jimmy clattering about in the kitchen downstairs, and the smell of the sizzling sausage was tantalizing. He'd waited weeks for this day. When he came down the stairs, however, he saw only one place set at the table.

"Jimmy!" he called. "Jimmy, I asked for two places this morning."

"You sure did, Boss," Jimmy replied, stepping into the doorway holding a spatula. "But your son was up when I was, and he grabbed a bite before I even started cookin'. He said somethin' about an auction in town he had to go to. He told me to tell you he'd be back real soon—real soon. He said to make sure you knew that. Definitely by lunchtime, he said, definitely. Real soon."

The father said nothing, but sank down in his chair and buried his face in his hands.